Ava Rising

Also by G.E. Nosek

Ava of the Gaia
Book One in the Ava of the Gaia Series

Ava Rising

G.E. Nosek

To…

AD, JW, HJP, CM, KN, IA, your enthusiasm was
infectious and your editing incisive.

My Trinity friends, for welcoming me into your joyful
chaos with open arms.

Chapter 1

Ava rose slowly out of unconsciousness, ushered by the twinned scents of grease and sugar. *Somebody made me breakfast in bed*, she thought with a smile. Her eyes fluttered open to behold an unfamiliar mountainous landscape. The earth was swirled in colors of brown and yellow and littered with pockmarks. And the air was laced with the smell of cinnamon…

She blinked and raised her head slowly from where it had been slumped on a diner booth tabletop, inches away from colliding with a cornucopia of breakfast foods and close enough to make those foods look like an alien landscape. Pancakes, cinnamon rolls, waffles and tater tots formed miniature mountains before her, with icing and syrup dripping down their peaks. What was she doing in a diner? She looked up from the mounds of food to find Lucas—his blue eyes staring anxiously at her.

Why did he look so sad? Had he found out about Owen? She knew she should have told Lucas sooner, but things with Owen had been such a whirlwind. Wait a minute, Lucas had found out about her and Owen months ago. What was going on here? Why did she feel so out of it? She shook her head, trying to clear the fog from her memory.

For the first time she got a good look at Lucas—the bags under his eyes were deep purple and he had a truly spectacular array of bruises across his face and arms. Had he gotten into another fight?

And then she felt it, the dull ache coming from her wrist, a drumbeat of pain every time her heart pumped. She shifted in the booth, slowly lifting her arm to assess the damage. She looked like some kind of cheap zombie

Halloween costume. Her wrist was wrapped in strips of torn white cloth, already fraying. Blood had soaked through the bandage in huge swathes. *Blood? What happened to me?* A single image bloomed in her mind, Lucas in his mid forties, shaking with rage and weeping tears of blood. No, not Lucas. Lucas's father. Why were his eyes bloody like that? She looked down at her bandaged wrist as a thought wriggled at the periphery of her memory, trying to unbury itself. She had done that. She had clawed at Lucas's father's eyes in an effort to protect Lucas.

Then came the onslaught of memories. Ava shivered—the terror of that night, the pain of Lucas's betrayal, and then his ultimate sacrifice of killing his father to save her—it was all too much. She felt herself begin to fade, willing herself back to the peace of unconsciousness. But then her head snapped forward violently as she remembered what had triggered the agony of that night.

"Lucas! My family? Owen? Are they alive? Did they make it?"

She saw Lucas whiten, saw his face tighten in agony, and she couldn't stand it. She tried to edge herself out of the booth so she could run, run far away so that the truth could never find her. But she was so weak. Lucas put a hand on her shoulder. She jerked back from his touch. It was like being raked by a live wire. Energy flooded through her body and her wrist stopped aching for a second.

"Ava, wait. You don't understand. Your family's safe, or that's what all the Ares communications that I've intercepted seem to be saying."

"But you looked so upset—" Her eyes widened and she covered her mouth with her good hand. "Oh, I'm so sorry. Your father…"

"It had to be done," Lucas said, stone-faced.

This time Ava reached across to grab one of Lucas's hands. There it was again, that flash of electricity.

She didn't speak. What could she say? Lucas's father had been trying to murder them both when Lucas had killed him. She couldn't mourn his death. But she could lament how much Lucas seemed to have aged in the last few hours.

Had it really only been six months since they'd met? She thought back to the first time she'd ever laid eyes on him, the ultimate predator, slinking down the halls of Roosevelt High her first day of junior year. From that very moment, she had known it would end like this—in death. There had never been any other option for the two of them. She was Gaia; he was Ares. She was sworn, as her forebears had been sworn for seven centuries, to protect the Earth and maintain the balance of nature. And Lucas—as an Ares his mission was to cement the supremacy of man and eliminate any threats to the ascendancy of humanity. As nature retreated before man's roads and guns, black-smoke factories and industrial development, the power of the Ares grew and the Gaia found themselves as prey. They were now outnumbered and outmaneuvered. And this boy sitting across from her, with his high cheekbones and blue eyes, the splash of freckles across the bridge of his nose only visible in the sunlight, and his incurable bedhead—he was on the opposite side of that war. He had been sent to destroy her because she was an Alpha Gaia—a member whose connection to the Earth was magnified beyond that of anyone else in her Order, allowing her to command nature's strongest forces. Within her lay the power of the hurricane, the tidal wave, the volcano and the quaking earth. It was a power that frightened her—and it was growing.

But he had made a choice last night. Her life over the life of his father. Her survival over the protection of his Order. Yes, he had almost killed her. She couldn't forget that. But she also recognized that she would have been willing to do the same to a member of the Ares if her Order had so commanded.

She blew gently at an errant curl, her breath making the strand of hair float lazily. She could tell by Lucas's faraway gaze that he was having a similar internal dialogue—troubled by doubts and questions but focused on assessing their new situation. On the one hand they were two seventeen-year-olds ostracized from their respective orders and on the run for their lives, who had only settled the question of whether or not they wanted to kill one another within the last twenty-four hours. She smirked. But on the other hand, Lucas had, after admitting to his secret Gaia powers, just done the one thing to irrevocably prove his commitment to her. And they had both just saved each other's lives. Smiling shyly at Lucas, she reached out hesitantly for his hand. The energy pulsed between them, warm and comforting. Ava could feel the heat building right beneath her skin and knew her cheeks must be scarlet. The only place that wasn't feeling warmer was her arm, which was feeling cool and numb—the pain in her arm had again disappeared, leaving her in peace for the first moment since she'd awoken.

Lulled by the calm of the moment, Ava watched as a tendril of smoke curved lazily upwards from Lucas's shoulder. Realizing the import of what she was seeing, she grabbed clumsily for the cup of coffee in front of her and dumped it over Lucas's right shoulder.

"What the—" Lucas sputtered as he rushed to save the newspapers covering his side of the diner booth from the onslaught of coffee.

"You were on fire," Ava said. Lucas just looked at her incredulously. She said again, "Your shirt was on fire. Look at it."

Lucas pulled the sleeve of his shirt towards him so he could inspect it more closely. When he looked back at Ava, there was a hint of fear in his eyes.

"Did we do that? Is this our punishment for last night, for breaking the battle lines between the orders?" He looked at her with a sad smile. She read the sense of doom hiding in the lines of his face; it was etched in the small arch of his eyebrow and the slight curl of his lips. "Now we can't even touch without setting one another on fire?"

She looked away from him, trying to hide beneath her mountain of hair. His question echoed in her mind—*did we do this? Or did I?* After all, if Lucas was right and she was an Alpha Gaia then the strength and power she drew from the Earth would be amplified beyond that of anyone else in the Order. And yet she had no idea how to control that power. Her Order had told her so little; her family had kept so many secrets. She had never asked, feeling only too happy to play human in the suburbs and remain blissfully ignorant. Looking back on it now, it was clear that her peers in the Order, like Owen, had known much more than she. And yet she had never questioned the discrepancy. This ignorance made her a danger to herself and the people around her. If she were a conduit for unimaginable power but had no tools to channel it, she was a live wire, energy sparking dangerously out of her. She examined the skin of the hand that had set Lucas on fire. It was blistered, but otherwise ordinary looking—was it now a weapon? Would its touch set everyone on fire? She stuffed it into her pocket.

Lucas caught the motion. His face softened. "It's not your fault," he said.

Ava looked at him, pushing her hand even deeper into her pocket. "How do you know?

"You've always been the Alpha. Last night may be the first time you realized your true power. But realization alone wouldn't change everything." He shook his head. "No, whatever this is, it's something we've caused together."

Ava looked down at the food, slowly withdrew the hand from her pocket and reached half-heartedly to pluck a tater tot from the top of the mountain. The movement created an avalanche of fried potatoes, causing tater tots to bounce and roll wildly across the tabletop. Lucas frowned and once again moved to swat them away from his newspapers.

Ava's lower lip trembled and she whispered, "I'm so sorry." Lucas looked at her expectantly before she continued, "What a mess..." Her speech was garbled and snot began to run down her nose to comingle with her tears. "All those delicious tater tots..."

"Ava," Lucas said, his voice stern but reassuring. "They're safe. All of them." His words only made her sob harder. Even through the fog still clinging to her brain, she couldn't miss the irony—here was Lucas trying to reassure her about the safety of her family, while he must be reeling under the weight of guilt from killing his father and putting his own family in danger. She wiped at her tears with her hair, swallowing her terrible guilt down with her salty tears. "How do you know?" she asked, her voice cracking.

Lucas looked purposefully down at the newspapers. Ava followed his gaze—he hadn't just been saving his morning read from the onslaught of coffee and tater tots, there were dozens of national newspapers in front of him. She recognized some, *The New York Times*, *The Washington Post*, and *The Wall Street Journal*, but there were many more.

"But those wouldn't have any news of our orders..." Ava said, trailing off, and then adding with a rush, "unless you're looking for obituaries." That wouldn't make any sense—it had been less than twenty-four hours since she'd heard from her mother, and there was no way obituaries would have appeared already. But so little made sense anymore and the terrible fear from the night before had not yet dissipated from her body; it was still careening through her, leaping at the slightest prompting. She had learned to control her fear and her anxiety but could not rein them in while bone weary.

"No," Lucas said. He hesitated and Ava understood that he was loath to disclose the secrets of his Order. "We use newspapers as a way to communicate to the entire Order, from the lowest ranks to the highest, spread all over the world. Kind of like the 'reply all' button on an email. Nothing too secret, obviously, but it's handy for quickly communicating bare bones info."

Ava couldn't stop from cursing under her breath. "All this time?" She studied the newspapers with painstaking attention, careful to keep the last of her tears from spilling onto them. Lucas had taken a pen to the large sheets of paper, slashing at certain phrases, circling letters, and drawing thousands of connecting lines between them.

She smiled ruefully. This new revelation made the war between the Gaia and the Ares seem so laughable, so like a game. And yet her blood-spattered clothing said otherwise.

Lucas let a wry smile escape. "Don't feel too bad. We are the smart Order, not the dancing-naked-in-the-forest Order."

Ava snorted for a moment, glad for the break in the tension. Then suddenly the coffee cup trembled in her hand—a flash of memory—she remembered the feel of the mud beneath her feet, the rain sliding gracefully down her body as she had danced with Owen out in the woods. Her brain was still sorting the real from the unreal.

Her tone turning serious, she asked, "What does it say?" She tried to snatch one of the papers from the table, but Lucas grabbed her hand, giving her a reassuring look.

"Apparently there was some kind of skirmish. The Ares chanced upon a training group of young Gaia. There were lots of casualties but," he added quickly, "I'm pretty sure all of them were from my side."

Ava exhaled sharply, then remembered herself and shot Lucas an apologetic look. "Any news about your father?"

"None. Which is strange. Either they don't know yet, which is highly implausible. Or they're keeping it quiet for some reason. Or…" Lucas trailed off, his face whitening.

"He's dead, Lucas."

They paused for a moment, and Ava awkwardly shoved a whole pancake into her mouth to avoid speaking. When Lucas didn't break the silence, Ava asked, "So does it say where this big skirmish went down?"

"No. As I said, they keep the details pretty scarce—nothing that would be dangerous if it accidentally fell into the hands of the Gaia."

"Here, give me those papers."

Lucas rolled his eyes as he handed them over, saying, "I'm telling you, Ava, there's no way you're going to be able to read the code. Each Order has its strengths, and mastery of language just happens to be one of ours. Don't take it personally—"

"Found it!" interrupted Ava.

"What—" Lucas spluttered.

Ava silenced Lucas with an expression of triumph, gesturing for him to look at the article she'd found:

Big Island of Hawai'i, Hawai'i Feb 16 - Kīlauea Iki erupts without warning, claiming several lives. The eruption of Kīlauea Iki Crater began around 4:00 PM on February 15, 2014 and lasted several hours. Within minutes, the eruption centered on four vents in the southwest corner of the crater. Experts report several episodes of lava fountaining with heights estimated to reach as high as six hundred feet. The eruption coated the crater in at least thirty feet of lava.

The unannounced eruption is believed to have claimed several lives. State authorities are working to corroborate eyewitness accounts of hikers in the path of the crater's eruption. Officials have declared a state of emergency, closing the area to visitors. Scientists at the Hawaiian Volcano Observatory are in the process of determining how monitoring equipment failed to detect the eruption and its seismic precursor activity.

Kīlauea Iki is a popular tourist destination, with visitors flocking from all over the world to explore the crater.

Ava looked up—Lucas was still scanning the article, brows furrowed in confusion. She jumped ahead quickly, looking for something that might bolster her theory. Excitedly she jabbed a finger at a paragraph further down the page. "Here, look. This is the key."

Lucas looked at her quizzically for a long moment. Ava could see his skepticism but evidently he had decided to humor her because he bent his head once more to join her in reading the designated paragraph.

Two eyewitnesses to the crater's eruption appeared on local television to describe what they had seen. Lucas Canning, thirty-five, and Alison Ginsburg, twenty-nine, of Arlington, Virginia described their account of the eruption. Ms. Ginsburg detailed her experience: "It was unreal. The lava—I guess that's what you'd call it—shot straight up into the air and then seemed to fall down onto several precise spots on the mountain. It was the craziest thing! My partner and I got our binoculars out and we could see a group of tiny dots moving away from the lava—we were kind of horrified because the dots looked like people." Mr. Canning recounted his experience: "The strangest thing of all was the noise the volcano made just before it erupted. It sounded for the all the world like the shriek of a woman, like an angry shriek. We could hear it through the deafening noise of the helicopter. I never would have expected a volcano to make such a human noise."

Experts consulted on the unusual timing, scope, and noise of Kīlauea Iki's eruption were all puzzled.

Lucas turned his head to face Ava. "I don't get it. What does this have to do with your family?" Unless…" he trailed off, his gaze troubled.

"Did you see that part about the volcano sounding like the wail of a woman? That was no natural eruption," Ava spoke rapidly, her eyes bright. "Volcanoes are my grandmother's specialty. I'm betting she or one of the other Elders was leading a group of Gaia children through the Ritual of Fire when the Ares attacked. The rest of my family and scores of other Gaia would have come to protect the young. We don't normally like to lump so many young Gaia together, but there are so few Elders left to teach…" Ava trailed off, feeling guilty about sharing so many of the Gaia's secrets. She saw the wounded look in Lucas's eyes at her hesitance and distracted herself by dunking a tater tot forcefully into the ketchup on her plate.

"What do you think happened?" Lucas prompted.

Ava reminded herself that Lucas too was incredibly invested in the fate of the people on the volcano. "Let's just say, if I were with the Ares and I had confronted my grandmother on top of one of the largest raw sources of power on the planet when she was desperate to protect the young Gaia in her charge, I would get the hell out of there."

"Speaking of getting the hell out of places…how are you feeling now? Are you well enough to travel?"

Ava caught a flash of emotion in Lucas's eye, something she couldn't quite identify. "Of course, why?"

"You haven't been…well," Lucas murmured in reply.

She glanced down at the bandage on her wrist— obviously she hadn't been well—and waited to see if he would elaborate. Finally he continued, "Er…you've been screaming…a lot."

Ava blushed. She had no memory of screaming. Quickly she assessed the various aches and pains coming from her body—the drumbeat of vicious pain still emanating from her wrist, the various but quickly fading bruises, and a new ache from her right hip. She ran a finger along the source of this new pain—the answering pulse of agony told her it was a raw burn. When had she burned her hip? Is this what had made her scream out?

Lucas mumbled, "I didn't want to stop, not yet, not so close to…But I thought some food and familiar surroundings might…calm you."

Now she understood the veritable feast surrounding her. "You certainly ordered enough food," she said kindly.

It was a gentle rib, one meant to make him smile—she couldn't bear seeing him look so vulnerable, so guilt-ridden.

He played with the scrambled eggs in front of him solemnly. "To be honest, I didn't know the first thing about Gaia healing…and I thought…I thought you might not make it through the night. That I might've killed you when I fed you some of my energy."

Ava felt another rush of pity for the man, the boy really, sitting across from her—what a lonely, frightening night he'd just endured.

Lucas shook his head. "Let's get out of here. I can take first turn at the wheel."

"Sure," Ava said quickly, eager to make up for the pain she had caused Lucas in some small way. "Wait a second. What car are we taking?" she asked suspiciously.

"I don't know yet…what's your favorite color?"

"Lu-cas. You know how I feel about stealing."

"How do you feel about dying?" he muttered darkly.

Ava was shaken, taken aback by the quicksilver change in emotion.

Lucas shrugged apologetically, and said, his voice much softer, "You've already driven in one stolen car today. Why not make it two?"

"To the parking lot," she said with forced levity. As they were standing to leave, Ava made to grab a fistful of tater tots and pancakes with her bandaged hand.

"Ava," Lucas said with a groan. "Don't you dare stick those bandages into that food. Not after I spent God knows how long trying to figure out how to sterilize them."

Ava rolled her eyes and bent her head down to grab some food with her mouth instead.

Chapter 2

The American countryside had passed by in a blur as Ava and Lucas had fled westward—alternating between napping and driving. Ava had chosen a roomy RV from the diner's parking lot for their escape vehicle after seeing the "Save a cow, eat a vegetarian" sticker on its windshield. They had spoken little after the diner, both intent on fleeing the demons haunting them, real and imagined. But after a day of near silence, Ava had calmed down long enough to start thinking about their next move. Between the focus in his eyes and his vice-like grip on the steering wheel, it had been clear that Lucas had some notion of a plan in mind. It had taken her another twenty-four hours to wheedle it out of him—he kept pretending to be asleep while she drove. Of course, she had known he wasn't. But she hadn't wanted to push too hard, not after everything he'd been through.

Finally on day two, he'd confessed his secret intention—he wanted to find his mother. The conversation had been nearly unbearable—Lucas almost breaking down several times as he explained that he needed to find his mom. That it was imperative he get to explain what he did and why. Given the haphazard nature of the their flight—stealing a new escape vehicle every couple of hours, scarfing chips and candy, and never taking their feet off of the gas—it had been as good a plan as any. But Ava had hesitated, until Lucas had sealed the deal by telling her his mother was in Australia. Australia—one of the last bastions of Gaia dominance. Lucas had explained that the Ares would be monitoring airports across the country, but might not be expecting them to pop up on the west coast—so far from where they'd last been seen. So they were heading for San Francisco. And then on to Australia.

Now she was curled up in the passenger seat of their newest stolen car staring at the moon—a gaudy exhibitionist preening against the stark landscape of the desert. She caught a glimpse of a sign welcoming them into Utah and realized she must soon take control of the wheel if she were still intent on her detour. The speedometer had inched upwards as they traveled. As the journey progressed Ava had regained some of her energy and by the look of the newfound flush in Lucas's cheeks, he had as well. With some of their energy returned, they could rely on superhuman reflexes as they careened along the highways. But a flood of renewed energy wasn't the only reason for their increasingly hurried pace. Ava could feel the anxiety seeping off of Lucas. It was filling the vehicle like a slow-moving fog, tendrils curling and searching and pushing at her—she felt herself gasping for breath against its claustrophobic force. She didn't want Lucas to know she was tuning into his emotions but she couldn't take it a moment longer. She pushed a button to lower a window in the car, allowing the soothing night air to rush in and cleanse the insidious fear. Lucas looked over at her and she smiled guiltily—it was clear from the embarrassed flash in his eyes that he knew exactly why she had rolled the window down.

Ava whispered to the wind, calling it to wrap itself around her head and face like a scarf. It would not be a sufficient barrier to block the emotions leaking out of Lucas, but it was worth a try. She had been attempting for days to shut herself down from Lucas's thoughts and emotions, to give him the privacy to grieve and process in his own way. But over the last several months she and Lucas had developed a unique emotional bond, borne of the intensity and polarized nature of their relationship, that allowed each to remotely sense the physical presence and read the emotions of the other. Recently it had even allowed Ava to pick up whole images and memories from Lucas's mind—the more salient the memory, the more intense the connection—like an antenna picking up the neighbors' cable TV. Since that terrible night at Lucas's,

Ava was picking up not just the occasional thought, but a flood of unwanted images and emotions. More than once, Ava had woken up screaming from a catnap in the passenger seat—haunted not by her own thoughts but by Lucas's. She had lied to Lucas, saying that she was having nightmares about her family and Isi, unwilling to talk about the images that she had accidentally plucked from Lucas's mind. Gruesome images. In one, a blood-covered Lucas stabbed his father—particularly unnerving because Ava experienced the act through Lucas's eyes, seeing the rage and betrayal firsthand. In another, a group of young Ares circled a terrified little girl, who looked like a member of the Gaia, with cold eyes and knives held high. In another, Lucas's father drew a hot poker from the flames and pressed it into the skin of Lucas's stomach.

The double onslaught of her own emotions mixed with Lucas's was becoming too much. She could taste the corrosive quality of the guilt rolling off of Lucas and it left her nauseous. And fear, always the fear.

She knew Lucas must be terrified of the Makhai. And with good reason. The Makhai took their name from the ancient word for the Greek god of war's battle daemons—savage spirits that reveled in violence and bloodshed. They were the militant wing of the Order of Ares. Their goal was to wipe out the Gaia. And when Lucas had killed his own father, he had also killed the Makhai's leader, martyring him instantly. In short, Lucas and Ava were now on the run from a well-trained, iron-willed, dogmatic group of killers. The force of Lucas's fear was contagious—she too wanted to flee, to disappear from the grasp of these heartless warriors. But two things held her back. Two things made her sweetly suggest to Lucas that she take over driving and then wait for him to fall asleep before turning off the highway and guiding the car further into the desert. One was the knowledge that Lucas would have a much better chance of surviving the next several months if he could learn to master his Gaia powers. The other was the small object in her pocket, its warmth radiating through the material of her jeans—a warmth that seemed by turns sinister and protective. But she planned on telling Lucas about only one of these things and she knew he would be less than receptive, which is why she quickly and quietly parked and then moved catlike around to the hood of the car.

She stared intently at the machinery in front of her, straining to remember the rudimentary automotive lessons her mother had given her. Placing a tentative hand on the engine, she felt the gasoline shiver excitedly at her touch. She exhaled in surprise at the unexpected movement, checking quickly to make sure Lucas was still asleep. She shook her head; of course she should have anticipated such a reaction. Gasoline was after all a derivative of ancient plant matter. She whispered to the ancient life force, preparing to corrode the engine in front of her. At the last second she stepped back, her hands trembling. Whatever it was that had Lucas running so scared, had seeped into her own psyche—she wasn't prepared to leave the two of them alone, irreversibly stranded in the desert. Pushing back the fear, she quickly modified her plan. After a moment of toying with the engine she removed the spark plug and hid it behind a rock formation—nobody would be leaving this place against her will.

Chapter 3

While Lucas slept, Ava did a quick scouting of their surroundings—the darkness of the February night hiding her form as she moved silently across the desert. She traced her fingers over the alien rock formations, admiring nature's carnival—the twisting and looping structures like giant contortionists frozen for all time in red-hued glory. Each touch brought a new memory—Isi, Owen, and she playing hide and seek among the rock formations, giggling as her grandmother, Lena, taught them how to burrow deep beneath the sand if they ever needed a makeshift refuge. Thankfully these were her own memories and not Lucas's, but still, the last few days had been consumed by reminiscing. Maybe she and Lucas were doomed to a life sustained by memories—forever on the run and physically cut off from one another.

She shivered, and with determined hands, reached into her pocket to draw out a silver necklace. Dangling from the chain was a circular pendant shaped like a miniature Earth, the land and water wrought of jade and lapis lazuli. A delicate silver dagger was affixed on top of the Earth-shaped pendant to form what looked like a primitive peace sign. She flinched, waiting to see if the necklace would burn her hands, but the metal remained warm to the touch rather than the white hot it had burned before.

Her mind went once more to the memory of her grandmother presenting her with the necklace, searching every moment of it for a clue to the necklace's unexpected behavior over the last week. Her grandmother had said the stone would help channel dual sources of energy—power drawn from the Gaia and Ares. What had been her grandmother's exact words? *You are holding an alliance stone. One that was created more than half a millennium before you were born. Can you feel its power? Whoever wears it…will find members of both orders called to them, drawn by its ancient promise.*

Ever since her grandmother had given her the necklace she had kept it close, puzzling over the mystery of its power. Lena had warned her not to wear it and yet her grandmother had never taken the necklace off—so wearing it alone could not activate the stone. What was its true trigger? Ava had carried the necklace in her pocket since seeing her grandmother—unwilling to risk wearing it and yet unwilling to leave it unprotected. Before that terrible night several days ago, she had thought that she was merely a messenger, guarding the necklace until she could safely transfer it to another member of her Order in the future. But now, now that Lucas had revealed that she was a so-called Alpha, Ava was not so sure. She wished her grandmother had told her more but realized, looking back on the memory, that her grandmother had not really understood the necklace. Gaia lore had passed on the story of the necklace's immense power, but because of the fissure between the orders, alliance stones hadn't been used to channel energy in centuries. It was strangely comforting that her grandmother had trusted her to work out the puzzle of such a powerful object on her own. Lena had believed in her.

She rubbed her hip, wincing as she realized the raw burn there had not yet healed. At one of their infrequent pit stops during the frenzied getaway of the last several days, Ava had slipped into the bathroom at a gas station to wash up. There she had studied the odd burn on her hip— the source of the pain she had felt back in the diner. Examining the raw flesh, she had realized that the burn was the perfect imprint of the alliance stone. The necklace seemed to have awoken. But when and more importantly why? She had gone over those hellish twenty-four hours over and over again in her mind. Some event—shucking her powers, putting her life in Lucas's hands, attacking Lucas's father, being mortally injured without her powers, learning the truth about her identity, or discovering the new and terrible energy that cackled when she and Lucas tried to touch—had caused the alliance stone to burn the mark into her skin and she had been too terrified and full of adrenaline to realize it in the moment. Or she'd been unconscious, lost to the world, as Lucas carried her from his burning house. Either way, she was left terribly confused about the meaning behind the burn. But it was clearly no coincidence. Desperation was a powerful temptress, and desperation was what had led Ava to the middle of the desert, far from anyone who might be alerted to the power of the alliance stone. She took one last look at the necklace and moved to clasp it around her neck when she heard the faintest noise behind her. In a flash she tucked the necklace safely back into her pocket and whirled around.

Lucas was holding the spark plug she had removed from the engine and looked ferociously angry.

"You want to tell me what's going on, Ava?" he said, swinging the spark plug in his hand, his tone casual but threatening. He stood silhouetted by the rising sun, his eyes sunken, every muscle in his body taught with tension.

Ava cursed under her breath and raised her hands in a calming gesture. She breathed in deeply, summoning the soothing power of the ocean to channel the energy towards Lucas—

"Stop," said Lucas, his tone brokering no dissent. And Ava immediately released the energy, hardly daring to breathe. The only other time she had seen Lucas like this was when he had first brought her to his house, when he had still been prepared to kill her. It turned her insides cold.

"I'll ask again. Why are we here? And more to the point, why did you feel the need to hide this little gadget?" he asked, shaking the spark plug in emphasis as he spoke.

Ava immediately regretted her spark plug subterfuge. There was nothing for it, the truth was her best friend now. "You need to train," she said.

"*I* need to train? Since when do you get to decide these things unilaterally? And then sabotage our only means of escape?" Ava caught a flash of an image from Lucas—the same faces that haunted all of his memories. Cold-eyed and lethal-looking—they must be the young assassins of the Makhai. Which would explain Lucas's fury at their unannounced detour. She stayed quiet, concentrating.

"Do we not trust each other?" he asked, sounding genuinely wounded.

But Ava couldn't answer. She was deep in concentration. She had taken one of the images captured from Lucas's mind—the one with the Makhai circling the girl. She closed her eyes in focus, changing the memory, shaping it in her mind like some kind of telepathic Photoshop. She crafted the image so that the Makhai and their fiery knives were frozen in blocks of ice before they could do their deadly work. Then she left the reworked image dangling in the forefront of her thoughts, injecting it with the anguish she felt looking at the little girl at the mercy of those dead-eyed warriors, and hoped that Lucas would pick up the image like she had been accidentally snatching so many of his.

Suddenly, Lucas rocked back as if he'd been hit in the face and the spark plug dropped from his hand with a clink.

"You took that from me?"

Ava knew he was talking not about the spark plug, but about the memory, the one with the little girl. He slammed a fist into the rock structure next to him. Cracks formed like an exponentially expanding spider web from the spot of the impact. She watched in fascination as the massive rock structure—the top reached almost forty feet up to the sky—began to wobble from the structural instability and the whole thing began to fall down on Lucas in slow motion. He glanced up at the commotion but didn't move. Ava rushed to block the falling rock, but Lucas barked, "No," and turned his face up towards the structure, a smile hovering on his lips. Just as the first smaller shards of rock were raining down on his exposed skin, the larger pieces hurtling to accompany them, Ava cried out, exhaling forcefully like a geyser as she did so. The wind shot out from her lungs, gathering power as it sped towards Lucas. Upon reaching him, the wind knocked him through the air to land twenty feet away, out of the path of the rock structure that crashed down to the desert's surface a split second later.

Lucas did not get up for a long time. Ava knew he could not be seriously injured and understood— sometimes in life you just have to lie down in the dirt.

"That little girl?" she asked finally.

He shook his head mournfully. "They made me watch. She was a daughter of one of the Ares. It was a brutal winter that year and the deer kept nosing around her house looking for food…which wouldn't have been terribly out of the ordinary, except they only came to her house…and they came in droves. I'm sure she was trying to stop them, to keep them away, but when you're young…it's hard to control."

Ava winced, realizing Lucas was speaking from experience. That this little girl could have been him.

"One day a gang of Makhai, the younger, vicious ones, caught her surreptitiously feeding the deer and they went crazy." Bitterly, he added, "I was five years old." They sat there in silence for a long time.

Finally Lucas turned to Ava and said, "So you really believe we can fight?" She caught it again—his hesitation. There was something about the Makhai that he wasn't telling her, something that scared him deeply.

She nodded, smiling reassuringly and then raised her hand as if to give him a high five. When he raised his hand half-heartedly back, clearly afraid to touch her, she called on the water molecules in the air to align. They leapt to her command—Lucas's hand, now encased in a block of ice, thudded harmlessly against hers.

He smiled at her then, a true smile, and Ava breathed a sigh of relief. Her intuition had been right—the only way to get Lucas to trust her on this was to show him the potential of his Gaia powers.

She flicked her wrist dismissively and the ice melted instantaneously, dissipating into the air as Ava freed the water molecules back to their spontaneous dance.

"Ready to learn about the power of water?"

"Water, huh?" he replied. "I'm not so sure about the Gaia manner of training. It's like your Elders got drunk and watched a bunch of old *Captain Planet* episodes. Water…Air…Fire…"

Ava let out another breath, and this time her shoulders actually dropped from where they'd been tensed up halfway to her ears. Lucas was engaging in the rhythm of witty banter. She had come to recognize it as a sign that he was holding his emotions together, at least momentarily.

He added, "At least they didn't get drunk and watch *The Wiggles*—or your Order would have been even more obnoxious than it already is."

Ava just smirked. A falcon came crashing out of the sky to swoop by Lucas's face, its talons brushing dangerously close to his skin.

Ava giggled and said, "I didn't call him, I swear."

"Well he shouldn't be attacking me now, right? Now that I'm a…"—he grasped for the right words, obviously uncomfortable with the concept—"now that it's clear that I have some Gaia blood in me."

"I think it might have been a joke. But you're right, when the animals come to accept you as one of the Gaia, they will never do anything to harm you." She whistled and the desert bird came to rest on her shoulder, his iridescent eyes staring back at her with keen intelligence. She rubbed its head gently. "Right?" she said to the bird and he squawked in agreement.

A mixture of longing and revulsion played out across Lucas's face. Trying to regain the earlier levity, she quickly launched back into banter, "So which one of the *Captain Planet* heroes would you have wanted to be?"

"Heart," Lucas said immediately.

"Um. Have you ever seen the show? 'Cause Heart was clearly a pu—nk."

"Whatever. You're just jealous."

"Of Heart? Are you serious? Now Dora the Explorer, that's another story…"

"Of course you liked Dora the Explorer."

"What's that supposed to mean?"

Instead of answering her question, Lucas asked one of his own, "How are we going to train with water in the middle of the desert?"

"You can only know a thing by knowing its opposite, little grasshopper," Ava said, tapping Lucas playfully on the chest, and then, realizing her mistake, instantly withdrawing her hand.

When Lucas just looked confused for several seconds, Ava continued, "No, I'm kidding, I never understood that crap. The canyon's just another twenty minute hike."

They hiked in silence for the next twenty minutes and then stopped as the rough trail they were following ended at a sheer cliff. Forty feet down lay a blue river—winding through the red-hued landscape like a psychedelic serpent. The sheer walls of rock rising up from the water were striped through with a multitude of colors, as if a little kid had taken the crayons from one end of a box and scribbled his way through the pinks and salmons and roses into the bricks and deep crimsons.

"We're going whitewater rafting," Ava announced, turning her back to the water to size up Lucas's reaction to her comment.

Lucas looked around suspiciously. "Where are the rafts?"

Ava smirked and without turning her head, launched herself into a backwards somersault off of the cliff. Her joyful laughter rang up throughout the canyon after her as if to drive home the depths of her cheekiness.

Ava kicked powerfully to stay in place as the water tugged at her playfully, craning her neck to see up to the top of the cliff where Lucas was now slow clapping. "Congratulations," he shouted down at her, "you have officially out Ava'd yourself."

"Not gonna lie. I was kind of waiting all day to do that."

"I hate sounding like a broken record. But you know being on the run for your life? You're doing it wrong." As he said it he stripped of his shirt. Ava tried not to stare too long at the muscles in his torso. Free of his jeans and shirt, Lucas catapulted himself off of the cliff in a graceful dive.

When he surfaced from the dive, Ava smiled playfully and said, "Not bad, not bad at all." She could see Lucas struggling as the water began to drag him downriver towards a particularly vicious patch of rapids.

"So, what should I do now?" Lucas asked. He had turned himself around in the water to face Ava and was clearly fighting not to be dragged away.

Ava crinkled her nose. "Gimme a second...I had only planned as far as my epic entrance into the water."

Lucas had now been swept a good thirty feet away from her. She heard him release a spate of indelicate words and a mumbled, "Are you kidding me?" before she saw him crash rather spectacularly into a boulder.

Fanning her hands out to tug on the currents of water around her like springs, she shot downriver towards Lucas. After a few seconds, she willed the water to crest into a wave that deposited her on the flat surface of the boulder that Lucas was now clinging to the edge of with a scowl. Ava looked down at him from the top of the rock, noting his wet hair and tired eyes, and suddenly felt a rush of pity. It had been such a long day and she had just tossed him into the water as if it were a warm bath.

"Sorry. I genuinely thought desperation might trigger some of your powers."

His frown deepened as he continued clinging to the rock. "Imagine—"

Ava had to drag her eyes away from the muscles bulging in his arms to look into his eyes as he spoke.

"—if I had taught you how to work with fire by pushing you into the flames."

"You're right. I'm sorry. Let me try again." As she spoke, she reached down for his hand. He looked at her uncertainly—she wasn't sure if he was afraid of the weird thermal energy they'd been producing or if he was still angry about what she had done earlier. She gave him a reassuring look and grabbed his hand with her own, pulling him up next to her on the rock. "Maybe we won't catch on fire while we're in the water."

"Water—I'm liking it more already," Lucas replied, giving her his most forward smile.

Ava shook her head, laughing. "It likes you too," she said, releasing his hand to gesture at the water from the top of the boulder, bending the ancient force to her will. A churning wall of river water rose up in front of them, slowly condensing into a sinuous pillar that bent towards them invitingly. With another gesture from Ava, the top of the pillar hollowed out slightly, leaving a large, inverted space as big as a soaking tub for Ava and Lucas to climb into. They sat there for a moment, Ava watching Lucas's mood change—she could tell from his grin that he was feeling what she was feeling, the cool embrace of the water, its constant shifting movement like a thousand tiny fish brushing against her skin.

"I can't tell you how to summon the water, Lucas. I know it's frustrating. But I want you to feel it. Feel the movement, feel the chill, feel it sliding along your skin setting your nerve endings giddy with refreshment and energy." As she spoke, the pillar swirled and spun, like the tilt-a-whirl at an amusement park. The red hues of the canyon whirled around them and the alien rock structures seemed to dance in the world's most glacially paced ballet—gracefully sliding and bending in the sunlight as the speed of the water pillar increased.

Lucas still looked rather pale from his earlier misadventure in the water, although he seemed giddier by the moment—with each swooping arc the water pillar was picking up momentum. Without thinking, Ava inched her hand into her pocket. Just as her fingers touched the warm metal of the alliance stone Lucas lost his balance on the pillar and slid into Ava, gripping her forearm, the same one tucked into her pocket, to steady himself. Ava's eyes widened at the impact but nothing seemed to change. And then, with a sonic boom, the water pillar exploded into the air. Neither of them was expecting the motion and both got bodily slammed by the geyser of water as it shot upwards hundreds of feet.

Ava had by this time freed her hand from her pocket, breaking the connection with the metal. But she was totally disoriented—*I probably have a concussion*—thrown off both by the sudden change in direction and the alien feeling of not moving as one with the water. It was beyond her control. She looked around, trying frantically to locate Lucas as the water continued its skyward ascent. They were at least two hundred feet up now. And then Ava heard it—a hissing sound as a jet of boiling water exploded next to her. Ava shrieked, trying to roll away from it. *What was happening? Why would the water behave this way?* As she spun away from the heat she caught sight of Lucas—now looking like the little kid whose parents had let go of his bike unexpectedly leaving him to wobble and fall. And then came a moment of relief, as the boiling pillar of water drew back from them, a yoyo that had hit its zenith and had to snap back to earth. Relief was quickly replaced by fear. Without the force of the water behind her, Ava had now reversed course and was plunging towards the ground totally disoriented. Out of the corner of her eye she could see another free-falling form. As the ground rose up beneath her—the bloody crimson of the landscape now an ominous foreshadowing of her future— she heard the anguished shriek of the falcon echo throughout the canyon. Feebly she sucked the air into her lungs, preparing to blow it out just enough to slow hers and Lucas's descent. But before she could exhale, a streak of blue darted out of the red below and enveloped her. Two smaller pillars of water had twined out of the river canyon, like the long sinuous arms of a jellyfish, to catch her and Lucas as they fell. The tentacles of water held for a moment, trembling under their weight, before collapsing.

Lucas and Ava dropped the last couple of feet to the ground, where they lay sputtering and coughing.

Ava pressed her back into the warmth of the desert beneath her, as if to erase the memory of the water's betrayal. Experimentally she called to the earth and felt a rhythmic pounding beneath her—at least the earth still had her back. She looked over at Lucas—it was he who had summoned those tentacles of water to save them. She had not reacted quickly enough. But as mortal peril was quickly becoming their norm, the fear soon dissipated, leaving a burning curiosity about the necklace and pride at Lucas's achievement in its wake. From her spot on the ground she raised her hand into a triumphant fist. "Desperation as motivation—it worked. I just had to crank up the danger a notch."

"Best. Teacher. Ever." Lucas's words were mumbled as he struggled to speak while coughing the last drops of water from his sodden lungs. Finally he regained his composure and turned to face her. "Your acting's not too bad either. It really looked like you were going to crash into the ground and die. Or at least break all of your bones. How'd you get the water to explode like that?" he asked, a hint of glee in his voice.

"Well, actually…"

"We were going to crash into the ground and die if I didn't do anything? Worst. Teacher. Ever."

Wordlessly, Ava drew the alliance stone out of her pocket, holding it up to the light so Lucas could see it properly. He examined it slowly, clearly noticing the strange pulse of energy it was emanating. "What is it?"

Ava quickly explained all that her grandmother had told her and then sheepishly admitted that she had touched it while they were in the water.

"But you're touching it now?"

"I know. The water didn't explode until I was touching you and the necklace."

Instead of seeming upset, as Ava had expected, Lucas seemed excited, even jubilant. "So we have a weapon now," Lucas said, nodding his head enthusiastically.

Ava scrunched up her face in disbelief. "Well, if you can call something that just launched us to the brink of death on a geyser of scalding water a weapon, then yes, we have a weapon."

"Oh, is this like a guy-girl thing? We like our guns and our trucks and our powerful machines. And you like being in control."

"Yes, totally a guy-girl thing. Nothing else could possibly explain why this little stone, which has now literally and figuratively burned me twice could make me uncomfortable." The shriek of a desert bird rang out again, and Lucas caught Ava's eye, pretending to shiver in fear.

She caught the glint in his eyes. "Why does it delight you so much to tease me with your faux-misogyny?" She moved to playfully poke him in his chest before stopping abruptly in her tracks. She backed away from him, trying to cover the awkwardness of the movement.

He answered, "Well once a woman has saved your life twice in as many months, faux-misogyny is all you have left."

Ava smiled at him, serious now. "Thank you for today. I would have gone splat," she said, clapping her hands together for added effect, "if it weren't for you and your newfound Gaia powers."

They stared at each other soberly. Ava hoped for something to break the tension of the moment and Lucas must have been thinking the same thing because he darted a hand forward as if to grab the necklace. "Can I hold it? No? Can I at least touch it?"

Ava shook him off, assessing the sorry state he was in—wet, rumpled, and half-covered in red grit. She hoped she didn't look as bad as he did. "You need a real bed tonight."

33

"You need a shower," he replied, grinning at her. She knew that grin. Lucas continued, "And as it so happens, so do I. Perhaps we could save water—"

"Separate rooms," Ava barked. "We're staying in separate rooms," she added more gently. "How much further is San Francisco?"

"For a mere human? About fourteen hours. For me? Eight."

"Perfect, let's drive for the rest of the day and get a good night's sleep in San Francisco. And then—to Australia," she said, sticking her hand out towards the horizon theatrically.

Chapter 4

Ava jolted out of bed to the sound of pounding on her door.

"Ava, it's me, I'm going to break into your room now."

She groaned into her pillow. Sleep had been a welcome relief from the unending emotional roller coaster of the last week—despair, terror, carefully crafted witty banter, wash, rinse, repeat.

She rolled over but refused to actually move into a vertical state without further explanation. Whatever was happening it clearly wasn't dire; Lucas was being far too casual. The click of the doorknob informed her that Lucas had indeed followed through on his threat to break into her room.

"Is that drool?" Lucas asked, looming over her prone . form.

"No," Ava answered quickly. She craned her neck, spying a large stain of what was most certainly her drool on the pillow. "I haven't slept this soundly in weeks," she said defensively.

"So that's why you insisted on separate bedrooms. You're a drooler."

"That's not a word," she replied, pretending to rise to his bait.

Lucas's tone turned more serious. "There's something I thought you should see." He held his iPhone up and she moved to a sitting position on the bed, muscles suddenly tense.

Lucas had a video queued up from their local news station. The image, embedded under the heading, "Has the Salem witch hunt returned to Massachusetts?" was pixilated but Ava could tell right away that it was Natasha in the thumbnail.

"If they've touched a hair on her head I swear to God—"

Lucas cut her off by pressing play on the video.

The camera was focused on a local news reporter who was speaking from her desk while Natasha's school photo was featured prominently in the background. "Hello, I'm Monica Leming and tonight we have an intriguing story out of Brookvale, Massachusetts. You've all heard of the mass hysteria surrounding the Salem witch trials of seventeenth-century Massachusetts. Now it seems history may be repeating itself. A local teen has had her house, car, and locker vandalized." The camera cut to show images of the vandalized objects, each covered dramatically in crimson spray paint. "The pranks vary in their exact phrasing but all have the same terrible message—"You'll burn, witch." The image behind the reporter changed to show the phrase scrawled across a locker. "Authorities are taking the acts of vandalism extremely seriously, exploring a number of angles. One source has informed us that authorities have not ruled out the possibility that the acts are racially motivated. With more on the story, we have Bill Drewbank's interview with the victim."

The video cut to a middle-aged man holding a microphone next to a fiercely scowling teenage girl. He smiled insipidly at the camera, asking his question without bothering to glance at Natasha. "Ms. Lopez, can you tell us a little bit about your state of mind after these terrible incidents? Do you feel that you can now empathize with the women targeted by the original witch trials?"

"Um…not that I don't respect your hard-hitting news coverage, but don't you think comparing a few words scrawled on a locker to the Salem witch trials, where dozens of women lost their lives, is a little melodramatic?"

This got the reporter to finally turn and truly look at his interviewee, but he couldn't manage to get any words out through his obvious surprise. Smelling blood, Natasha continued, "I mean for a generation practically weaned on *Harry Potter*, 'witch' is the ultimate compliment. Hermione Granger is the definitive badass." Natasha looked like she could continue on this subject for a long time, but her expression changed suddenly; it was clear that she had remembered her surroundings. Somewhat less enthusiastically she added, "I could do without the burning part, but—"

By this point the reporter had regained his composure and interjected, "That seems awfully cavalier, Ms. Lopez. I'm sure your parents are less enthused—"

Natasha managed to grab the microphone from the reporter and stare directly into the camera as she spoke, her eyes flashing with intensity, "What I am much less cavalier about is the disappearance of my friend Ava Fae. Neither she nor her family has been heard from in several days and nobody seems to give a damn—"

Drewbank wrestled the microphone back from Natasha at this point and the hand of someone off-camera grabbed the riled teen and steered her firmly out of the picture, but not before you could hear shouts of, "She looks like a cross between a really tall Jennifer Lawrence and the Little Mermaid!"

"A cross between Jennifer Lawrence and the Little Mermaid…that is remarkably accurate," Lucas muttered with a smile as he returned the phone to his pocket.

"Feisty, no wonder you two get along so famously. It's all over the internet right now. Those reporters will think twice before interviewing anyone on live television again." He slapped his knee in appreciation.

Ava returned the smile, mimicking her friend gleefully and bouncing on the bed, "Hermione Granger, the baddest witch in town. God I love that girl." Carried by the energy of the moment she did a few graceful flips on the bed, and then pulled out of her last spiral to belly flop onto the mattress and bury her face in the pillow.

Her face muffled by the cushion, she asked, "Wait, the Ares wouldn't actually hurt her, would they?

She turned to find Lucas shaking his head. He said, "Besides, this video clearly shows that she can handle herself."

Ava digested this for a few moments and then responded, "Don't get me wrong, if biting wit could defeat the Ares, then Natasha would be the ultimate weapon. Unfortunately biting wit cannot parry a knife." After a pause, she continued, "I mean Nat dropped out of judo when they wouldn't let her wear her *Finding Nemo* costume in the dojo. She's half blind without her glasses. She never wanted to watch old re-runs of *Buffy* with Emily and me. When we asked her what her spirit animal was, she said it was a baby sloth." Ava drew the next part out dramatically like a lawyer delivering the knockout punch of her closing argument, "She wears slippers outside all the time, *as if they were shoes.*" Pausing to take a breath, she added, "She has literally no way of protecting herself."

"Ava, your lip," Lucas said as he headed for the small bathroom attached to the hotel room. Ava licked her top lip—the metallic taste of her own blood filled her mouth. Perversely the taste made her smile. *Serves me right for leaving Natasha like that.*

Lucas returned from the bathroom with a damp washcloth and when Ava didn't pull away from him, he gently blotted at the blood. "You got some serious teeth on you, lady. More like a cross between Jennifer Lawrence and a narwhal."

Ava looked at him, eyes still slanted in despair.

"Narwhal, that got your attention didn't it? You and the animals, huh?" He shook his head, grinning. "Anyway, now that I have your attention, this right here," he said, pointing at the blood on the washcloth, "is exactly what the Ares want. The whole stunt with Natasha was probably orchestrated by them. They have plenty of media contacts they could have manipulated to ensure she got airtime. They want to bait us out of hiding."

"Well, it's working."

"They would never kill a human. Harassment is as far as they'd go."

"Right. The Makhai would stop at harassment. That makes sense given the memories I've taken from you." Ava pounded the mattress with her fists. "Don't you dare patronize me, even if you think it'll keep me safe. If you're wrong I'll lose another friend."

The evocation of the Makhai had stopped Lucas in his tracks; he was glassy eyed. There it was again—base fear.

"Lucas, what is it? Tell me," she added gently.

"Nothing."

He was lying, Ava could sense it. And he must know that she realized he was keeping something from her. But there were things she was keeping from him, so she didn't push.

"I'm sorry, it's just that neither of us seems to know our orders as well as we thought. The earth shot us like cannon fodder into the air the other day—it rose against me. And you...obviously haven't acted like your Order thought you would," Ava murmured.

Lucas was quiet for a moment, his fingers playing with the hotel matches he had stolen. He twirled them artfully, lighting them with a snap of his fingers.

Finally he said, "This isn't the work of the Makhai. If it were, the video you just watched would have been about the brutal murder of a young high school student."

Ava shivered. Lucas looked down at her—the look in his eyes made her shiver again, but not out of fear this time. She waited—barely daring to breathe—to see what he would do next but he just reached behind her and ever so gently tucked the bed sheet back around her shoulders. He was careful, so careful, not to touch his bare skin to hers and Ava sobbed inwardly, longing for that touch like a potted plant in desperate need of watering from a derelict owner.

Once the linen barrier was in place he moved his hand up and down her back soothingly. He whispered, "I know you feel guilty," and the way the words caught in his throat as he said them, Ava understood that guilt was an emotion he was all too familiar with at the moment. "I know you hate that you had to leave Natasha behind. That you might have put her in danger. But"—his hand stopped in its place resting firmly in her lower back as if to emphasize his point—"we're going to get out of here to somewhere nice and safe. And then you can write a long letter to Natasha explaining everything. And I promise to move hell and high water to get that letter to her."

It was a small promise but Lucas spoke so earnestly that she felt safe in his words.

"Ok, you know the Ares better than anybody else. What can I do to protect her?"

"What we're already doing. Getting out of the U.S. They know she won't be of any use tracking you down when you're in another country."

"Alright, let's go get our disguises." She stood up from the bed and started looking around for her clothes. "We're leaving today."

Chapter 5

Struggling to rush up the Lyon Street steps in San Francisco in her tight skirt and heels, Ava collided with a tall man sporting large sunglasses and a mane of white blond hair. *Sorry, dude, only Lucius Malfoy can pull off that look.*

"Sorry," Ava muttered, this time out loud, as she brushed past him, now dead-set on getting her disguise and getting out of the country.

She felt a hand tap her butt and she spun around to face the Lucius Malfoy impersonator, yelling, "Are you kidding me with that elf-man? Creeps like you keep women from feeling safe in their own neighborhoods. You tapped my ass, and normally I would return the favor by kicking yours. But I'm in a hurry, so I'll just give you a preview—" she had been lifting her leg to deliver a swift kick to the man's groin when she choked on her words, "Lu-cas?"

In response, the man jumped in the air and clicked his heels together in a sideways kick—a leprechaun gleefully celebrating his trickery.

As he completed the action, Ava felt a rush of pride and success streaming off of the white-maned figure, confirming beyond a shadow of a doubt that this was indeed Lucas. Ava studied Lucas's disguise—meanwhile he began moonwalking up the hill and then broke into an impressive rendition of the Running Man. Besides the flowing blond hair, he had also lightened his eyebrows, created blond scruff on his chin, and somehow shaded his face so he looked much thinner. He was dressed in a threadbare suit and had procured a series of rings for his fingers. His transformation was complete. He looked like a struggling magician; Ava wouldn't have given him a second glance it she hadn't bumped into him. By the time she had finished her survey Lucas had transitioned into an elaborate pantomimed reenactment of Neil Armstrong planting a flag on the moon.

She giggled. "Ok, ok, I get it. You fooled me." When he didn't stop his hijinks, she tossed her head and ran a hand through the thick sheen of black hair cascading over her shoulders. "What do you think of my disguise?"

The Gaia generally eschewed human disguises, preferring either to camouflage themselves when in natural settings or tease humans into such a state of confusion that they didn't need a disguise. Being in costume felt both illicit and thrilling—it might qualify as even more fun than Halloween.

Lucas looked her up and down, much more slowly than was necessary. "Definitely unrecognizable as Ava Fae."

Ava pumped her fist. "Success." Scratching at one of the voluminous fake eyelashes now attached to her eyelids, she smiled at Lucas. "You may call me the master of disguise. Or just Dr. Disguise, whatever rolls off the tongue more easily."

"Well, Dr. Disguise, I'm not sure how to break this to you, but although you don't look like Ava Fae, you've chosen to conceal yourself by dressing like a *Rocky Horror Picture Show* enthusiast."

Ava looked down at her tight black skirt and corset, platform boots, and heavy makeup and realized the truth of his statement.

"Like I explained before, the disguises have a very specific purpose. We'll be able to charm our way through the airport no problem. But we need to make sure that nobody afterwards can describe which way we went or what plane we were on—that the Ares can't track us by interviewing people at the airport."

Lucas moved his face to within inches of Ava's and an eyelash dislodged from her eye, wafting breezily to the ground as if it were snowing in *The Rocky Horror Picture Show*. "I have to stand at least ten inches away from you just to avoid being poked by one of your new eyelashes." Lucas rubbed his forehead in frustration. "Why exactly did you think dressing like that would attract less attention at the airport?"

Plucking the other eyelash off with rather more force than was necessary, Ava frowned at Lucas. "We *are* in San Francisco."

Lucas looked at her in disbelief for moment and then chuckled.

"Ok, ok," she said. "So I'm not the master of disguise. But I wanted to practice."

"I'll tell you what your first mistake was."

"Tell me."

"You bought that whole outfit 'cause you wanted to wear the wig. You saw that luscious drape of a wig in the costume shop and you just couldn't resist."

Ava grinned ruefully. "How'd you know?

"It happens to the best of us," Lucas said, shaking his head in remembrance. "Ninth grade. Seduction exercise with my father. We went to get our garb for the exercise and I saw it. All party in the back, serious in the front— that mullet was calling to me."

Ava giggled. "So did you rock the mullet? I bet you could've pulled it off."

Lucas frowned, his expression suddenly distant. "When my father saw me clowning around with it in front of the mirror he smiled at me. Like he understood the joke. And then, I watched his reflection in the mirror. With that smile plastered on his face the whole time, he picked me up and shoved me straight into the mirror. When the salesperson ran back, he pretended to be tending to my wounds. And he gave her that same smile. Always that smile. To the teacher asking about my bruises, to the Elders asking about my progress, to the parents of friends who asked why I couldn't sleep over." Lucas shivered. "I was picking glass out of my scalp for days afterwards."

Ava dug her fingernails into her palm but didn't say anything. What could she say? The best way to help Lucas was to get them the hell out of the country. They walked in silence for twenty minutes, heading towards the Golden Gate Bridge. Their plan had been to walk around the Presidio, first testing their disguises on one another and then gauging how much attention each was attracting as they went. But there weren't many people out and about to attract attention from. It was an unusually chilly day for February and the air was heavy with moisture. Ava amused herself by tracing her fingers through the air, calling tendrils of fog to follow her gestures as if her fingers were mini jet planes trailing clouds of exhaust.

"Avaaaa," Lucas drawled in frustration, pointedly eyeing the wake of fog trailing from her fingers.

She considered tracing out "sorry" in giant looping fog letters before quickly nixing the idea. An image of fourteen-year-old Lucas covered in glass stilled her itching fingers.

Lucas let out a long sigh of disappointment. Ava turned to him, saying, "What did I do now?"

"It's not you." He gestured at a sign posted near the entrance of the park. Ava read it quickly:

Attention visitors:
The Golden Gate Bridge is closed to pedestrian and motor vehicle traffic until further notice.
We apologize for the inconvenience.

Ava nodded. "Oh, that explains why there are so few people around today. I remember reading something about this last week. A northern stretch of the San Andreas Fault ruptured and I think it damaged the bridge."

"Another natural disaster caused by your grandma?" Lucas asked with a smile.

In reply Ava just offered Lucas her best Cheshire cat grin.

"This bridge is a work of art," Lucas said, his tone reverent. Framing the bridge between his outstretched fingers, he added, "Look at those crisp red lines standing as a triumph of humanity."

Ava snorted but Lucas continued, undeterred, "A veritable temple of human engineering, crafted from the finest American steel. Did you know that each tower contains six hundred thousand rivets?"

Without thinking, Ava replied, "Rivets and steel are nothing against the power of the Earth." Lucas gave her a questioning look, clearly surprised by the ominous nature of her tone. Ava was surprised herself. She shivered and whispered, "Let's keep moving."

A half-mile later Lucas twitched. "Ava, I swear to God…"

"What?"

"Don't pretend you haven't noticed."

"Noticed what?" Ava said as she gently shooed away a bee that had landed on her shoulder.

"That," Lucas replied, pointing at the bee. "They're following you. The whole hive."

"Oh." Ava looked surprised. "I didn't even notice." She smiled ruefully. "They like to rest on my shoulders for a few moments when they have a long journey to search for nectar."

Lucas rolled his eyes and nodded his head to the left where a little boy and his parents were huddled on a blanket eating a picnic lunch. The little boy was watching Ava with wide eyes.

"Oops."

"Yeah, humans are afraid of bees, Ava. They tend to notice when they're around." Lucas shrugged his shoulders and stopped walking abruptly. "Maybe we should just leave. The whole point of this little outing was to see if your disguise was ready for the airport," he said, gesturing at her outlandish garb. "And between your homage to *Pretty Woman* and your shoulders serving as some kind of halfway house for the bees of the Presidio, I would say we are not prepared for the danger of the airport."

Ava put her hands up in a gesture of surrender. "No. I'm trying I swear."

Lucas looked at her expectantly.

"I know I keep messing up." Ava kicked at a clump of dirt for a few moments and then turned to look Lucas squarely in the eye, talking quickly, "Imagine you spent your whole life playing soldiers with your friends and it was really fun and really exciting but you could always just go back to your house and stop playing whenever you got tired. That is what my life has been up until these last few weeks. I sat at the feet of my Elders, dazzled by these epic tales of danger and heroism that made me yearn to be a warrior of my Order. I got to explore these powers—the kind of powers that all little kids dream of having—while frolicking in the woods with a merry band of animal companions. But I never faced real danger." Ava kicked the dirt clump viciously; it exploded into a cloud of dust. "And now it's like somebody has armed me with a bazooka and dropped me in a war zone…I'm just waiting for my friends to come back and play soldiers with me."

Lucas's face softened slightly—the anger replaced with confusion. "Why did they do it? Why did they leave you so unprepared?" The way he asked, it was clear it was a question he'd been puzzling over for months.

Ava looked around for another mud clump to kick. Finding none, she looked up to meet Lucas's gaze. "I think…I think they loved me too much. They got so focused on making sure I was happy in the present that they ignored the truth of my future."

"How *human* of them," Lucas said with the ghost of a smile on his lips.

Ava shrugged, matching his half-smile with one of her own.

Lucas shook his head and pointed to the bridge, which was now less then a mile away. "If you can get your bee posse to disperse and somehow manage not to attract any more attention while we're walking through the park, then we'll go straight to the airport." He grinned at her, almost but not quite nudging her in the side as he said, "Gotta stop being such a Queen Bee."

"Remember what I said about you and puns—you're un*bee*lievably bad at them."

They traded offensively bad jokes and enjoyed the beauty of the park as they moved towards the bridge. After a few moments, Ava found herself walking several steps behind Lucas. She scanned the trees around her looking for a squirrel or bird with whom she might be able to convince Lucas to practice his empathy.

With her senses fully focused on the natural world, Ava reveled in the beauty of the park. These moments of quietude were scarce. As she drank in the shimmering pattern of golden light and vivid greenery spreading out around her like an iridescent spider web, something tugged at her consciousness. Shaking it off as the inevitable anxiety that accompanied a life on the run, she tried to refocus on the vegetation surrounding her. But the feeling stayed with her, gnawing away at the back of her mind— she must be picking up on Lucas's anxiety about the airport. She focused on a particularly lovely tree—its boughs swooping and dipping gracefully. And then, in a moment of terrible clarity, it dawned on her. She screamed inwardly and her feet faltered, but she gritted her teeth and forced herself to keep walking as if nothing were wrong. Plastering a smile on her face, Ava caught up to Lucas and whispered, "They're gone…all of them. All of the animals are gone."

Lucas looked at her for a moment—from the quick movement of his pupils she could tell that he was scanning their surroundings to ensure the accuracy of her statement. Then she felt fire explode up her arm as Lucas grabbed her wrist. A picture of the Golden Gate Bridge bloomed in her mind and he whispered, "Run."

Her body pitched forward to obey his command, every muscle straining to escape the lifeless stretch of park. But then she jerked to a halt, her stomach muscles screaming in protest, and grabbed Lucas's hand, shouting, "Wait!" in her mind. She gestured at the fog ahead of them and hoped that Lucas understood what she wanted to do. Channeling her energy to connect with the water of the bay, she whispered to the hydrogen and oxygen atoms, stirring them into a frenzy. Her fingers trembled as she tried to concentrate through the fear—she felt terribly vulnerable without the animals as her eyes and ears.

She heard Lucas gasp. She opened her eyes to see a dense curtain of fog gathering in the bay, leaving all but the highest point of the bridge obscured. The cloud of fog began to churn towards them, obfuscating everything in its path until the entire world was shrouded in gray. Only when it had fully enveloped them did Ava take a breath. She had called the fog so thick that she could not see Lucas through its embrace but she could feel the terror rising off of his body. The fear spiked and Lucas yelled, "Run!" this time abandoning any pretense of subtlety.

And Ava ran. Terrified by the disappearance of the animals, she shot off towards the bridge, her golden hair streaming out behind her. She couldn't see anything through the gray and only had the roughest sense of Lucas's location. She tried to hone in on him by tracking his emotion like some kind of primitive sonar. But everything was so confused. She pushed her body faster and faster away from that terrible place behind her. Her fingers itched to call the wind but she forced herself to conserve the rest of her energy after having expended so much to summon the fog. Even without calling it she felt it stirring through her hair, pushing on the skin behind her knees, encouraging her to move ever faster. She could feel the roots of the trees beneath the ground, pulsing with encouragement and the steady rhythm calmed her from the initial terror she had felt at the disappearance of the animals. The park's creatures had fled without warning;

she couldn't imagine what would have caused them to desert her.

She felt her skin prickle and out of the corner of her eye she saw a blinding flash. Just ahead of her and to the right stood an oak with flames licking up its trunk to the branches—the fire burned unnaturally bright and hot and an acrid scent filled the air. She heard distant shrieks as the people in the park saw the blaze and felt bile rise in her throat at the destruction of the ancient life force. Clearly the Ares were not afraid of making a scene.

She had been warned many times by her Gaia teachers, especially her grandmother, that her connection with the natural world could be a liability. As an Alpha, her connection would be magnified many times over. But even so she hadn't expected the connection to be so visceral— fire shot through her own trunk, spreading to her limbs as it had done with the oak. She was overwhelmed by vertigo as she tried desperately to keep up her pace. Her heart raged for the needless destruction of the oak and cold sweat poured down her body.

Another blinding flash—this time to her left. This tree was even closer and the heat rising off of the billowing flames was oppressive. She stumbled slightly and knew it was only moments until she collapsed from the agony of fire skidding across her nerve endings. But she pushed herself to run, drawn by the soothing tug of the ocean water in front of her. She could see the red of the bridge rising like a target. When the third flash was to her right she felt a terrible dread. *They're corralling me. They want me to go towards the ocean, too. But why?*

She fell to the ground as she felt the roots constricting in torment below her—her legs twitching uselessly as pain screamed along her synapses and paralyzed her muscles. The wind that had been swirling through her hair was more aggressive now, tearing at her clothes, egging her into action. She gathered it around her and thrust it towards the sky. For two painful seconds nothing happened and Ava could feel the lurking malevolence of her Ares pursuers close in on her as the flames consuming the nearest tree flared higher. Then a splash of water the size of a quarter hit her head and the sky opened as if someone had run a butcher knife through it. Thunder rumbled as water fell in thick vertical tubes towards the ground. There was an angry sizzle as it extinguished the flames all around her and Ava felt relief flood through her. As the fire faded, the pain in her limbs began to subside and her mind cleared momentarily.

At that moment, Ava realized that this chase through the park was merely the prelude to the action. She pulled herself bodily from the mud, which released her with an unhappy squelch. She had a moment to look down at the imprint she had made, realizing she had sunk a full three feet into the ground as the earth had tried to bury her in protection, before the wind behind her shrieked with fury and propelled her through the sheeting water. There was nowhere left to go but the bridge and she hoped like hell that the mud, rain, and wind would be able to slow her mystery attacker for a few seconds. Lightning forked in jagged patterns above her as she hurdled the construction barrier and started sprinting across the bridge.

A hot flash of terror tore through her and it took her a confused moment to realize that it was Lucas's fear she had picked up and not her own. And then she felt a surge of relief—Lucas was on the bridge as well. But her relief was short-lived. A huge steel cable tore off from the bridge with a shriek and swung dangerously close to Ava's face. She cursed under her breath. *You've got to be kidding me.* She shivered as she sprinted, feeling disoriented without the pulse of the earth beneath her—a sixth sense to guide her through danger. This was why her attackers had been herding her towards the bridge. With the Ares' command of metal, the structure was a mile-long weapon—to cage her, crush her, burn her.

Pain shot up her leg as she sank into a molten steel sinkhole that had appeared in front of her without warning. With a cry she dragged her leg free as she felt the steel tighten around the limb. She was only getting further away from land and her energy source as she sprinted. A spray of steel erupted in front of her. She threw an arm up to cover her face and felt the molten metal splatter against her skin. As she slowed, distracted by the burning spreading up and down her arms, a body hurled itself onto her back. She hit the bridge with a thud and immediately used the momentum to roll with her attacker, struggling to gain the upper hand. But she was too exhausted from the exertion of calling the storm earlier in the night, and the attacker forced her onto her back, pinning her against the floor of the bridge.

She scratched and bit, sinking her teeth into the attacker's neck, using moves that would inflict maximum pain with minimum energy as she figured out what to do next. As she fought to clear her mind, the attacker managed to clamp a huge hand around her throat and slam her head into the bridge. Trapped beneath the figure she could do nothing but stare at her attacker—it was then that she saw them, the cold, emotionless eyes from Lucas's memories that had been haunting her sleep. *The Makhai.*

She inhaled sharply—she recognized this man. He was one of the warriors who had surrounded the little girl with Gaia powers. He was older now, but the straw-colored hair and moon-shaped scar on the side of his left eye were unmistakable. He had killed that little girl. His eyes seemed to brighten as she weakened—he was feeding on her pain, clearly invigorated by the violence he wrought. No wonder Lucas was afraid.

She felt the metal grow hot beneath her, smelled the singe of her hair, the breath caught in her throat as the hand squeezed tighter. She would pass out soon from the heat and the pain and the lack of oxygen. As she faded, the elements around her grew more frantic, wind howled

50

along the bridge, lighting tore across the sky again and again like the finale of a fireworks show. The sheer power of the natural display jogged her memory—what was it that the sign had said? *Attention visitors...the Golden Gate Bridge is closed...until further notice.* It had been damaged by seismic activity. If only her grandmother were here—she would be able to summon the power of the quaking earth.

An agonized cry pierced her waning consciousness. She couldn't tell if it was Lucas or another attacker but anger surged through her at the thought that Lucas's nightmares about the Makhai were becoming reality right in front of her powerless form. With no energy left to act, she opened her mind totally to the natural world, becoming a permeable membrane. It was a dangerous strategy—she would feel every act of destruction inflicted on the natural world around her—but she needed the Earth to feel the full force of her anger and desperation. She needed the emotions to filter down into the depths of the Earth and be amplified a thousand times back.

Nothing happened for a few seconds and Ava's eyelids fluttered closed as the heat overwhelmed her. She felt a tremor beneath her...the bridge was moving. *No, the earth below the bridge was moving.* And then came another tremor.

With a terrible shriek of ripping metal, the bridge rent in two, mere feet away from Ava and her attacker. He was thrown off of her by the violence of the movement. Scrambling for a handhold as their section of the bridge tilted precariously towards the ocean, he was left dangling below her. Ava, who had had an instant to anticipate the action, had secured herself to the bridge above her assailant. She had a moment of satisfaction as she watched shock bloom on his face, followed almost immediately by base fear, before the wind slammed into him and knocked him from his tenuous perch into the water below.

Straining her muscles to get a better view of the falling body without falling herself, she wondered if she should follow him into the water to finish the fight. She had no doubt that his Ares-enhanced limbs and organs were strong enough to survive the fall and he seemed by no means down for the count.

A violent cracking sound interrupted her deliberations. Ava peered down at the bay below and gasped. The section of water directly beneath the path of the falling man had hardened into a thick sheet of ice. She looked wildly around for Lucas. *Had he made the ocean ice over like that? When had his Gaia powers gotten so strong?* But after several seconds of scanning what was left of the bridge she realized with a sickening thud that she was alone. She watched the bloodstain spreading out from the prone form across the already melting ice. With a whimper she emptied the contents of her stomach on the bridge. So much for playing soldier. She had killed a man without even trying.

She looked down at the blisters covering her skin and hurled herself with reckless abandon over the edge of the bridge, unmoved by the consequences of her action. But she was not to feel her self-inflicted punishment; as she dropped closer to the surface, a wave of water thrust up to catch her before gravity could do its deadly work. She fell against the pillar of water and immediately tendrils of it broke up and curled around her to soothe burning skin and extinguish smoking hair.

She stayed in the water's embrace for a long time, feeling the evil heat seep slowly out of her, drawn by the ocean's healing touch. She heard the haunting call of a humpback whale in the area, questioning and worrying as any overprotective mother. Ava begged the whale to stay away. Who knew how many more attackers were in the area? Hot shame snaked its way through her as she thought of the body lying on the bloodstained ice. She tried to make sense of the last few moments of the fight. How had she caused the earthquake without trying? Had other people been injured? She hadn't wanted to save herself and Lucas like that. Not like that.

Tentatively she opened her mind to the earth below her, gently probing the layers of rock with her senses. She held her breath, terrified that even this slight action might trigger more unintended consequences. Apparently her body was now a very uncontrollable and very dangerous weapon. Pushing away her fears, she pooled her focus, determined to understand what had happened so she could learn to control her power in the future. She refused to live life as a liability.

After several minutes spent exploring the tectonic plates and testing the earth, she had constructed a rough timeline of the events that had triggered the bridge's destruction. It seemed that the seismic activity that had damaged the bridge the week before had been merely the first wave of movement. The fault had been poised for another earthquake—her energy must have tipped the delicate balance. She breathed a small sigh of relief. She hadn't so much caused an earthquake as precipitated one that was already coming. But even from her underwater haven she could hear the harsh wail of sirens emanating from every corner of the city. She imagined the ambulances and fire trucks racing to save people and property and could barely breathe under the new load of guilt that had settled over her like a weighted blanket.

She closed her eyes for a moment, gathering the ocean water around her like a cocoon, a tangible barrier to escape from the pain and shame and fear. She must have nodded off in the rare peace of the moment because when she opened her eyes the bridge looked no bigger than her hand in the distance. She clucked sternly at the water around her for dragging her so far afield and beckoned for a current to speed her back to the city. The water churned reluctantly at first, clearly unhappy at the prospect of returning her to the source of danger, but it eventually relented and she soon found herself deposited on a small beach bordering a grassy field. She lay there in a sodden heap, too exhausted to even right herself. The sound of sirens washed over her, each one hitting her like a slap in the face. She let the overwhelming sadness rise up over her—an emotional flare shooting into the night that Lucas could find and track if he were anywhere in the vicinity.

Chapter 6

A full hour passed before she could sense Lucas coming. He emerged out of the darkness; when he got close enough she could see that he was nursing a black eye and various scratches and burns. Her stomach turned and she wondered if he too had killed his attacker...or attackers. He came to stand over her, and she could tell from the movement of his eyes and faint hint of concern emanating from him that he was scanning her body for injuries.

"Excuse me, ma'am, I'm going to have to write you up a ticket." He stroked an invisible mustache, doing his best impression of a traffic cop. "Your left taillight is out...and you broke the Golden Gate Bridge."

From her position on the ground she started laughing and crying—snot mingling with her tears to streak down her face. "It's not funny."

"It's a little funny. You were being attacked by one person, *one person*," he said, holding up his index finger, "and your first instinct was to unleash an earthquake to bring down the *Golden Gate Bridge*." His voice was equal parts wonder, reproach, and excitement. "This is why we can't have nice things."

At this Ava began to laugh in earnest.

Lucas continued, "Was it because I called it a triumph of human engineering? Because if so, I just want you to know that the Pyramids are garbage—definitely not worth a trip to Egypt—"

"It wasn't me. The earthquake. It wasn't me." She hadn't wanted to tell him her theory yet—God knows they didn't need anything else to worry about—but the words had bubbled up before she could stop herself.

Lucas looked at her in disbelief. "Who was it? Your grandma again? She can't cause all the natural disasters in the world, Ava." His tone turned more serious. "You know I was just teasing you before—your power is actually incredible. It was really kind of a brilliant maneuver—"

"I'm not being modest," she cut in sharply. "I think it was *she*—Gaia. I think Mother Earth has decided to enter the battle herself." As Lucas continued to look at her, incredulity written all over his face, her words tumbled out faster and faster. "I didn't kill him. I didn't want to kill him…It didn't even occur to me to ice over the water to break his neck as he landed…I heard it…I heard the sickening crack of his body snapping like a twig as he landed."

"Slow down. Mark is dead?"

Ava eyes widened. *Mark?—Lucas had known their attackers.* "Yes." She wiped her snot away as she continued, "After the earthquake, which I swear I didn't cause, the man attacking me lost his balance and tumbled off the edge of the bridge. While he was falling the water below him iced over and…"

"And you're sure you didn't communicate subconsciously? Maybe you'd seen another Gaia warrior try that move before and so it was filed away in your mind? Somewhere deep down? It wouldn't be impossible—the natural world seems to be responding to even your most fleeting of thoughts."

"I've never seen that 'move' done before. And it's not something I would just think of. It's so…twisted."

A siren interrupted them; the sound and what it signified suddenly left Ava feeling claustrophobic. "Let's get out of here," she muttered and put a hand up in the air, motioning towards Lucas to help her up. Hesitantly he did so. As soon as she made contact with his skin she flinched violently away from him. The same burning energy had ignited at their contact, but there was something else, something even more disconcerting. She turned and dry-heaved.

"What's wrong?" Lucas asked in concern, moving towards her.

"Stay away from me," she barked.

Lucas put up his arms and retreated in confusion. Ava swung around to confront him. "I can feel the satisfaction seeping out of your pores. You wanted this to happen." Accusation was thick in her tone.

When Lucas didn't say anything to defend himself, Ava took a step forward and shoved him, making sure to connect the skin of her palms with his bare forearms. The skin on skin contact was like steel striking flint—sparks jumped from the point of friction and drifted lazily to the ground. Ava watched the neon specks with satisfaction for a moment and then shoved Lucas again, harder. This time there was a full shower of sparks. Lucas backed away a few feet, his face impassive.

Ava said, "You dangled us out as bait and I barely made it out alive. I ki—somebody died because of me." She cursed under her breath. "*I broke the Golden Gate Bridge*," she echoed Lucas's joke, but this time the words didn't seem nearly so funny. "And potentially brought a city to its knees."

Lucas returned her stare with no pity in his eyes. "Did you really think nobody else was going to have to die for us to live?" His voice was taut with anger. This time he took a step towards Ava. "Did you know the person you killed? Did you know the name of his wife? His newborn daughter?" With every word, the muscles in his neck tightened a little more.

It was a strange moment. Ava was already angry but she was also picking up on the rage flickering through Lucas's body and it was building in her, coaxing the flame of her own anger. And it felt delicious to be shouting and kicking and pushing. So Ava raised the stakes. She closed the gap between them and raised her arms to shove Lucas again. "Then why did you make us do it? And why didn't you tell me about your plan?"

Lucas grabbed her hand, blocking her forward motion. He held onto it firmly as Ava tried to pull away. "This was the only way. You've heard the rumor that the Ares can read the future? We can…in a way. By knowing every bit of data about a person, every material fact about his environment, we can predict exactly how a person will react in a given situation long before that person knows what he'll do. This is especially true for our own members, who we've monitored since birth and put through a rigorous series of personality and aptitude tests." Lucas sucked in a breath. "I have one and only one trump card in my race to escape the Makhai. The Ares don't know me like they thought they did. And until they recover those last bits of data, until they trace the Gaia blood in my lineage, and fill in the blanks—I can move unnoticed. Like I'm off-map in a videogame. They were expecting me to slink quietly out of America. And so I had to draw them out, so we could get rid of those who were trailing us here—where your power would be at its zenith. If they had ambushed us in the airport we wouldn't have had a chance. You started to see it today with your bees and your fog—you leave a phosphorescent trail, Ava. I needed that to draw them out."

As he had been speaking, their hands had burned hotter with energy. The sparks had turned into flames, which were now licking up their arms.

"But…think of all the people that might have been hurt in the earthquake. What if some of them died? I didn't want this." The last part came out as a wail.

"You don't think more people will be hurt if the Ares succeed in wiping out the Gaia?"

Ava was silent.

"We have to go now, while the Ares are in disarray. While I'm still essentially invisible—unpredictability is our only chance. And you have to follow my lead. We need to leave no trail at the airport—it's critical that they not know where we're going next. We need the head start."

Ava made to pull away, but Lucas held tightly to her arm. "I'm serious. This could be the most dangerous part because we'll have nowhere to escape to." He looked at her solemnly as the flames licked up their arms. "Are you with me?"

"I'm not *not* with you."

He nodded and pulled out of their embrace, watching as the flames disappeared into the darkness. "Good enough for me," he murmured.

Chapter 7

Ava turned her head to stare at Lucas, who was soundly asleep cocooned in several of the courtesy blankets provided by the airline. He had removed his blond wig, exposing a new buzz cut. She had the most intense desire to run her fingers through the short bristles. But she didn't want to wake him—it was a miracle they'd made it this far and he needed the rest.

After hurriedly changing out of their flame-eaten clothes, they had charmed their way through the airport and into first class seats on the next flight to Australia. She had kept her head down, sending calming thoughts around her, leaving scores of sleeping people in her wake. It had taken all of the discipline she had not to look over her shoulder every second, terrified of finding another set of emotionless killer eyes among the crowd. But Lucas had absolutely insisted on the point and she had decided to trust him for the moment. The half hour of waiting after they had boarded the flight but were not yet in the air had left her drenched in sweat. She examined the bloody marks on her arms where she had dug fingernails into skin to keep from jumping out of her seat, escaping from the

Makhai ambush she was sure would come while they were sitting ducks on the runway. But Lucas had been right—the plan had gone off without a hitch. He had nodded off moments after takeoff—it was the first time she had seen him truly relax into a deep slumber. She didn't really want to know what had made him so desperately afraid these last few weeks, haunting him as he tried to sleep, but maybe it would finally come out over the next fourteen hours of forced repose.

Lucas whimpered softly in his sleep like an exhausted puppy and Ava couldn't help but smile. The smile didn't quite stretch across her face—a spurt of jealousy blocked its path. Although she had dutifully kept her head down in the airport she couldn't help but overhear snatches of news coverage from the TVs dotting the terminal. It had all been focused on the destruction wrought by the earthquake. An earthquake she had triggered. She snuck another glance at Lucas. His fear seemed to have receded but her burdens had only grown. She wouldn't be sleeping that deeply for a long time.

It was true that first class had infinitely more legroom than coach, but the proximity of Lucas's body was still disconcerting. Ava turned away from his sleeping form, which was letting off a pulse of warmth with every heartbeat, to look down at the Pacific Ocean stretching out below her. It was midnight blue now but would soon be sparkling azure as the plane headed west. She was so very far from the earth—a feeling that usually made her panic but today made her feel strangely giddy. She had escaped, at least momentarily. A knee knocked into hers gently and she turned to find Lucas rubbing the sleep from his eyes. The giddiness she felt was reflected in his smile.

"We've crossed through the wardrobe to Narnia, at least for a little while. For the next fourteen hours we can be whoever we want to be," she said with a toothy grin.

Lucas replied, "Do you have any idea how advanced the technology is in these new 777s?" He ran his hand lovingly over the plastic of his armrest. "This is so exciting." He rocked forward in his seat. "I'm going to go ask the flight attendant for a tour."

Ava's smile faltered. Lucas must have noticed because he replanted himself in his seat. "Or I could stay here and talk to you about Narnia."

"It was a metaphor," she replied with a mock scowl. "It felt like we were entering a parallel universe, a parallel universe where we might have more *freedom*," she said, arching her eyebrows suggestively, "to act like teenagers."

She felt a wave of attraction roll off of Lucas at her words and fairly pin her to her seat. "Hold your horses, cowboy. We have to test my theory slowly."

Lucas turned to look at her, his face the picture of innocence. "What do you mean?"

"I mean…" Ava trailed off, flustered. "It seemed like your body might…like to join me…in my seat." It was the best euphemism she could muster in the moment.

"Let me guess. You think I'm turned on by my proximity to you. But whatever you think you just felt coming from me wasn't for you. It was for her," he said, pointing to a pretty brunette in the row next to them.

Ava kicked his foot.

"I'm serious. I'm not a mood ring."

"Congratulations," she replied dryly.

"Listen to me, Ava." He smiled playfully and continued, "Consider it a trade. You listen to me and I'll listen to you talk about your strange obsession with children's fantasy books."

Ava kicked him again. "It was a metaphor," she repeated through drawn lips.

Lucas's tone turned serious as he said, "You have a very strong sense of empathy…I've come to understand that the Gaia experience empathy in tangible form…you can literally see and smell and touch the emotions of the people around you. And it's beautiful to watch you connect with everyone from the elderly woman walking down your street to the pigeon fluttering to collect your crumbs to the cricket serenading you at night." Ava blushed with pleasure at the compliment. Lucas continued, "But you have the emotional nuance of a sledgehammer."

Ava leaned forward to interrupt, "Wh—"

But Lucas put his hand up. "Let me finish. Today, after the attack on the bridge, you sensed my satisfaction that my plan had worked. If you had taken a moment more you might also have felt my terrible sadness, my guilt, my overwhelming fear for your safety. You have to give me," he said and then gestured at the people sitting around him, "you have to give all of us more credit. The world is not so black and white."

She realized the truth in his observations and inched towards him.

He seemed surprised at her easy acceptance but recovered quickly and continued, "You know you're not the only ones who can read emotions. The Ares can too, we just do it a little differently. We put great weight in the disconnect between the data we collect from humans and the actions they take." Ava stared at him intently not yet understanding what he was getting at. Lucas pointed to a woman in her mid-twenties three seats over. "Look at that woman in 6F. Her pupils are dilated, she's sweating profusely, and she hasn't unfolded her arms in the last two hours. She's terrified of being on this plane. But she's here." Lucas looked at Ava expectantly. "What does that tell you?"

"That she's a millennial—I've heard they're a masochistic group."

"No. It means she got up the nerve to get on this plane even though the whole time she'll be worried that the plane will malfunction and crash into the sea below and the surviving passengers will be picked off one by one by sharks, forced to watch as their fellow passengers scream as they get eaten alive."

"That is unbelievably specific," Ava replied.

"I know. We had a *very* long wait in the bathroom line before takeoff. But, do you know why she got on the plane?"

Ava shrugged.

"Because her grandmother is getting remarried to her newly discovered soul mate and she doesn't want to miss it. And that is why the Ares revere humans—for the gap between their immediate comfort and their resulting actions." He nodded solemnly and continued, his voice taking on a mock serious tone, "That brave woman risked death by plane-crash-induced shark attack to see her grandmother marry the soul mate she met playing baccarat."

Ava giggled.

"But seriously, if *that's* the fate she thought she'd meet and she still set foot on this airplane..." he trailed off, shaking his head admiringly. "I think that's really brave."

Ava was left momentarily speechless. It was endearing to see Lucas speak with such veneration for their fellow passenger.

When she didn't say anything, Lucas continued, his voice dropping all hint of flippancy, "You know what else I know?"

Ava didn't know what to say. There were so many secrets yet untold—which one had he discovered?

"You don't have to be here. On this plane."

"You're right. I could be down there chilling with the sharks, waiting for planes to crash so we could feast on anxiety-prone millennials."

He ignored her attempt at levity and continued, "If I went back to my Order they would torture me for information and then they'd kill me. Some of the Order's old guard would protest, but with the Makhai in charge— I'm as good as dead." He paused. "You, on the other hand, you would be taken back. The Elders might feign anger, they might even be truly angry, but you could return to them. Instead you're here with me." He bumped her knee gently with his own to underline his point. "Which means that you're either here for my sake, or because you think staying with me can somehow bring about peace between our orders and save the people you care about." He gave her his widest smile yet, exposing all of his teeth and making his dimples stand out like diamonds in the sun. "But I like to think it's mostly for me."

He was right of course. Even if she hadn't been quite so honest with herself or quite so assured of her Order's forgiveness, she knew deep down that they would never kill her. At first she had been so caught up in the need to flee that she hadn't analyzed all of her options—whether she should stay with Lucas or try and make a break for it to return to the Gaia. And then with each passing day, each terrible event, a little voice in her head had grown more insistent. *You don't have to stay here. You could be safe and warm in the protection of your Order. You don't owe Lucas anything.* But she couldn't leave. And Lucas with his surprising display of intuition had identified why. She stayed because her retreat and safety meant certain annihilation for the Gaia—she had to end the war, especially now that she knew she was the Alpha. And she stayed for him.

Gnawing on her index fingernail, she wondered how this little revelation would change their power dynamic. Did he have leverage because he knew she felt compelled to stay with him? Or did she have leverage because he was the only one who had nowhere else to go? Why exactly had he told her now? Was it a sign that he trusted her or was it a test?

While she thought she studied his face. The shorn locks of his new buzz cut made his features stand out even more starkly—the blue eyes, the cheekbones, the light trail of freckles across the bridge of his nose. He stared back at her, letting her study at her leisure. And then at some point she stopped thinking, she stopped breathing, mesmerized by the sudden flush in his cheeks, the slight uptick in his pulse, the widening of his pupils.

Lucas moved his face until it was only inches away from Ava's. "Of course, sometimes all you need is the emotional nuance of a sledgehammer." He stroked his index finger lightly along the inside of her wrist. Ava didn't dare breathe. Savoring the light touch she searched for the telltale coil of smoke rising from the spot of contact. When it didn't come, hope exploded in her chest. She hadn't said anything before but she had thought this might be a possibility. She had hypothesized that while aboard the airplane more than thirty thousand feet above the Earth's surface, they might be far enough away from the Earth's pull that whatever power was causing this burning reaction would be too weak. This flight could be a temporary respite—allowing them to snatch a few hours of affection. Hesitantly, she reached a hand out and ran it through Lucas's shorn hair. He reacted like a cat to her touch, arching his neck towards her hand to maintain contact and purring happily. She waited once again for the burning sensation. She could feel the tension in Lucas's neck under her hand—he too must be waiting for the inevitable disappointment.

When it didn't come, Ava moved her hand down to Lucas's face to trace the hard line of his cheekbone. And then he was kissing her—he had closed the gap between their bodies and wrapped his arms around her. For Ava, it was like catching her breath after a long run. To be without human contact for so long, to have wanted nothing more than a reassuring touch. As they kissed, they explored familiar but long withheld places on each other's bodies—Ava trailed her fingers over the coiled muscle of Lucas's back, moving slowly, trying to memorize the feeling to sustain her for the lonely months they had ahead of them.

The plane vibrated slightly, buffeted by the wind. Ava ignored the movement, shutting out the external world to focus more fully on the task at hand. The plane seats made for awkward positioning and Lucas was essentially lying on top of her, his hands cradling her body as he kissed her. She moved to nestle more deeply into his chest, trailing fierce kisses along his neck.

The sharp ding of the plane's speaker system sounded, and a voice crackled over the loudspeaker: *Ladies and gentlemen please return to your seats and remain seated with your seat belts fastened. The plane has encountered some unexpected turbulence.*

Ava heard what the other passengers did not—a hint of real fear in the flight attendant's voice. The plane was shaking more violently now; unlucky passengers who had not yet returned to their seats were staggering and stumbling down the aisleways, trying desperately not to land in anyone's lap. The wail of a toddler rang out from somewhere behind Ava and Lucas. Other children joined in—the jarring movement of the plane was frightening. And yet, Ava could not pull herself away from Lucas. They kissed, and with each second of intimacy Ava drew hope, warmth, energy, and reassurance.

The voice rang over the loudspeaker again: *Ladies and gentlemen, cabin pressure is dropping. Please remain in your seats and stay calm. Air masks will begin dropping shortly. For parents and guardians, secure your air mask first before assisting loved ones.*

The plane was now being jolted so violently by the wind that glasses in first class were rolling off of trays and smashing, luggage was coming loose from overhead compartments and connecting with unlucky passengers, and people sitting were knocking into their neighbors, tossed around like dolls by the impact.

Abruptly Lucas pushed her away. "It's us."

She looked at him in disbelief. But as soon as the two parted the violent jolting of the plane ceased.

Ava slumped back in her chair, defeated. The explosion at the canyon, the unexpected earthquake, the icing over of the bay, and now this. It seemed undeniable—Mother

Earth had decided to join the party. And apparently she loathed Ava's boyfriend.

They looked at each other nonplussed. "What should we do with the next ten hours?" Ava asked, deflated.

Lucas leaned his elbow on the call button, not letting off until a harried flight attendant finally arrived. "We're going to need all the chocolate you have back there. And cake, lots of cake," he added.

Several hours later, Ava lay slumped in her chair half-heartedly rubbing her stomach and brushing at the crumbs scattered across her body. Lucas licked chocolate off of his fingers while flipping through one of the catalogues from the backseat pocket. "Ava, you've got to see this," he said. "They have an egg-poaching machine that doubles as a blow dryer."

"Enough," she said, grabbing the magazine out of his hands. "We've wasted most of the flight already."

Lucas gave her an injured look.

"Well, the first part wasn't a waste. But I didn't need to eat my weight in ice cream….On second thought, that part wasn't a waste either. But we need to strategize."

"Yes, I love strategizing." Lucas's eyes were a little glassy. Ava chalked it up to all the sugar he had eaten. "Strategizing is what we Ares do."

"Perfect. You start," Ava prompted.

"Ok. Should we start by talking about the part where I put my mouth on your mouth and that almost brought down a jumbo jet?"

"Nope. Don't sidetrack the strategizing," Ava said, only half serious. But she really didn't want to think about how kissing Lucas had almost caused a large object to fall from the sky.

"Don't sidetrack?" He nudged her. "This isn't just about us anymore. Something…someone has changed since the orders splintered. The planetary balance has shifted. You and I," he murmured, gesturing at their slumped forms, "we crossed some kind of sacred boundary."

Ava refused to be shaken from her point. "So we figure out what changed."

"By?"

"By re-tracing history. What really made the orders explode from an uneasy truce into all-out war? World War Two is the key. I know it."

There was a spark of recognition in Lucas's eyes.

"What, what is it?" Ava asked.

"Well, obviously, that's when the Makhai were formed."

"Right, because of my great-aunt. The other Alpha…" she trailed off, thinking about the violent fate of her predecessor.

"I think there's more to the story." Lucas was quiet for a few moments. He ran a hand restlessly through his hair. "Have you ever heard of Rommel?"

"The Nazi commander?"

"Well, yes. He was an officer in the German army during the war. But he was also a member of the Ares. World War Two was an ugly time for our Order."

Ava gave him a look, as if to say, *now is not an ugly time?*

Acknowledging her look, he continued, "I know, but that was the true start of the ugliness. The Ares were experiencing serious infighting with a small but militant wing of the Order who wanted to support the Third Reich in the war. The crackpots insisted that Hitler was leading the world towards the ultimate evolution of humanity." Lucas shook his head, clearly embarrassed. "Luckily, the vast majority of the Order was incensed at such dangerous and ignorant hatred. Rommel was from that wing of the Order, the less crazy one. And he conspired to assassinate Hitler and end the war. But the Ares were besieged both by their own militant members and by the scheming of the Gaia, and Rommel's attempt was foiled." Lucas paused. "After the scheme's failure, he was forced to take his own life. Rommel's death and the prolongation of the war left my Order incredibly bitter. The Makhai capitalized on that bitterness, riding the wave of resentment against the Gaia to power. They painted the Gaia as dangerous ideologues, willing to sacrifice the good of humanity for some trees."

Ava shook her head. She didn't want to believe it. That her Order might have precipitated its own demise. The myth she'd been taught did not match this sordid tale. A voice crackled over the loudspeaker: *Ladies and gentlemen please return to your seats and fasten your seat belts. We are beginning our descent. If you'd like to reset your watches, it's one minute before 8:00 AM in Melbourne and it looks like a beautiful, sunny day.*

Although she was desperately curious to know more about Rommel and the Ares' infighting, there were more pressing matters to attend to before they landed in beautiful, sunny Melbourne. "The Makhai. All roads lead back to them. What's so special about the group? What is it that you're so afraid of?"

Ava rocked back away from Lucas, her neck snapping like she'd been slapped across the face. A split second later Lucas muttered in surprise. He had spilled his glass of apple juice all over himself. Before she could sort out what was happening, Lucas muttered something about napkins and darted towards the bathroom at the front of first class.

Ava took a deep breath, shuddering at the force of the emotion that had just slammed into her from Lucas's body. She shook herself like a soggy dog shaking off excess water. But to no avail—Lucas's fear clung stubbornly to her skin.

A voice crackled over the loudspeaker, *Sir. Sir, please return to your seat.* A moment later, the voice repeated itself, the formerly perky Australian accent now sliding into distinct displeasure, *Sir, return to your seat at once. The plane has entered its descent.*

Ava laughed bitterly to herself. *Good luck with that, lady. This particular passenger does what he wants.* She couldn't believe Lucas had pulled something so amateur—spilling his own drink to avoid explaining the source of his fear. And yet, it was effective. Unless she chased him down and burst into the bathroom, no doubt causing the poor flight attendant to collapse in a fit of apoplexy, she wouldn't be able to pry any more information out of him.

Lucas finally obeyed the flight attendant's command and returned to his seat moments before the plane skidded to a landing on one of the long runways stretching out of the central hub of Tullamarine Airport. He shoved a pile of chocolates into her lap with a wink and an apologetic smile. *At least he knows he's an idiot.*

Ava thought about pushing the candies onto the floor. But Lucas's evident terror had inspired in her more pity than anger. Plus, she thought pragmatically, it was not the chocolate's fault that Lucas couldn't open up to her more. As the plane made its slow trek to the terminal, Ava bit happily into a chocolate stuffed with raisins and almonds and vowed not to let Lucas's strange disappearing act ruin her happiness at having successfully evaded the reach of the Ares. They were safe, for now.

Chapter 8

Stepping out of the Melbourne airport into the sunlit morning, Ava felt like she had completed her journey into a parallel universe. It was the end of February, the dead of summer for Australia, and the combination of hot sun blanketing her exposed skin and the feeling of having successfully escaped from America left her smiling broadly. The air was warm but threaded through with a cooling breeze, and the space outside the terminal was dotted with what looked like miniature palm trees. Everywhere she looked were clumps of happily reuniting family and friends—each wearing some version of cutoff shorts, a tank top, and oversized sunglasses. The logical side of her brain knew that members of both orders were surely still looking for them. But the animal side stretched happily in the sunlight and itched to get into a pair of cutoff shorts of her own. Here, ten thousand miles away, in the opposite hemisphere, and with a sudden switch from the chilly weather of America to the blinding sunlight of Australia, all of the horrible things that had happened in the last several months felt very far away. She looked over at Lucas, who was blinking happily in the summer warmth. Pushing aside an intense longing to grab his hand, she said, "Let's go find your mom."

They hailed a cab and Lucas directed the driver to head towards Federation Square.

"So, you know Melbourne well?" Ava asked.

"Pretty well."

"But I'm guessing your mom doesn't live in the city?"

"I don't think so. This is just the best place to start looking for her. Although I'm rather hoping I can get her to come to us," he said, clearly impressed with himself.

Ava raised her eyebrows. "How?"

"Still working out the kinks in that plan…"

"No newspaper code?" Ava asked with a superior smile.

"Everyone can read the code," he said dismissively.

"I know. It doesn't seem like a very secret way for a secret order to communicate."

"I have an old friend here…"

"We can't trust anyone in your Order."

"He's not an Ares," Lucas said, clearly amused by the idea.

"So how do you know him? The childhood you've described doesn't seem very conducive to making friends outside the Order."

"It wasn't conducive to making friends. But for one glorious summer Greg was my…" he trailed off, a hesitant smile playing at the corners of his mouth.

"Your…?" Ava asked, eyebrows raised.

70

"My wing man, for lack of a better word."

"I thought you said he was an *old* friend. Who needs a wing man when they're a kid?" Ava pantomimed an impression, saying, "Excuse me, Katie, you're looking lovely today. You should come see what my friend Greggy is building in the sand box. It's a work of art."

"Okay, we're not that old of friends. But I told you, my father started my training early." Sadness flashed in his eyes when he said it but he recovered quickly.

Ava felt a pop like the sealing of a Ziploc bag. Lucas had walled in all his emotions from her and she knew better than to pry.

"Well let's find this Greg character then."

The taxi deposited them at Federation Square, which was humming with energy even at mid-morning. As they moved away from the car, Lucas struck an exaggerated pose—pointing his fingers into fake guns like he was a member of Charlie's Angels. "We're going to have to take evasive action. Are you ready?"

Ava giggled, happy to be playing toy soldiers again.

They moved quickly through the city, weaving along sidewalks teeming with people on this beautiful day. Melbourne had an incredible energy to it. Colorful graffiti arced across the brick alleyways, clearly welcomed by the city dwellers—great big crabs and sunflowers and dancing sea creatures could be seen, as if all the subjects of a Van Gogh painting had escaped their frames to dance across the city walls. These fantastical creatures lent a textured effect to the downtown. There were two layers of city dwellers—the silent spectators gazing down from the walls on the parade of citizens meandering past, and the citizens themselves, each competing in an effort to look ever more lively. Fragrances were layered, with sporadic hints of eucalyptus, spicy curry, and grease mingling with the omnipresent scent of coffee. The city center was crowded with towers, grand stone buildings, and bubble-shaped structures, making it look like an alien species had colonized sections of the stately city. Like a pop star executing a dramatic onstage costume change, one layer of the city would quickly dissolve into another wildly different layer. Frenetic markets washed into gorgeous parks into lines of outdoor restaurants. All of this gave Melbourne a chaotic warmth the likes of which Ava had never before encountered.

They were looping back through and around neighborhoods, slipping on and off of trams to confuse whoever or whatever might be following them so Ava had plenty of time to take in her surroundings. While she did, she noticed how many female, and many male, heads turned to gawk at Lucas.

"Now *you're* doing it, Lucas," Ava whispered, mimicking the tone he always used to chide her when she subconsciously attracted the natural world to her.

"WHAT? Where?" Lucas looked around wildly. Ava remembered the immense effort it had taken Lucas to suppress his Gaia powers for so many years and realized that she had just inadvertently played into his biggest fear.

"Sorry, you're not attracting any animals to you. Or you are, but they're all of the human variety."

Lucas opened his mouth to reply but he was preempted by an automated female voice announcing, "Swanston Street stop. All doors will open. Swanston Street."

"This is us," Lucas said, beckoning towards Ava as he moved to the open tram door. Ava stepped down from the tram and took in her surroundings. Restaurants and storefronts lined one side of the street and the other housed a dignified stone building with ivy covering its front—maybe a library or a government building of some sort. She could see the faint outline of towers in the distance, and as they walked up the street towards the stone building, she realized there must be a whole complex of stone buildings extending behind it. She gestured at the compound and asked, "How does this fit into your plan?"

"I have brought you to the best place on Earth." He looked at her expectantly, unable to contain his smile. "College."

Ava stared at him, nonplussed.

Lucas asked, "Where were you trained to hide from members of the Ares?"

"In a crowd."

"What kind of crowd?"

"Well," Ava said, pausing to think, "we learned that a mass of emotions can mask you from anyone following you. The larger and more emotionally charged a crowd the better. So a sports arena full of sobbing football fans or…"

"Or a place where thousands of teenagers live together, eat together, *shower together.*"

Ava's eyes lit up in understanding. "College."

Lucas echoed her, "College."

As they moved towards the ivy-covered stone building, Ava confirmed her previous prediction. Extending behind the dignified building was a warren of stone buildings intermixed with patches of green space. As they walked, Lucas shot her a playful smile and turned around, walking backwards.

Affecting a posh British accent, he said, "And over here we have the college crescent. Around this lovely oval sit the storied colleges, affiliated with the University of Melbourne. The oldest residential college was founded in 1872."

As Lucas continued with the charade, gleefully pointing and pantomiming like a hyperactive octopus, Ava raged internally. Lucas's father had recognized this playful chameleon quality in his son. He had tried to take it and twist it into something dark. Thankfully, Lucas seemed to be uncovering the original without the cloud of his father hanging over him. Perversely, as Lucas became more sure of himself on this adventure of theirs, Ava became less.

She looked up to find Lucas staring at her expectantly. Ava tried to cover her inattention by playing along. She clapped happily and said, "I knew it. You've taken me to Hogwarts!"

They walked along Tin Alley, which seemed to be some kind of main thoroughfare for the University of Melbourne and Ava couldn't help but stare at the students streaming past them. A short distance down the Alley, Lucas walked confidently through a gate that opened onto a wide expanse of grassy field surrounded by a ring of stone buildings. Before he entered he turned to meet Ava's gaze and said portentously, "Soak this in. This may be the only shot at college life we get."

Ava had a moment to reflect on this ominous pronouncement before quick as a flash Lucas was smiling impishly again. He gestured at the grandeur in front of him, whispering reverently, "Trinity College."

Ava had only a minute to wonder how they were going to find this Greg character among the thousands of university students on campus before Lucas waved down a blond boy walking across the grass.

"Is that Greg?" Ava asked.

"Nope, but…he'll know who Greg is."

"How do you kn—"

Lucas cut her off to greet the blond boy, "Hey, how's it going? I'm on old friend of Greg Hitcham, do you know which room is his?"

The person smiled widely. "Oh Greg, yeah. Does he know everyone in America as well? He's in that one," he said, pointing to the third floor of a gorgeous old stone building. "But I'd give him a moment to put his pants on after you knock. Not too fussed about wearing them in the summer."

"Thanks, mate."

"Cheers," said the blond boy as he sauntered off across the green.

74

"I think I'm going to love Australia," Ava whispered under her breath, staring at the back of the towering blond as he moved away.

***

Just as the blond boy had warned, it took Greg a moment to answer the door after Lucas and Ava knocked. But he had apparently not been using those minutes to put pants on, because he answered the door in his boxers.

"Lucas," Greg said warmly and immediately grabbed him up in a bear hug. Ava had a half second to feel slightly left out before the strapping redhead turned and engulfed her in a hug, pulling her off of her feet and into the air in his strong embrace.

After he'd set her back down and released her from the hug, Greg stuck out a hand to shake and said, "I'm Greg."

Although she felt like the handshake was somewhat superfluous after the massive embrace, Ava decided to humor Greg and stuck her hand out in response.

"A fellow ginger. And a lovely one at that," Greg said with a warm smile.

Ava sputtered. Somehow the accent made it sound charming and not corny. "Ava. Nice to meet you, Greg."

He gestured at the lower half of his body. "Sorry about the no pants—"

"Are you though, Greg?" Lucas asked with a glint in his eyes.

Greg shoved Lucas playfully, and they began wrestling in the hallway. Ava had a feeling that this ritual would last a long time, and although it was a welcome sight to see Lucas goofing off with a guy friend, she decided to explore the college while the two old friends got reacquainted. Plus, maybe the blond boy would be back.

She ran her hand along the smooth mahogany wood of the immense banister wending its way through the heart of the old dorm, imagining the decades of college kids who had run, walked, and glided up and down the same stairs. She could sense them here still, the long dissipated emotions of those past generations. The place had a nostalgia hanging over it. But not the bad, melancholy nostalgia. The imprint of years of youthful exuberance and camaraderie lingered in the air, a tangible sensation. Ava, who was not feeling particularly young and who had never felt more lonely, had a fleeting fantasy of staying here—enrolling at an Australian university and taking part in the rituals depicted in the graying photographs crowding the walls. As she stepped back into the outside world, the blinding Australian sun woke her out of reverie. She stopped for a moment and tilted her head up to the sky, imagining she was a sunflower soaking up the sun's rays. Within moments, some of her exhaustion and anxiety began to evaporate.

"Are you lost?" asked a black-haired girl. Ava couldn't help gawking; the girl was dressed in a onesie—what her grandmother might call footie pajamas—in the form of a giraffe, complete with a hood shaped like a goofily grinning giraffe head.

"What, um. Yes. Completely," Ava replied.

Even if she didn't hear the note of despair in Ava's voice, the Australian girl must have heard Ava's accent because she immediately nodded her head in understanding. "Ah, an American exchange student. I'm Jules. I can take you to where the others are meeting down at the pub."

"The pub. That sounds lovely. But I should probably find my…boyfriend."

"You've got a boyfriend already? What've you been in Australia—less than a week? You don't waste any time, do you?" Ava thought the other girl seemed rather impressed. But then the girl added, "Although it's rather more fun without one."

Ava giggled, immediately warming to Jules. She didn't have the emotional bandwidth to explain that her previous declaration about being lost had been more of an existential musing than a statement about her geographic location. Plus, she quite enjoyed being mistaken for the new American exchange student.

"Can you tell me? Where is everyone?" She and Lucas had been counting on a horde of teenagers to cover their tracks from anyone who might be following them, but the dorms seemed distressingly empty for such a lovely afternoon.

"Oh, right. It does seem a little quiet doesn't it? But don't worry, the freshers get here tomorrow."

"Freshers?" Ava asked, brows furrowed.

"The people starting their first year at college. Like you."

"Right. Like me." *If only it were true.* Shaking her head quickly, she added, "Well thanks, Jules. Off to find the old ball and chain."

Before she could make it all the way across the grassy expanse a group of college students waved her enthusiastically over to a picnic table. One of them, a tall boy with a mop of curly black hair, said, "Join us for a glass of cordial."

Cordial—it sounded so quaint. Ava's mind was filled with images of *Downton Abbey* and afternoon tea. She was startled by the day-glow green of the drink handed to her when she sat down at the picnic table. Suddenly realizing how parched she was, she tilted her head back and downed the glass of cordial.

She put the glass down to claps and low whistles of appreciation. "Girl can skull," one of the Australians muttered, clearly impressed. Their excitement was contagious—Ava blushed, feeling an excessive amount of pride. There was only one thing to do—she put her cup back out, gesturing for it to be refilled. After she had finished several more glasses of cordial, to the delight of her fellow picnic table crew, Ava felt comfortable in the knowledge that some truly beautiful friendships had been born out of her cordial conquest. The group of them chatted companionably, watching an orange sun set over the many towers of the stone dorms. At one point it looked like one of the towers had impaled the sun, causing it to bleed fiery crimson into the sky.

Lucas found her there as dusk was settling. After greeting the crowd of college students, Lucas turned to Ava, saying, "Greg said we can crash on his pullout couch."

Ava looked at him wistfully. "You don't have enough friends for us to start setting fire to the rooms of the few that do you have."

"It's a big pullout couch. We wouldn't have to touch at all."

"Or Greg and I could share the pullout couch and you could take the bed," Ava offered innocently.

Lucas screwed up his face. "You know what, let me talk to Greg again. I'm sure we can find another couch for you."

Ava grinned. "Don't you think his and my genes would combine to create beautiful ginger babies?"

"Greg and I will share the pullout couch," Lucas blurted out.

"No it's ok actually. I think I'm going to sleep in that oak tree," Ava said, gesturing at a massive beauty at one end of the quad.

Lucas burst into laughter. "Stop."

Ava's face remained impassive.

"In the tree? Won't that hurt your back?"

"Remember that one time you told me I was the most powerful member of an ancient and deadly order? So no, it won't."

"Fair enough. If you change your mind, Greg and I will be spooning in room 301."

Smiling, she waved him off to play with his friend. But Lucas didn't move. He stood staring gleefully at her.

Ava looked from the massive oak—its limbs reaching at least sixty feet into the air—and back to Lucas. "I'm not going to climb it while you're watching me with that stupid grin."

"What? Come on! I've just never seen you be such a dirty hippy—" Lucas stopped midsentence, distracted by an army of possums scurrying out of the darkness to his left. Swearing, he hopped away from the horde of rodents.

When he looked back up, Ava was lounging happily on a branch forty feet in the air. She was lying with her back against a sturdy horizontal limb, hands behind her head, and her feet propped up on the massive trunk.

Lucas sputtered, "Are you kidding me? You dirty...sending those terrifying devil rodents to violently attack me." He pointed at her, a mock frown across his face. "You better watch out lady, I'm coming for you. Australians are master tricksters. I've learned from the best."

With a great creaking shudder the oak tree trembled, sending a cascade of leaves to the ground. Ava grinned. She was just about to pretend to shiver at Lucas's threat, but the oak had beaten her to it.

"Did the tree just—"

Ava cut him off, "Goodnight, buddy. Have fun with Greg."

"Goodnight."

Ava let out a sigh of relief as she watched Lucas amble over to one of the dorms. At last she was alone to puzzle over her newest problem. The cordial drinking stunt had not been solely about impressing the Australians. She ran the back of her hand against her forehead experimentally. Her skin was still hot to the touch. Not terribly unusual given that the temperature had hovered in the nineties all day, except for the fact that Ava didn't experience weather the way other humans did. The Gaia stayed comfortable, clothed or unclothed, until temperatures reached the very extremes of the spectrum. Her grandmother used to say with relish, "Cockroaches ain't got nothing on the Gaia."

Being overheated was a new and uncomfortable feeling. Indeed, any kind of physical discomfort was rare. Her body was strong and its healing power was unparalleled. She'd never experienced the common ills of humanity—colds, sunburns, chicken pox, or the flu. Why did she have to start now? Was it some kind of body development? *I've already been through puberty.* She ran a hand over the curve of her hips as she pondered the new health distraction. *Definitely been through puberty.* What if this were some strange side effect of being the Alpha? What if she had to go through a second puberty as she evolved? Her mind spiraled in anxiety; it was late at night and her brain was free to worry without being rudely confronted by reality. She wished she had access to a computer to look up her symptoms as she had seen so many of her high school friends do when they got sick. But she knew from watching Natasha's searches on the internet—frantically pursued after a particularly nasty case of hives—that the search would just "reveal" that she was beset by flesh-eating bacteria. If you searched long enough, it was always flesh-eating bacteria.

Lucas was nowhere nearby, so she couldn't blame the claustrophobic unease on him. She was not accidentally stealing his emotions—this anxiety was all her own. Sighing, she pushed the new worry deep down inside—it would have lots of company with all of the other worries she'd been accumulating of late. If she couldn't solve the problem, she could at least make herself more comfortable. Concentrating on the water of Port Phillip Bay, which was only about ten miles away, she called a cool breeze to wrap itself around her and soothe her burning skin. Even with the makeshift solution, she didn't manage to drift off until the sun was rising over the dorms' towers.

***

It's the eye of the tiger…it's the thrill of the fight…rising up to the challenge of our rival. Ava looked up blearily from where

80

her face had been pressed into the bark of the tree branch. From the position of the sun she knew she couldn't have been asleep for more than an hour. And yet despite the early hour, *Eye of the Tiger* was now blasting from every corner of the grassy quadrangle. Unable to resist, she sang along for a chord—voice raspy as sandpaper—and punched her arms into the air. The birds, which descended on the oak to take shelter in the tree throughout the night, erupted into the air.

"I'm not that bad," she said defensively. Just like it had the night before, the oak tree shook for a brief moment, once again causing a cascade of leaves to fall to the ground. But this time she had the distinct impression that the tree was shaking with laughter—at her.

It dawned on her that the song was a cue of some sort—probably a rallying cry for these "freshers" everyone kept talking about. In which case, she had better climb down from the tree before anybody noticed her eccentric choice of sleeping arrangement. The thought came a moment too late. She was just setting a foot down to begin her descent when she saw them—a mass of teenagers streaming forth from all of the dormitories ringing the quad, as if the buildings had projectile vomited the entirety of their occupants simultaneously. They were all dressed in neon green—so bright Ava had to shield her eyes for a moment—and heading straight for her.

They moved ever closer, laughing and chatting, some dancing to the music, a few throwing in the random cartwheel as they walked. Excitement dueled with tiredness on their faces and all had lost the battle against bedhead. She caught sight of Lucas in the pack of freshers, shimmying anxiously, as if he were trying to shake out a bug caught in his shirt. He must be worried about her. And then next to Lucas, she caught sight of Greg. Rather than a neon t-shirt, he was dressed in full jester regalia down to the tips of his pointed shoes and the bells on his many-peaked hat. *This place is mad. Absolutely barking mad. And I love it. But how to get out of this tree?*

Jules, the girl who had been dressed in the giraffe onesie the day before, began clucking at the freshers to assemble around Greg. Still groggy, Ava panicked that she would be left behind from the day's festivities and miss out on Lucas's plan.

She shimmied quickly and quietly down the oak's trunk until she reached a branch about fifteen feet off the ground. There were no more lower branches for footholds and she didn't want to shimmy down the trunk like a rogue black bear chasing errant campers. She planted her feet on the branch, checked to make sure there was nothing below her, and sprung into a double backflip out of the tree. She landed in the middle of a crowd of freshers and looked up to find hundreds of surprised eyes trained on her. Panicked, Ava sunk into an exaggerated bow. There was dead silence for several seconds. Then Greg ran over, the bells on his hat tinkling merrily as he sprinted, and lifted one of Ava's arms up in a gesture of triumph. "What do you know? We got one crazy American student this year!"

The crowd of freshers erupted into cheers and Ava breathed a sigh of relief.

Jules sauntered over and nudged Ava's elbow playfully, saying, "Americans really do love to make an entrance, huh?"

Ava tried to smile at Jules but the utter stupidity of her plan was beginning to dawn on her. She looked around for Lucas, afraid to see his reaction. Something soft hit her on the shoulder. She darted a hand out to catch the object and realized it was one of the neon tees. Whirling around, she caught Lucas's eye. The tenor of his mood was clear; she made a mental note to avoid him for the next couple of hours.

The gathered freshers began a ritual of "stretching"— led by Greg, the ritual was largely a pretext to get a hundred teenagers to look as ridiculous as possible. Giggling hysterically as she did another awkward hip circle, Ava felt a wonderful sense of community with all the other people who looked like idiots around her. As she dropped into another lunge Ava pondered one of the great mysteries of the universe—why did making yourself look as idiotic as possible with a group of strangers always seem to forge an indelible bond? She smiled, wishing Sheba could join her in the aerobic shenanigans—the bear would have a field day. Although she'd probably try to muscle in on Greg's jester job and the two would have to wrestle for supremacy. At the image, Ava felt a pang of nostalgia. She pushed it aside and tried to find her way back into the goofy rhythm of the moment.

Next, the group of rowdy teenagers packed their way onto the trams running by the college and set forth towards downtown Melbourne. As she attempted to pry herself loose from an overstuffed tram, eventually carried forward through the doors by the force of other excited freshers, Ava realized the genius of Lucas's plan. As far as she could see, streaming out of all the other tramlines in the city were thousands of teens from different colleges dressed in various shades of garish neon. *Today, we're invisible.*

As they ran from landmark to landmark, carousing and singing and rolling on the ground at each one, from Federation Square to Flinders Street Station to the Melbourne Cricket Ground, Ava tried to keep an eye on Lucas's activities. But more than once she was distracted by the jubilant spirit of Greg or Jules. She did manage to catch him sneaking away from the main cluster of students several times, and it seemed clear that whatever his plan, Greg was privy to it.

One of their last stops was the State Library of Victoria. On the street outside of the library Greg instructed the students to practice their "stretching" routine from earlier that morning, preferably by drafting willing passers-by to join them. The students spread out along the street looking for potential partners and Ava eyed a fierce looking elderly woman with a puff of blue hair. As she moved to greet the lady, she heard a whisper in her ear, "Stall the group here for a moment, please."

Half turning to catch Lucas's eye, she responded, "How do you suggest I do that?"

"I'm sure you'll think of something," he said with a leer and a wink at her chest.

She turned to find Lucas sliding into the library, now without his neon shirt, and sighed. Turning back to the group of college students, most of whom had already performed the requisite hip circles and were ready to move on to the next challenge, she tried to catch the group's attention by clearing her throat. A few eyes turned towards her. *On to plan B*. Breathing deeply, she reached inside of herself, summoning her pheromones to dance and swirl, turning on her Gaia charisma, and cleared her throat once more. This time faces began to turn towards her like sunflowers towards the sun. She began, "Four score and seven years ago…"

After finishing up with the Emancipation Proclamation, she moved on to Kennedy's inauguration speech. Just as she was saying, "And so, my fellow Americans: ask not what your country can do for you, ask what you can do for your country," she caught sight of Lucas emerging from a crowd of people near the front of the library, his neon shirt on once more.

He moved around until he was right behind her. His breath on her neck, he whispered, "Really? This speech?"

"What?" she sputtered defensively. "They loved it. So much so that I thought I'd give them a little taste of Eleanor Roosevelt next. What'd you expect me to do—flash them?"

Lucas grinned. "No, of course not. Where'd you get that idea?"

Ava glowered at him.

"Oh you mean before, when I winked at you? I was merely intimating that you should speak from the heart. And besides, I thought that if you were going to go with a Kennedy, you'd at least go with Bobby."

She narrowed her eyes at him. "Ok, bud. I see what you did there." Her voice dropped and she asked, "Did you get what you needed?"

Lucas flashed her a thumbs-up signal.

***

After chasing the preternaturally energetic form of Greg (was he some lost son of the Gaia?) through the city for half a day, Ava was ready to collapse in a heap when they finally returned to the dorms. But the Australians had other plans. They herded everyone into a large room in the basement of the central hall to watch a footy game. Ava soon learned that footy, or Australian rules football, was an exceedingly confusing and exciting game played by athletic Australians in exceedingly small shorts. This was a sport she could get behind.

Jules sat down next to her, companionably offering her some crisps. She explained the rules to Ava and Ava was soon laughing and cheering along with the rest of the crowd.

At one point early in the game, Jules laughed so hard her drink shot out of her nose.

"What's so funny, Julesy?" shouted Greg from the other side of the massive couch.

But Ava never got to find out. At that moment, Lucas strode to the front of the room, laptop under one arm. She could feel the energy he was churning into the crowd—he was pouring on the excitement. "Friends. We have been slandered." He held up the laptop, pointing to the headline on the screen—"Rare book disappears in chaos orientation week. Students to blame?" Accompanying the headline was a bird's eye picture of a mass of students in the streets near the library, sporting the full spectrum of neon colors.

Lucas read out a few lines from the article, "The library's rare copy of *Beauty and the Beast*, dating from 1898, disappeared as a mass of students descended on the city's landmarks in the annual ritual of college orientation."

Ava watched as Lucas riled the students up over some imagined slight in the article for the next ten minutes. He finished by saying, "Friends, post about this story— everywhere. Share it near and far."

Forty pairs of eyes nodded docilely as Lucas spoke. Ava moved uncomfortably in her seat. She had done what Lucas was doing many times—calling on her innate charisma to convince and manipulate people—but it looked distinctly unsettling to watch it done from the outside. Finally she understood his aim—he wanted the story of the book's disappearance to spread like wildfire, far enough to reach even his mother, wherever she was hiding.

As Ava was getting up, Jules asked her, "What are you wearing to the party tomorrow night?"

Ava hesitated.

"You're coming to the party right? It's the fluoro party."

"Fluoro?"

"Fluorescent, silly. You definitely don't want to miss it." Seeing Ava's hesitance, Jules continued, "You better come. I have high hopes for your dance moves after the stunt you pulled this morning."

Ava smiled noncommittally as she moved away from Jules. But her insides were exploding in excitement. *A party. Dancing. Freedom.*

She sidled up to Lucas, parting the crowd of students who were surrounding him—furiously texting and tweeting and emailing as he encouraged them. "So you stole *Beauty and the Beast*? And the college students got blamed for it," she said, shaking her head.

"Don't look at me like that. I'm going to return it. Greg and I have it all planned out."

"Oh good, drag Greg into it." Ava put a hand to her forehead, shaking her head once more. She sensed something from Lucas, something she had felt before—a whiff of satisfaction. Her mind flashed back to the moment on the bridge, when she had pushed him so hard she had drawn sparks from his skin. But this emotion was less potent, less sinister. She nodded and said, "You tipped the story."

Lucas smiled and shrugged. "What can I say? News doesn't make itself."

"That's the only thing news does," Ava replied dryly. "I don't get it. Do you have some kind of secret obsession with dancing candlesticks?" she asked, changing the subject.

"Maybe," he said, wiggling his eyebrows suggestively but he couldn't hide the sorrow in his eyes. "It was my favorite book growing up. My mom read it to me every night—the non-Disney version. No dancing candlesticks in that one." He paused, furrowing his brow in worry. "If she sees it, the news about it being stolen, she'll remember." He added softly, "She has to remember." He covered his evident doubt with a wide smile as one of the Australians reached to high five him.

Gesturing for Ava to follow him out of the basement, he said, "The good news is it's done—no more sleeping like a dirty hippy. In a tree. With only the possums for company. Now we can move on to somewhere less urban, more protected."

Ava's face fell. Surprised at how disappointed she was at Lucas's suggestion, she turned to him, asking, "Don't you want to stay a little longer? I mean, we are relatively safe huddled in this seething mass of teenage emotions."

Lucas's eyes lit up in delight. "Well what do we have here? Little Miss Hippie *loves* college. She can't bear to leave." He paused, thinking about Ava's suggestion. "Trust me, I don't want to leave either. But I'm not sure what point there is to staying. My mother would never come here. We'd have to be somewhere more isolated to have any hope of drawing her out."

"If I said I wanted to stay for a dance party, how much less seriously would you take me?" she asked, ducking her head slightly.

He bent his own head until he could look straight in her eyes again, peering out from beneath dark lashes. "No less seriously, Ava Fae. We can stay one more day. It'll give me time to stock up on provisions." Ava nodded a silent thanks to Lucas—she was sure he didn't need any more supplies and the flimsy excuse made her smile.

Lucas rubbed his hands together in anticipation. "Now, let's go get you an outfit for the party." His voice resuming its usual mischievous tenor, he added, "After the *Rocky Horror Picture Show* disaster, I'm definitely not letting you go shopping alone."

Chapter 9

What is it with Australians and neon? Ava wondered as she scanned her surroundings. In keeping with the theme, the dance floor was covered in fluorescent paint splattered in mesmerizing patterns. She had had a feeling that the college students would really commit to the costume aspect of the party and she was not disappointed. There were people in full-body suits made of neon spandex intermixed with students who looked like they had just dunked themselves in colorful paint, as if the raucous graffiti of Melbourne had come alive to dance and play. One girl had even woven hundreds of glow sticks into an elaborate turtle shell apparatus—now a glowing beacon of fun as the girl spun and spun on the dance floor. Ava looked down at her own outfit and beamed, giving herself an internal high five. *Nailed it.*

Jules, dressed in a tank top and shorts and covered in tiny multicolored dots of neon paint—a living breathing pointillism portrait, ran over to her. Ava had a moment to marvel at the beauty of the costume before Jules grabbed her arm excitedly and said, "No, bud. You *didn't*. You dressed as—"

"Abraham Lincoln," Ava interrupted, smiling self-contentedly.

Jules looked at her appraisingly for a moment and said, "The beard's a good look for you. But what does it have to do with the theme?"

"Abraham Lincoln is always theme appropriate," Ava said with gravitas.

To her credit, Jules just shrugged happily. "Why isn't your boyfriend dressed as Mary Todd Lincoln?" Jules asked, gesturing at Lucas, who was currently wearing paint spattered overalls—over a bare chest—and a white mask. The mask looked like it was carved out of plaster—but it didn't have any pupils and the mouth was frozen in a chilling smirk. The effect was made somewhat less scary by the fact that Lucas was already jumping around frenetically with Greg, who was dressed as a giant egg, in their best estimation of dancing.

"You know your way around Civil War-era American history," Ava said, stroking her fake beard appreciatively. "Very impressive. Lucas does love Mary Todd, but he was enthralled by that mask at the costume store. As were most of the people here it would seem."

"Kind of creepy, right?" asked Jules.

"Very creepy. Abraham Lincoln is kind of freaked out."

"He and I both. You realize you just addressed yourself in the third person…as if you were Abraham Lincoln. You don't think you might be taking it a little too far?"

Ava smiled broadly and grabbed Jules's forearm. "Abraham Lincoln would like to dance now." Jules shook her head with a laugh and led the way towards the dance floor.

The dance floor had been constructed outside beneath the graceful sweep of the oak's branches. With the earth throbbing beneath her and the music pulsing through her veins, Ava felt totally in her element. Through half-closed eyes she watched the whirling gyrating forms around her, mesmerized by the colorful lights flickering over the dancing masses. Flashes of glow sticks popped in her peripheral vision, adding to the colorful chaos. Desire and joy swirled around her, rising off of the dancing crowd and sliding along her skin beguilingly. Fanning herself, she broke away from the crowd and headed towards the refreshment table set up at the far end of the quadrangle. Miniature lanterns had been strung all throughout the branches of the trees encircling the grassy courtyard. Disoriented by the emotion of the evening and enchanted by the thousands of glittering lights illuminating the elegantly arching limbs, Ava once again felt like she had crossed into a parallel universe. One where only this quadrangle existed, protected by an unbroken circle of light. Her shoulders sagged as she relaxed totally into the escape of the moment and hurried her pace to get some water and return to the joyful, numbing embrace of the dancing crowd. This night of youthful exuberance—where teenagers coalesced in a mass of mutual abandon—would be fleeting, and she didn't want to miss a moment of it.

A string of eight or nine college kids had their arms out parallel to the ground and were winding their way across the quad, laughing tipsily. Ava rolled her eyes—a conga line, really? But upon closer inspection, she realized that they were pretending to be flying in an airplane, as children do, arms propped out like miniature wings and waving wildly. At the front of the line was a student pantomiming like an airplane ground crewman, waving the string of students to their next destination. Ava inhaled deeply and released her breath, directing the expelled air towards the feet of the group. She heard a shriek of excitement as the group was lifted a few inches off of the ground by the air current and she shook her head, smiling. There were more shrieks of laughter and a muffled, "Take a picture!"

She had given them a story that would surely become college legend—the day nine tipsy college students willed themselves into levitating through sheer youthful enthusiasm. To the next generations who would fill this space and admire the graying photographs, this would be her legacy. The thought suddenly made her sad. Ava wouldn't appear in any of those photographs lining the wood-paneled halls of the college. Being on the run meant leaving no imprint in any photo, in any city, in any life…

"What can I get you?" a boy asked, jolting her out of her reverie. She recognized him from the crew who had been sitting at the picnic table the night she had chugged her body weight in cordial and she gave him a wide smile.

Ava eyed the drinks lined up across the table. Although the drinking age in Australia was eighteen, and Ava would be turning eighteen soon, she hadn't even attempted to wrangle an orange wristband denoting that she was of age. Given her emotional state the last several days, she hadn't been keen to add alcohol to the mix. She thought about grabbing a soda, but as the now familiar thirst was haunting her again, she thought better of it. "Just water, please."

"No cordial this time?" the boy replied with a cheeky grin.

Ava grinned back and grasped the cup of water the boy held out to her. Somebody whispered in her ear, "You shouldn't be here." Ava didn't recognize the voice. She wondered which of the older student advisors had come over here to prevent her from drinking underage. It felt nice, being protected.

Without turning around she held up one hand—sans wristband—and the other, currently clutching a glass of water. "Don't worry, this isn't alcohol."

When this announcement was greeted with silence, she turned around. She saw that the person behind her was wearing one of the same white masks Lucas had chosen as a costume. She pushed down a shiver at the lifeless look of the mask.

"Who is that under the creepy mask?" she drawled in a singsong voice, attempting to be playful despite her apprehension.

The masked figure didn't respond. From behind the veneer came the voice again, "You shouldn't be here, Ava."

"Look I promise, it's not..." she trailed off, suddenly feeling very alone and very vulnerable—where was Lucas?

The figure spoke again, voice low, murderous, "So easy to kill. Just like Isi."

At the invocation of her slain best friend, Ava's breath caught in her throat and her vision momentarily went black. She tensed her muscles, ready to lunge at the figure, when she gasped. A crowd of masked figures had gathered behind the one talking to her. They each raised a pointing finger at her and whispered in unison, "You shouldn't be here, Ava." The emotion rising off of them was threatening. Ava's eyes bounced from one masked personage to another, frozen by the cold emotionless pits of the eyes, so like the eyes of the Ares killers from Lucas's nightmares.

"Lucas!" Ava screamed, freeing herself from her momentary paralysis and sprinting back towards the dance floor. Knowing he wouldn't be able to hear her over the music but hoping her emotional panic would alert him to her distress, she kept running and screaming.

A hand grabbed her shoulder and Ava spun around, muscles tensed for a fight. She blanched as she saw the white mask before recognizing the figure's worn sneakers as Lucas's shoes. She grabbed Lucas's arm without slowing her sprint and began dragging him towards the gate that would release them onto Swanston Street.

Lucas didn't ask; he just followed her at full speed, tossing his mask as they ran. The hand she was holding grew hotter and hotter as they sprinted but she ignored the heat shooting up her arm. They barreled through the pedestrians out enjoying the weekend night, careening wildly through the streets. Ava glanced back and caught a glimpse of Lucas's confused face—they were sticking to the major pedestrian arteries of the city rather than losing themselves in the smaller side streets, going towards the city center not away. She hoped she remembered how to get to her chosen destination from their first day of elusive maneuvers that had taken them all over the city.

She cursed under her breath and pulled up to a stop. They were on Princess Bridge in the heart of Melbourne's central business district. Ava had been trying to get to the park with the boathouses she remembered from before, but she had led them here instead. She looked around at the throngs of pedestrians and tourists out enjoying the lovely evening and then gave Lucas an apologetic look. He had a moment to mouth, "Not again," before Ava pushed herself quickly and quietly over the railing and into the river below. From beneath the water she heard a splash and Lucas sunk gracefully to where she was suspended in the murky river. She motioned at him to back away from her. Clasping her arms above her head like an Olympic figure skater, she spun gracefully. The water rippled away from her spinning form, leaving a globe-shaped space in its wake, a giant bubble beneath the river hidden from the world above.

Lucas's face was filled with wonder as he glanced at the sphere surrounding them, trailing his fingers along the wall of water. The water rippled at his touch before moving back into position, holding the globe shape.

"Why didn't you start with this when you were teaching me about water?"

Ava thought back to Lucas's spectacular run-in with a boulder during their whitewater rafting excursion and screwed up her face apologetically. "It's not a real Gaia technique. I taught myself to do it when I was younger. It's where I hide out when I want to get away."

"What are you trying to get away from this time?"

Ava explained what had just happened as Lucas's expression grew ever more grim.

Finally, Lucas said, "On one hand, it's vintage Makhai to manipulate humans, to use them as if they were puppets. But this was so much more passive. It seemed more like a warning. Sure they get a rise out of terrifying people, but knives are way more effective at that than people whispering at you."

"I'm not sure about that. The energy rising off the masked figures—*they hated me.*"

"But the message? Again it really doesn't fit the Ares' M.O."

As they continued talking Lucas began to run around the globe, bouncing gently off the walls. Getting closer to Ava, he whispered, "Teach me? Teach me how to do this."

"I will. I promise." She looked away from him as the water began to churn. "I just need to get as far away from here as possible first."

Lucas frowned, saying, "But Greg—I didn't get to say goodbye to…what is it, babe?" Lucas put a hand up to his mouth as if he had just said the filthiest swear word in the world. "Oh my God, I'm sorry, it just slipped out…"

Ava giggled through the tears that had begun to fall. "Oh, *babe*, if you have that reaction every time, you can say it anytime you want. You look like you've just eaten dirt."

"It'll never happen again," Lucas said earnestly. He reached a hand out as if he were just about to brush her tears away. This was a new game he liked to play— pantomiming the affection he wished he could show her if it were not for the new curse of fire impeding their every touch.

The thought made Ava cry harder, her lower lip trembling. "I'm sorry you won't get to say goodbye to

Greg. I just—they mentioned Isi. Said I was just as easy to kill as she was. Did they torture her like this? Foreshadow her death in cruel moments?"

"No, Ava. No." He scrunched up his face in concentration and gestured at the water. A tendril unfurled, stretching out from the wall of the bubble like a disembodied limb. It snaked around Ava—mimicking an arm wrapping around her shoulder.

She managed to smile through her tears, and offer a silent clap at Lucas's performance. Then, a steely look in her eyes, she pushed the arm of water away, as if shrugging off an annoying suitor, and moved slowly and deliberately towards Lucas. She had become accustomed to the sound of Lucas's heartbeat over their last several weeks of constant companionship. A moment before it had been steady—the only steady thing in Ava's new life. But now it was beating a staccato rhythm—pounding out its excitement. Ava hooked a finger into one of the belt loops of his paint-splattered overalls, giving him her best wicked grin. The staccato sped up even more quickly—now the speed of a hummingbird's wings. She hooked another belt loop, and tugged him towards her—pressing her body into his. She snuck a kiss. But it was a fleeting victory. After a few seconds the bubble shivered and collapsed, extinguishing the small fire consuming their clothing.

As they sputtered to the surface, Lucas turned to her in wonder. "What was that?"

"A small act of defiance."

"Well...Vive le revolution!" Lucas yelled, jamming a fist in the air and swimming back towards her, hunger in his eyes.

Ava backtracked in the water, giggling. "That's quite the French accent you have, Monsieur." She fanned herself—the motion only half in gest. *When did it get this hot?*

"Merci, Madame." He pursued her through the water, the predatory glint in his eye growing brighter.

"Sorry, bud. That fire made me all hot and bothered. And not in a good way. I'm boiling."

Hunger turned to concern. Lucas offered, "Let's get further out in the water. We won't stop until you feel safe." He held her gaze until she nodded. Glancing at his overalls, he added, "If only I had chosen a more aerodynamic version of fluoro apparel."

Ava looked down and realized she was still in full Abraham Lincoln regalia. She had tossed the beard while they were running, but the three-piece suit was hanging heavy in the water. She shrugged, grinning at the absurdity of the moment and said, "Oy, Mary Todd, be a dear and help me get my jacket off before we go."

"Sure thing, Abe. Just let me finish editing that Proclamation you asked me to look over—your comma use is a bit erratic."

They were smiling as they started swimming up the Yarra River towards Port Phillip Bay. It wasn't much, but as Ava swam she held onto the smile and savored the memory of the brief kiss—it was the best rejoinder to the masked man she could muster.

Lucas kept his promise. After reaching the bay they hugged the coast, swimming through the night. Lucas swam with eyes wide—clearly fascinated by all of the underwater creatures that were attracted to the two strangers with Gaia blood. Dolphins joined them one or two at a time throughout the evening. By the time the first light of dawn broke, they were surrounded by an honor guard of hundreds of them.

Lucas was not as adept at calling the water to boost him as he swam and his stroke faltered as the miles churned by. When he looked like he might collapse from exhaustion, a dolphin swam close and offered him her dorsal fin for support. Lucas looked at Ava questioningly.

"I know you don't like it when humans ride on—"

Ava interrupted him, "Sabreena offered you a lift of her own free will. I would take it if I were you, or you might offend her."

"Oh thank God." The stoicism slid off of his face as he rubbed his calves vigorously. "And thank you, Sabreena." He stuck a hand out of the water to shake Sabreena's dorsal fin like he might shake a human hand in appreciation, grasping the appendage awkwardly.

Ava shook her head, giggling. "Nope. Try again."

But the young dolphin saved him any further embarrassment by nudging his chest affectionately with her rostrum and squeaking encouragement.

"I don't believe it—you're blushing. Smoother than butter when it comes to interacting with the human ladies, but one friendly offer from a dolphin and you've devolved into a blushing schoolboy."

"Shh…" Lucas whispered. "Don't ruin my credibility with Sabreena. Interspecies coolness is harder than it looks. Cleopatra is one of the few animals who can pull it off with such ease." He rubbed a hand across his chin in embarrassment. "Was that the dolphin equivalent of going to shake when the cool kid is going in for the fist bump?"

Ava didn't answer, distracted by Lucas's previous comment. *Cleopatra.* The name stung. *You shouldn't be here, Ava.* Whoever they were, the masked figures were right. She shouldn't be here. Hiding from danger. So far from her family, her friends, her canine best friend—Cleopatra. *I'm here for a reason. This is to protect them,* came an answering voice in her head. But it didn't feel like it at the moment as they swam for their lives. Pushing the thought from her mind, she dug her arms into the water aggressively and sprinted through the ocean.

Several miles later Ava switched to backstroke so she could check on Lucas while they traveled. She smiled at how carefully he was holding onto Sabreena, clearly trying to avoid causing any discomfort to the dolphin. Dolphin and man chatted happily and Ava noticed that Lucas's skin

97

had turned a rich brown in the Australian sun. Looking at her own pink skin, which was getting pinker by the day, she sighed inwardly.

When at last they grew too cold to stay in the water any longer, they extended their senses, probing the shoreline for a likely shelter. Upon finding one, they bid a quick farewell to their dolphin entourage and waded onto shore at a deserted looking sandy beach.

"Mr. President. Welcome to…this sandy beach that I don't know the name of."

Ava did a formal bow, her trousers drooping ridiculously from the weight of the seawater. "Thank you kindly. 'Tis a lovely spot. I feel very *safe* here." He had kept his promise; he had not stopped until she felt secure.

"Anything for you, Mr. President. Anything." The joking tone he affected didn't reach all the way to his eyes.

Ava shivered at their sincerity and blurted, "You look exhausted, Lucas. Get some sleep. I'll take first watch."

Lucas shrugged and scooped exhaustedly at the sand, before burrowing into the small indent he had created.

As he was drifting off to sleep, Ava whispered, "They're still here."

"What do you mean?"

"Our dolphin friends have decided to watch over us for the day."

Ava felt the pulse of contentment that fluttered off of Lucas at her words and it made her heart thrill. A smile played on her lips as her own eyelids fluttered closed.

Chapter 10

Something was following them. She could tell as soon as she woke up. Cursing at herself for falling asleep during her watch, she rolled over in the sand to find Lucas staring out to sea.

He turned to her and said, "We're being followed."

"I know. Can you tell by whom?"

"I'm trying…" As he trailed off it was clear that he was not succeeding. He stomped his foot into the ground, spraying sand into the air. Ava ducked to avoid getting any in her eyes.

"Watch it," Ava exclaimed.

"Sorry," Lucas murmured. "It's just…I'm a strategist. That's what I do. But I don't know how to strategize like this…with no data. Without knowing who's tracking us, I don't know whether we should set out by foot, or by sea, return to the city, or flee to the country."

Ava nodded, saying, "My family might be coming to find me. Or it could be the Ares…or the Gaia. Personally, I'm hoping it's not the former."

"Or it could be…my mom," Lucas said.

Ava looked at him in surprise. She hadn't considered that his mom might be following them. But given Lucas's prodigious talents it would make sense for his mother to be a powerful member of her Order. For someone of that age and skill, it wouldn't be difficult to track two young members. She shivered, hoping that Lucas's mother was not like his father.

Lucas must have caught the action because he said, "She's different."

Ava bit her tongue, not wanting to badmouth Lucas's remaining loved ones—there were so few. But it was no use. She'd never been one to hide her emotions. "How do you know? I mean I trust you, I do. Otherwise I wouldn't be here. But how is finding your mother really going to help us?"

"Do you think I'm a monster?"

"What? God, no, Lucas. You know that."

"My father was a monster."

"You're not your—"

Lucas interrupted her, "I'm not looking for your reassurances. I'm making a point. Where did my defiance

99

come from? Why did I turn away from the violence of my father?"

As Lucas spoke—his tone strident enough to convince even himself—Ava caught a flash of memory. She saw a very young Lucas—maybe four or five—clad in spaceship pajamas and curled on top of his covers like a puppy. His cheeks were flushed and his eyelids were fluttering as a lovely woman with a mass of dark hair stroked his forehead tenderly.

Ava jabbed a fingernail into her palm, trying to disentangle herself from the stolen memory and return to the present moment. She stared down at the sand, embarrassed to have snatched such a sacred snippet of his past, however unintentionally, and realized that Lucas was in the middle of saying something.

"—and we need to find someone in the Ares who will be sympathetic to our call for peace. Who better than my mother?"

Ava wasn't exactly sure what Lucas had been saying while she had been distracted, but that had never stopped her before. "Your mother…who was married to your father…who—"

Lucas cut in, "She'll understand. She has to understand." He said the second part mainly to himself.

"When was the last time that you saw her, Lucas?" she asked, trying and failing to keep the hesitation out of her voice.

Lucas didn't answer right away, which left a pit in her stomach. *He hasn't seen her in a very long time.* She kept going, even though the sadness in Lucas's eyes made her want to stop. She had to drive home her point. "Did she ever come to see you and your dad when you guys traveled to Australia?"

When he finally answered, Lucas's eyes were unfocused; Ava realized he was very far away. "Those trips were the most excited I ever saw my father…that was the closest I ever felt to being loved by him. He wouldn't let me out of his sight. He was manic on those trips, wanting to explore every corner of the city we were visiting." Lucas paused, still immersed in his memories. "I always felt so special on those excursions. I was still very young and had little control of my powers. In those days, as now, Australia was not friendly territory for the Ares; the land was wild and the creatures deadly. The Ares Elders tried to keep my father from bringing me on his trips." He smiled sadly, continuing, "But he absolutely insisted that I go with him…like he couldn't bear to be away from me for that long.

"I tried to be so good on those trips. I was sure that if I could just be calm on the plane and quiet in the hotel, he would realize how right he was to bring me with him. That I was worthy of his affection." Lucas's face darkened—the shadow of a long-ago confusion twisting his features. "But he only seemed to get angrier at me during those trips. I knew I must be doing something wrong, I just couldn't figure out what it was," he said, his voice plaintive.

Ava cursed Lucas's father in her mind. He had twisted him, starved him for love. But why? Why torture him with these trips—hold out fatherly affection as a prize that could never truly be won? Realization of a terrible truth clawed at the pit of Ava's stomach a second before she saw it reflected on Lucas's face.

Lucas met her gaze reluctantly, suddenly looking very tired. In his eyes she saw the once happy memories of his father slowly dissolving.

"Bait. He was using me as bait," he said quietly.

Ava didn't speak. A crab scuttled out of the sand and snapped its pincers at her—as if shaking a tiny fist. She shook her fist back. She marveled at the claw. Snap. Snap. Snap. She pictured several lines of string—thin as fishing wire—stretching from Lucas's waist to the earth as if he were a balloon in the Thanksgiving Day parade. In her mind she saw the crab severing one of the lines with its pincers—breaking one of the last feeble anchors Lucas

101

had in the world. Gone was any shadow of fatherly affection—even the rare moments of love had been a lie, another trick. Unconsciously she found herself shifting as if to block the crab from cutting any of her own precious strings anchoring her to this world. She hadn't yet reached out to her family, too afraid that any communication would lead them back to her and Lucas. Was that a mistake? Would she and her family survive the ensuing months to ever see each other again? If so, could they forgive her for her betrayal?

They sat in silence for a long moment, tracing designs in the beach, until Lucas rocketed upright, kicking sand everywhere. Ava covered her eyes.

"He was using me as bait!"

Brushing sand from her curls, Ava looked at Lucas, eyebrows raised in concern. "Right…we got that part. Are you feeling hot? Have you had any water today?" Her tone was kindly, like one she might use on a slightly confused grandparent.

Lucas waved his arms at her, physically pushing aside her condescension. "Don't you see? He was trying to lure my mom out of hiding. Which means my dad didn't know where my mom was. Which means that my mom ran away from my dad! Which means she might not despise me for what I did!" With each new conclusion Lucas's voice was rising—until he was left yelling at the empty beach.

There was so much confidence in Lucas's voice. Ava felt a little fire of hope springing in her own chest at Lucas's surety. Dousing it quickly—hope was not a luxury they could afford at the moment—she watched Lucas spring into a series of backflips along the sand, whooping jubilantly. Her crab friend was back and once again shaking his crab claw. It reminded her of a crotchety old neighbor who had shaken his newspaper at her and Natty when they'd played too loudly. She shrugged her shoulders at the crab, saying, "Don't look at me. There's only so much hope-crushing a girl can do in a day."

The crab did a frantic two-step back and forth in front of her, as if to urge her into action.

"Alright, alright," she said to the crab before turning and shushing Lucas half-heartedly. A laughable endeavor. By this point Lucas was wild with his own hope—it had consumed him like wildfire.

The dolphins—still keeping watch in the ocean—began to squeak in excitement. Lucas charged into the waves to receive their nudges of congratulation—the wide receiver running into a circle of his teammates after scoring a touchdown. The explosion of noise and emotion emanating from Lucas unnerved her.

At the clacking of claws, Ava rolled her eyes—launching into an internal rant. She knew it was crazy. Don't you think she knew it? Yes, from the memory she had snatched from Lucas, his mother had seemed to be a genuinely loving woman. But the fact remained that whoever his mother had been, she had married a monster. A monster who had tried to kill them both. They were searching for a woman whose husband had just been killed by her only son. They could not count on a happy reunion.

She opened her eyes to see that she was alone on the beach. No curmudgeonly crab to be seen. This was a new low. Either she was hallucinating crustaceans. Or she wasn't and was instead guilty of word-vomiting her deepest fears to the crustaceans she did encounter. *I've got to get out of here.*

At the thought, she saw Lucas and one of the dolphins begin racing across the sea parallel to the shore, applauded raucously by the rest of the pod.

Wading into the water, Ava yelled at the cheering group of man and dolphins, "Friends, sadly, I think we must depart."

***

Several hours and many miles later, two dolphins swam up beside Lucas and Ava offering to buoy them for a few miles. Seizing the rest break as an opportunity to get

Lucas's head back in the game, Ava asked, "So, where should we be looking to break camp for the night? Some of the dolphins have volunteered to scout ahead for us."

When Lucas just looked at her blankly, she added, "I don't want to travel too far today. We need to save our energy." *For whoever or whatever is following us.*

It took Lucas a few moments to reply, but when he did his eyes were focused, calculating, "Of course."

Ava breathed a sigh of relief—*he was back.*

"There are plenty of little beach towns up the coast. The perfect spot would be close to a beach town, so that I can sneak in and check the newspapers and international news channels, but far away from any wandering citizens or tourists." He paused for a moment. "And since we'll be away from the sea, and our lovely protective friends," he said, executing a little bow of thanks in the direction of the dolphins surrounding him, "we should look for somewhere else that gives our Gaia powers an advantage. I'm thinking a forest. There are a few national parks up the coast we could camp in."

Ava had stopped listening. He had said "our." *Our Gaia powers.*

From that point on Lucas was all business—seriously communicating with the two dolphins serving as scouts. For her part, Ava was enjoying being pampered by the dolphin pod. Many of the dolphins were traveling with their young calves, and their mothering instincts quickly extended to Ava. She couldn't hide the flush in her cheeks, or the rasp in her voice—now a constant reminder of her all-consuming thirst—and the dolphins fretted over her anxiously. They took turns nudging and bumping her affectionately throughout the trip.

Around mid-afternoon, Lucas turned to her with a smile. "They found it, Ava. The perfect spot to camp. Beach access to the forest is about two miles ahead."

Ava stopped herself from asking how exactly two dolphins had scouted out a forest, for of course they had communicated with other animals, animals that could walk and crawl and slither on from the beach to find the perfect place for them to camp. She had been getting rusty, locked away in Brookvale—cut off from observing and learning about the natural world. The dolphins would be offended that she had underestimated them.

As they neared the beach, Ava turned to their loyal friends and explained why they would need to part ways from this point forward. Although it would draw far too much attention from their mysterious followers to continue with their dolphin honor guard, Ava promised to keep the pod updated on their progress. To emphasize her point, she called to a circling albatross, which quickly descended and landed gently on her shoulder. "Jerome, here, will serve as a liaison."

One of the leaders of the pod nodded her head in understanding and squeaked in reply. Ava nodded sadly—Astrid, the matriarch, would be taking the pod on a loop far out into the ocean and back towards Melbourne in case anyone was following them. She felt suddenly bereft—the raucous affection of the dolphin pod had distracted her from the burden of her worries and she would be very sad to see them go.

As they headed back to shore, the dolphins squeaked in unison, the tone reassuring. Ava heard their message loud and clear: "We'll be watching." The words seemed to be magnified many times over as if all the creatures in the sea, and the very ocean herself, had made the promise. She almost felt bad for whoever was coming for them. Almost.

Chapter 11

It had been two weeks since they had said goodbye to the dolphin pod. The intervening days had been long, hot, and dusty. Thankfully Lucas had stolen them some provisions and less conspicuous clothing, so Ava was freed from the heft of the three-piece suit. They had been moving from campsite to campsite, working their way up the coast, never staying more than a night at any one spot. But progress had been much slower than expected.

The feeling of being constantly followed had taken its toll on them. Lucas had lost weight, his muscles now strained against his skin, and he had deep purple circles under his eyes. Ava knew she must look much the same. With each passing day, she'd gotten thirstier and thirstier. She had tried to hide the mysterious fever ravaging her body from Lucas, not wanting to add any more worries to his plate. But he must have noticed that something was off, because they had started travelling fewer and fewer miles every day, Lucas insisting that it was he who needed the break. But she caught him surreptitiously monitoring her.

And then today, without warning or ceremony, she had collapsed. The motion had been almost graceful—knees swaying and giving way to deposit her on the ground.

Thankfully, they had just entered South East Forests National Park—where their Gaia powers would be strong—when she fell. Now she was lying on the bank of a river waiting for Lucas to return from his scouting trip. He had warned her not to move, had said something about heat strike...no...that wasn't right. Heat stroke. That was it. No sooner had the thought crossed her mind than she got distracted by the feel of the earth against her skin. She trailed a finger along the dirt below her, mesmerized by the contours and whirls of the rocky ground. A curl stuck to the damp sweat on her forehead. She blew at it wildly, giggling. Quickly she grew frustrated when she couldn't dislodge it. She tossed her neck violently and forgot completely about her hair when she saw the clouds above her. So fluffy. They looked delicious. She reached a hand up to pluck one out of the sky and plop it into her mouth....hmm...ice cream. She closed her eyes and imagined scooping a giant spoonful of cookie dough ice cream into a bowl and then adding a scoop of salted caramel. She dug her hands into the ice cream, brows furrowed as sweat poured down her face. It was so hard, like trying to scoop rock.

"Ava, Ava, you're dreaming." Lucas's face loomed above her. "Something about your milkshake bringing all the boys to the yard." Concern dueled with laughter on Lucas's face as he bent over her.

Ava looked down—her hands were still attempting to burrow into the rocky outcropping next to the river. No wonder the ice cream had seemed so difficult to scoop. She snatched them back and cradled her bruised appendages on her chest.

"I don't have a milkshake for you, but I did bring something almost as nice." He pressed an icepack to her sweltering forehead.

At the rush of refreshment from the ice pack, she felt momentarily lucid. "Where'd you find it?"

"Game warden's cabin."

"What else did you steal?" She gave Lucas a searching look.

"Nothing. Just a newspaper…And this," he added, dangling a roll of duct tape in front of her, his eyes dancing with glee.

"Fourteen days," Ava said solemnly.

"What?"

"We've answered an important scientific question. Fourteen days—that's how long it takes to make a grown man swoon at the sight of duct tape."

"Says the lady who hallucinates about milkshakes."

"What? Are you telling me other people don't hallucinate about milkshakes? I'm pretty sure if you look hallucinate up in the dictionary its precise definition is 'to dream about milkshakes.'"

Lucas put a finger up as if he might shake it at her, and then proceeded to lick it and mime flipping through the pages of a voluminous dictionary. "Ah that's right, I see now. The pages were stuck together before. 'Hallucinate. Noun form, hallucination. A dreamlike state involving or related to shaken milk of the frozen delicious variety.'"

The straight face he had been maintaining soon crumpled into silent laughter, quickly progressing into something that couldn't be described as laughing so much as howling. Looking at the dirty, tired form of Lucas losing it next to her, Ava began to join in, her belly shaking in mirth. She stopped abruptly. Her skin was very pale beneath the flush of her cheeks and there was a heavy sheen of sweat on her forehead. She looked up at him in embarrassed bewilderment, like an elderly person who has lost her bearings for a moment. "What's happening to me?"

Lucas turned towards the river and called a long rippling tentacle out of the water. Holding it like a lasso he swung it to arc gently down on top of Ava. The water enveloped her entire body—leaving only her eyes, nose and mouth free from its swirling embrace.

"It's no use. I've been calling the air and water to cool me all day. I feel like the heat is coming from inside…like my organs are cooking," Ava said with a soft groan.

Lucas's brow furrowed at the graphic image. "I'm going back to the cabin. I saw a computer in there. An old behemoth but it'll do the trick. The internet will be able to shed some light on this."

"No," she called. Lucas turned back to her expectantly but she just mumbled something about "flesh-eating bacteria…" and then her head fell back against the earth.

Lucas looked at her in confusion. "That's it. Try and get some sleep, it should cool your body."

Ava mumbled something else, groaning with the effort.

"What was that?"

"I could teach you, but I'd have to charge," Ava whispered, her eyes fluttering as she watched Lucas trudge off into the trees. The forest suddenly looked very dark, she thought, as she drifted into a fitful slumber.

***

In what seemed like only a moment later, Ava was shaken awake for the second time that afternoon.

"Lucas," she cried in dismay. "I was just about to eat the blueberry treacle…" Without opening her eyes, she babbled on, "And I don't even know what treacle is…but it always sounds so delicious when British people talk about it…" she trailed off abruptly. She had opened her eyes to see not Lucas in front of her, but a small child. The little girl looked slightly frightened by Ava's behavior. Remembering her recent affair with the clouds and the ice cream rocks, she realized this could be another heat-induced hallucination—a dream within a dream within a milkshake dream. *Lacto-Inception.* But just in case, she wiped the drool off her chin and turned to face the forlorn girl.

"Sorry about that," she said sheepishly, "my dreams about baked goods can get rather aggressive." She said it with a smile, hoping to draw a laugh from the child. When it didn't seem to reassure the newcomer, Ava dragged herself up and onto her elbows, willing some color back into her face. She called the air to wipe the sweat from her brow and hoped that her humidity-affected curls weren't making her look like some kind of insane clown.

"Are you lost?" she asked gently. She and Lucas hadn't seen any tourists in the park but the woods had been alive with their presence—the birds, trees, and other creatures instructing them on which areas to avoid to remain unseen.

The breeze Ava had called to cool her brow was still swirling around her and it brushed through the little girl's hair, making her pigtails twirl like helicopter propellers. This provoked a faint giggle from the forlorn creature. She had been avoiding Ava's gaze before but now she stared straight into Ava's eyes and gave her a knowing smile—like she understood that the breeze had not been entirely natural.

Ava froze, hoping against hope that this was a hallucination. She'd never had a human detect her powers before. The girl's brown eyes were still fixed on her unblinkingly, as if she were throwing down some kind of challenge. Why did the child seem so much older than her years?

"Have you lost your family?" Ava tried again. This time the little girl grinned and shook her head. She moved closer to Ava, one hand outstretched towards Ava's curls, the other balled tightly in a fist. Too late Ava realized the little girl was hiding something in her closed fist and she jerked back instinctively as the child moved the closed hand towards her. But when the girl opened her tiny hand she revealed nothing but a leaf. God, she was getting jumpy.

The little girl gestured at Ava to look at her treasure. Hesitantly, Ava moved towards the outstretched hand and examined the leaf. It was a thing of simple beauty, the shape of a teardrop. Ava smiled at the little girl. But she didn't smile back, instead pouting and gesturing for Ava to look closer.

Small children have a way of bending adults to their will, and Ava was no exception. It was clear from the tiny dictator's enthusiastic gesturing that she wanted Ava to touch the leaf rather than just examine it. Ava pushed herself forward to oblige with a hesitant poke and then jerked back, spasms running through her body as if she'd been electrocuted. Greedily, she put another finger on the leaf and sighed contentedly as a rush of energy flowed through her. The leaf belonged to a Lifetree. She thought back to the Book of the Ancients, mentally flipping through its weathered pages. There it was, the Lifetree. She scanned the mental image quickly. Operating as the hearts of ecosystems, the Lifetrees were usually hundreds of years old. They were sacred to the Gaia—acting as both protected and protector. The trees drew energy from their entire ecosystem, and were powerful sources of fuel for the Gaia.

If this leaf were from somewhere in South East Forests National Park, which stretched for hundreds of square miles, it would be immensely potent. As the energy thrummed though her core, relief washed over her heat-ravaged limbs. She felt cool, collected, and truly lucid for the first time in weeks. With the newfound clarity she realized that this was definitely not a hallucination. And then, as a last wave of power shuddered through her body, the energy ran out.

Turning to look at the girl in wonder, she realized the brown eyes staring back at her belonged to the Lifetree. Or rather, the eyes belonged to the girl, but the centuries-old intelligence—illuminating them with that unearthly glow—belonged to the tree. Ava had read about this in the Book of the Ancients but had never seen it happen in real life. The bonding of Lifetree and human was exceedingly rare. The Lifetree could momentarily share awareness with humans, usually only very young children, children who were drawn to the beauty of the trees.

The book had made this symbiosis seem enchanting— children learning from a gentle life force hundreds of years old. But in person it was unnerving. She pushed the thought aside as the little girl gestured for Ava to follow her into the darkening woods. Although she knew Lucas would be terribly worried to return and find her gone, her desperation for further relief from her affliction drove her into the forest.

The energy supplied by the leaf had left her strong enough to walk behind the little girl, and the two kept a quick pace as they darted and twisted through the brush and trees. But Ava could not keep the heat at bay for long. She felt it seeping into her fingers and toes, sweat returning to slide down her back—a precursor to the fire that would eventually overwhelm her body. As she weakened, she dropped to the ground, crawling through the rough brush and soil. The little girl never slowed, and Ava found herself moving ever more frantically to keep up. She clawed at the dirt, thrusting her now ungainly body forward, forward towards freedom from the internal furnace consuming her organs.

And then finally she heard it, a soft keening in the wind. The haunting beauty of the sound made the hairs on Ava's arms stand up. The Lifetree was singing her home. A beat later she heard a gentle hum beneath her like the whirring of an air conditioning unit. Ava smiled—that was the sound of energy flowing towards the Lifetree and being pumped back into the forest. The heart of the entire ecosystem was pulsing steadily beneath her feet. She was overtaken by a wild urge to plunge a hand into the dirt and grab hold of a root like you would a power cord—sucking the energy meant for the rest of the ecosystem straight into her veins. Such an act would be sacrilege. Ava pushed the thought down deep, frightened by her desperation.

As she crawled another step, an otherworldly scent wafted over her, making her skin tingle. Eucalyptus, that hint of mint and pine with the faintest stirring of honey. Her senses were overwhelmed. Although her synesthesia made even quotidian interactions with nature sublime, never before had she felt such connection, such vibrancy. She scurried forward, on hands and knees, churning dirt everywhere, desperate now to catch a glimpse of this goddess of the woods. Remembering back to the worn print in the Book of the Ancients, she knew she should soon come upon a clearing, for although eucalyptus trees grow close together, all Lifetrees have a halo of space around them. Like a crowd parting for a monarch, the other trees of the forest grew slightly apart from the Lifetree.

When her miniature tour guide finally led her to the clearing she was not disappointed. The moon had appeared, casting a pearly light over everything before her. The trunk of the eucalyptus was massive—it would have

112

taken four of Ava to wrap her arms around it. The bark shone innumerable different shades of gray-green in the moonlight, as if it were continually moving, shifting its pattern and shape. Ava half expected an elven princess to descend gracefully from the branches of the tree. Already feeling better just being in the presence of the Lifetree, Ava pushed herself into a standing position and moved reverently towards the eucalyptus. She knew the ritual—she would introduce herself to the tree and she would ask the tree to borrow energy. She practiced the ritualistic words, words from the ancient tongue that tasted strange and powerful on her tongue, before reaching out to place her right palm on the tree.

She waited a moment, dizzy with anticipation. And then she howled, a primal sound torn from deep in her belly—her fury and dismay ringing out across the forest for miles. A giant beetle had landed on her arm. She looked up with dilated pupils and watched, helpless, as thousands more of the insects swarmed out of the tree. Every inch of bark was covered and she could feel the tree trunk creaking under the pressure. In the moment of asking for power, she had left herself completely open to the tree and now she was bonded to it.

She shrieked and writhed, brushing at invisible invaders she imagined boring into her skin, greedy to eat her insides and leave nothing but the husk of her body. The stench of death overwhelmed her and she fell to the ground, scratching at every exposed bit of skin she could find. Her insides were on fire and the scent of eucalypts enveloping her now seemed heavy and cloying—she was suffocating under its weight.

"Lucas," she shrieked into the darkness of the forest. She repeated the call again, "They're eating me!" She could feel creatures nibbling at her nerve endings, causing them to misfire and send tremors of pain throughout her body. The agony had left her unable to string two thoughts together—she couldn't tell where the bark of the tree ended and where her own skin began. She felt something slimy on her fingertips and held them up to see if she'd managed to crush one of the creatures attacking her. But she realized that it was only her own blood. She looked down to find that she was covered in long, bloody streaks—wounds wrought by her frantically scratching fingernails. But her mind, connected still to the tree, could not free itself from the terror of the thousands of murderous raiders. She felt something, a tiny sprouting of hope in her chest. *Lucas was coming.*

As her eyes rolled back in her head and her awareness faded into black she saw a figure emerge from behind the tree.

"You," she whispered. "How could you?"

Chapter 12

A tickling sensation across her eyelids raised Ava from unconsciousness. Memories rushed back to her, and she frantically tried to claw the invading beetles away from her face. But with a silent scream dying in her throat, she realized that she couldn't move her limbs. A quick inventory of her body told her that her legs and arms were stiff and immobile, but she could still move her neck and face. Opening her eyes, she took stock of her surroundings. She was lying on her back in the clearing about twenty feet from the Lifetree. Her hands were bound above her head. She was groggy, her system sluggish from the overwhelming pain of the tree's demise. Fighting to remain calm—and ignore the twitching sensation still assaulting her nerve endings—she peered to either side to determine what had caused the tickling sensation across her face. Out of the corner of her eye she saw a scorpion crawl over her right shoulder. She followed the path of the scorpion and blanched—before her was a scene straight out of her nightmares. Betrayal hit her like a punch to the gut for the second time that night.

For in front of her, Owen, one of her oldest friends and a fellow member of the Gaia, was kneeling over Lucas's motionless form. Ava couldn't decide which was more terrifying. The parade of scorpions Owen had summoned to converge around Lucas's unconscious body or the knife Owen was holding precariously close to Lucas's exposed skin. She made to shout but could only gurgle. *What was wrong with her? With Lucas?* The image of the scorpion flashed in her mind—had the venom paralyzed them?

Owen was too skilled a soldier not to have realized that she was now awake. But he wasn't paying any attention to her, which made Ava shiver internally, even if her limbs could not move. *He doesn't think I'm a threat. Me, the Alpha. What did he do to me?* She stared at him intently, looking for clues to his intentions. Although she was almost positive Owen wouldn't kill her, she knew the same was not true for Lucas. She was going to need to use all of her skill and wit to ensure he emerged from this predicament alive.

She studied Owen. His mouth drawn in concentration, he was tracing the point of the knife over Lucas's left wrist. Anguished at the thought of the point of that knife slicing into an artery, and overwrought from the exhaustion and terror of the last two weeks, her concentration scattered. With a deep breath, she forced herself to focus—to analyze the situation like she had been taught. Pushing aside her devastation that Owen was the one following them, and the second terrible pain that he had been willing to hurt her through the stunt with the Lifetree, she had to admit that Owen's actions were perfectly rational. From where he and the Order were standing, she had either run off with or been kidnapped by a member of the Ares. Lucas must be removed as a threat and she, the Order's most powerful weapon, must be returned to the fold. If Owen was acting rationally then

115

she had a chance. But she was confused by his current actions. Now mumbling to himself, he was still tracing the knife over Lucas's wrist, unable to settle on a point of contact. Occasionally he would shake his head in frustration and move to the other wrist.

While Owen was distracted, she called for the energy of the earth to warm her limbs from their paralysis. The responding pulse from the earth was weak but she could feel it building, gathering from places deep below her. Her arms tingled, coming to life, and she wiggled a finger experimentally.

Quick as a whip, a root, three inches thick in diameter, shot out of the dirt to slap her arm to the ground. Owen turned around at the last moment to catch Ava's look of defeat and then turned back to the tree to whisper something.

The energy had been enough to return her voice to her. "The Lifetree. She's collaborating with you," Ava said in disbelief. That's when the real terror set in. A Lifetree had been turned against her—had the earth disowned her?

His voice preternaturally calm and his face neutral, Owen spoke, "Yes. The Lifetree is very old…she's dying and she didn't want her death to be in vain. Her last act is to help the Order."

"How does killing us help the Order?" Ava spat, defiant despite her desperation.

Owen ignored her question. Instead he tore the front of Lucas's shirt roughly and held the point of the knife casually over Lucas's exposed chest as if he were holding a paintbrush over canvas. When he spoke, his voice was empty of emotion, "Ok it's just you and me here, Ava. I'm going to give you the benefit of the doubt. I'm angry, deadly angry." A twisted smile, full of bitterness and regret, appeared on his face. "Feel my anger."

The earth shuddered, tremors pulsed through the dirt, rippling out from Owen and she was suddenly swept away by a wave of rage and grief. She was drowning in it, suffocating, and she had no energy to protect herself, to shield herself from the mind-bending intensity of his emotions. She slumped back in defeat, riding the waves of wrath. Quickly she was pulled under by a vicious undertow of anguish. As she fought for breath against the weight of sorrow, a realization hit her. Owen's friends, maybe her friends, had died. Recently and horribly. For the second time that night she was bound to the sensations of another entity without protection and her mind could not hold much longer under the assault. But she was loath to appear weak, to ask for mercy before the time was right. Sneaking under that current of sorrow was something Owen couldn't hide—his lingering affection for her. She would have a chance to dissuade Owen. But only one, and now was not it. And so she waited, allowing his grief to fill her mind. Letting it suffocate her slowly.

Finally he spoke, "Cleopatra filled me in on that night. But I've come to realize that she left out a few key details. I've pieced together most of the *how* of the story." He turned piercing eyes on her. "But for the life of me I can't figure out the *why*."

His words grew indistinct, distant and then Ava blacked out, momentarily overwhelmed by the onslaught of Owen's grief. When she came to, Owen was in the middle of talking.

"—and then Lucas tricked you into shucking your powers and lured you into his house to kill you. This is where things get confusing. I guess he decided you would be more valuable to the Ares as a kidnap victim, because at least some of the forest creatures have reported that he charged out into the night carrying you while a fire raged through his house. The others have been strangely quiet, unwilling to cooperate."

"Owen—"

"Stop," he snarled. After calming himself down he continued, his voice gaining new emotion, "Your mother was devastated. She had given you a direct order…she had begged you to remain safe in your house. And then, *poof*, you disappeared. In the wake of your disappearance she learned you'd been fraternizing with the enemy for months, exposing your friends and family to unbelievable danger.

"So imagine my surprise,"—there was something dangerous, primal in his eyes; they glinted with a predatory spark—"when I caught your trail in Australia and found you, not kidnapper and kidnapped, but lovers." He let out a violent string of curses under his breath. "My God, after everything that happened, to find you running gleefully around Melbourne and dancing without a care in the world...I'll never forget that moment of betrayal."

She desperately wanted to ask what had happened. Who the Order might have lost. But asking would mean putting Lucas in unspeakable danger. Who knew what Owen would do if he had to relive that period of trauma and loss. So she remained quiet. She cursed this godforsaken war—once again it had caused terrible misunderstandings, and before the night was through it might claim more casualties.

"Despite all of that, I owe you one last chance to explain," Owen said. As he spoke she felt it quiver and pulse—his affection for her. How should she respond? How should she play it? Ava watched him, waiting for him to expose a chink in his armor, to unburden himself. She knew Owen—or at least she had known him, before whatever tragedy had befallen him. He needed to get these things off his chest. But there would be a way to make him see her side of the story if she timed it right.

"Your grandmother blames herself. She's tormented with guilt. I've been visiting her."

He didn't say it, but she could hear the omission in his voice—her grandmother was not alone in her torment. Owen too was burdened by guilt. Lucas had called her an avenging angel once. She had dismissed him then. But now she saw clearly the wake of destruction she had left in

118

her path. And she had only just begun. Could she handle this, this life of demolition? And what was it all for? Nothing. Nothing if Owen did the unthinkable and killed Lucas in cold blood right in front of her eyes. The knife was still poised over Lucas as he lay vulnerable, suddenly looking very fragile.

"You told her about the boy with the tattoo and she trusted you," Owen said and again she heard his unspoken words, *I trusted you.* "She didn't alert the Elders. Do you have any idea how the Elders reacted to being kept in the dark about their secret weapon? About you? Not kindly." He looked at her plaintively. "Your grandmother has grown very frail since your disappearance. She asked me, she begged me to bring you back safely."

Ava ignored this new and painful information and instead seized on Owen's spark of emotion. *Now, now is the time.*

She spoke clearly, determined to be heard this time, "He killed his father. To protect me." Owen barely raised an eyebrow. "He killed the leader of the Makhai," she added.

Although she hoped Owen would listen to her reasoning, she wasn't taking any chances with Lucas's life. He looked terribly vulnerable—bare-chested and bruised. Calling a very slow trickle of energy up from the earth she wiggled her toes, felt the life spreading through her feet and into her legs. She only needed a few more minutes.

"Did he tell you about the Makhai before or after he tried to kill you?" Owen asked, his voice taunting.

"No, it's not like that, Owen."

"Decades of intrigue, of cold-blooded murders. For God's sake, Ava, they killed the other Alpha, your grandmother's sister. And all it takes is one act of bravery, probably contrived, in front of you and the Makhai have suddenly neutralized the Gaia's greatest weapon."

Ava faltered. She had thought upon hearing her news Owen would pause, would turn to her and ask for a full explanation. Instead, she was the one left reeling. Doubts clouded her mind. She *had* been unconscious for the greater part of the evening when Lucas killed his father. But no, Owen hadn't been there that night. Neither Lucas nor his dad could have acted that well. Lucas couldn't have been pretending every singly minute these past few months.

She thought of their string of tender moments—in the river learning how to bend the water to their will, when he had showed such endearing affection for their fellow passenger on the plane, and the resulting moment of passion in the air. But then she remembered the night at the bridge—it was true that she'd never seen what happened to the Ares attackers. But no, there was something else, something Lucas couldn't fake. She hadn't wanted to expose his secret—it would have been a tactical advantage not to—but things were getting out of hand.

"He's one of us, Owen." She shrank back at the fury that rose in his eyes when she said "us," and immediately tried to correct her mistake. "He has Gaia powers."

This finally got Owen's attention. He rocked away from her.

Smelling blood, Ava pressed her advantage, "Wake him up and see for yourself. Don't take the coward's way out. Don't kill him in cold blood while he's totally defenseless."

Owen shook his head sadly. "I'm not trying to kill him."

Was he going to torture him first? Ava shivered, but this time her body was loose enough for the tremors to show. She cursed and tried to still her body but looked up to see Owen watching her with that predatory stare. Resolution written on his face, he turned back to Lucas and pushed the point of the blade into his left wrist, drawing blood.

"Don't," Ava said. She had thought she was whispering, pleading for mercy. But as she heard her voice echo through the woods she was astonished at how every syllable resonated with power. Her voice held the threat of a thousand years, of the earth itself. The realization filled her with a dark energy. "The tree may have joined your side, but all have not deserted the Alpha," she said ominously as dark clouds rolled in overhead—blocking out the pearly light of the moon.

Owen looked terribly sad. "So that's it. You really did choose him over us." The earth began to thrum with his energy and roots shot out of the ground like stakes to surround Ava.

In response, the night sky caught on fire. Or at least that's what it looked like as lightning forked in apocalyptic chaos above their heads. As if some goddess of lightning had raked her fingernails across the chalkboard of the sky, leaving great jagged trails of electricity in her wake. With an ear-splitting boom, lightning slashed into the ground several inches away from the Lifetree. Ava heard a hissing sound and smelled the acrid smell of burnt earth. Heat had been the bane of her existence the last several weeks, but this was her kind of fire. She couldn't bring herself to hit the eucalyptus straight on; instead she willed the lightning to strike in a circle around the clearing. Her threat was clear—there would be no escape for Owen or the tree if she so decided.

Owen shouted over the din, "Good. That makes you angry. Maybe you are still a sister of the Gaia."

In response to Ava's lightning strike, the roots that had been acting as stakes arced up and over her body and back into the earth on the other side, creating a wooden cage. With every moment it bent closer and closer to Ava, threatening to crush her beneath its heft. Water began to fall down in droves, drenching everyone, and sending the scorpions scattering. Lucas would not remain paralyzed long without their continued supply of venom and Ava concentrated on giving him a few more minutes to wake up and prove to Owen the truth of her words. As the rain splashed against her forehead, Ava hoped it might cool

Owen's temper—dampening his anger enough to prevent any further violence to the defenseless Lucas.

Whatever it did to Owen, it had no such effect on the eucalyptus; indeed, the Lifetree seemed to grow even angrier. The roots continued to constrict around her—a wooden ribcage pressing down against her own. A root snaked out and wrapped itself around her neck, pressing down hard against her windpipe. *It's trying to kill me.* The thought was more terrifying than the actual violence and it left her on the verge of a panic attack. It felt so wrong, so perverse for a Lifetree to attack an Alpha—like a mother attacking her own child—and it left Ava unable to think, to breathe without hyperventilating.

In desperation, she reached out to the tree to explain, to open her mind and demonstrate her pure intentions. Communicating with the environment was usually as natural as breathing—as instinctual as the eternal rhythm of oxygen in, carbon dioxide out. She was one with the organisms around her, an integrated part of the ecosystem. Deeper than that—she was the oxygen and the carbon dioxide, a part of the atmosphere and the earth. The transition between herself and the natural world was seamless, complex but unnoticeable, like the act of breathing.

But this time there was no response. It was like reaching a hand out with an olive branch to the Lifetree only to look down and find a bloody stump in place of the hand. She could not connect. She shuddered and gasped. Her breath came in great wheezing gulps and she coughed as the roots continued their downward thrust.

Finally Owen shouted, "Enough!"

The tree creaked in dismay. It didn't withdraw the roots, but it stopped pressing in to suffocate Ava.

Owen looked at Ava, then back to the knife in his hand, collapsing like a deflated balloon. "Don't you see, Ava? I'm trying to help you."

This earnest Owen was almost more frightening. He truly believed that torturing or killing Lucas would help Ava. *Had he gone insane with grief?* It wouldn't be the first time a Gaia warrior had been unable to process personal tragedy, submerging themselves in a primal, vengeful shell of their former selves. For the Gaia, grief was an all-consuming affair.

But he had protected her from the Lifetree. That had to mean something. She steeled herself to try one more time. If she could get Lucas to wake up...if she could just get him to wake up. Owen might understand—that is, if he still had any semblance of sanity. *But Lucas needed more time.* Injecting her voice with as much mystery as she could conjure, she dangled a morsel before Owen so that he would want, would need, to know more, "Can't you see what's right in front of you, Owen?"

Ignoring her bait completely, he dropped some of his own, "Can't you? Can't you see what he's done?"

In the process of asking the question Owen seemed to have worked himself up once more over Lucas's imagined sins. He shook Lucas awake roughly and asked, "Where are they?"

Lucas opened his eyes slowly. Obviously confused, he looked down at his bound arms and legs for a moment before staring up at Owen and his bloodied knife. He didn't so much as blink at the sight of the weapon. "You again," he murmured, like you might say to a neighborhood squirrel pestering for crumbs.

Ava inhaled sharply—the last time Lucas had seen Owen, the Ares warrior had essentially threatened the Gaia warrior's life while he was kissing Ava. All without Owen knowing. That kind of reminiscing was liable to get Lucas killed at the moment. But Ava breathed a sigh of relief—Owen hadn't seemed to pick up on the reference.

Lucas mumbled, "What are you on about, Captain Planet?"

Owen pushed on a spot on Lucas's arm, right below his tattoo, repeating his question, "Tell me. How do I get them out?"

At his touch, Lucas grimaced. Owen pushed harder until Lucas grunted in pain.

Ava screamed, "What are you doing to him?"

"I need to cut out the sangstones," Owen blurted, clearly frustrated.

Ava trembled. Owen had lost it. He had spoken nonsense, his pupils were dilated, and he wanted to cut something out of Lucas. Whatever the Ares had done to him in that last terrible assault had left him mentally unstable.

She felt for her connection to the lightning above, readying herself for whatever was to come. But then Lucas whispered, "You can't…you can't."

Ava looked back and forth between Lucas and Owen wildly. Lucas seemed to know what Owen was talking about. Owen wasn't crazy. Was she? Had she been made the fool for trusting Lucas again?

For the first time, Owen's face softened as he met Lucas's eyes. The Gaia warrior said, "The sangstones have to come out. Or this little suicide quest will be over before it starts."

The paralyzing agent had obviously worn off some, because Lucas began to struggle against his bonds.

"I wouldn't try it if I were you," Owen said calmly as he pushed Lucas to the ground. His actions were gentle, almost tender. "You missed the fun, but Ava has already been trying to do much the same as you with just as little success. And although I don't relish my mission—*I have my orders.*" He didn't look at Ava as he said it, but she knew the words were for her.

"You won't be leaving this clearing unless you leave without the sangstones," Owen added. It was clear from his tone that his mission had not specified whether or not Lucas had to be alive when he left the clearing.

The threat energized Lucas. He turned to Owen, and when he spoke his voice was taunting, "That was quite the move you pulled earlier tonight. With the little girl. So the Gaia manipulate children now? You're willing to become the Ares to defeat them?"

Ava's thoughts flashed to the little girl—what had happened to her after she had passed out? Owen stayed quiet—Ava could tell from his irregular heartbeat that Lucas was making him angry, and she hoped to God that Lucas had a plan. That he was not just poking the bear with a stick for the fun of watching him roar.

"I mean, she was so good at pretending to be terrified. Screaming and crying. And then when I rushed to help her, you blindsided me. That was a clever plan—kidnapping and hypnotizing a little girl. All so that you could torture the most powerful and beloved member of your Order? Ah, Captain Planet, the noble Gaia warrior." The sarcasm flowed thick as honey in Lucas's voice.

Ava expected Owen to lash out at Lucas's words, but he just looked miserable.

Lucas dug in, saying, "You must be proud of yourself."

"Pride?" Owen snarled. "Don't speak to me of pride. Does Ava know? Have you told her what you are? What you've done?"

It was Lucas's turn to fall silent. Owen whispered a command to the tree, and the roots withdrew enough so that Ava could see both of them, could meet Lucas's eyes.

Owen turned to face her, asking, "Do you know what a sangstone is, Ava?"

"Leave me out of your games," she replied bitterly.

A twisted smile came onto his face. "You don't know. He didn't tell you." Owen paused. "I've been following you for a long time. And I've noticed that the two of you never touch. Which is strange because even from a couple of miles away I could tell that you want to. Badly."

He had her attention now—she was riveted. Was Owen going to explain the source of the strange fire that erupted when she and Lucas touched?

"And then I realized. You can't touch, can you?" Owen laughed. "Gah, the irony. Two lovesick puppies betray their orders only to find that their very touch now causes them physical agony."

"Let me guess—heat, sparks, fire. Haven't you been wondering why?" Owen asked, clearly enjoying himself now. "Poor little Ava, desperately trying to figure out why. While all the time...this one knows...he knows why." He nudged Lucas with his toe.

"No," Lucas said in disbelief. "It can't be."

"Do you want to tell the rest, Lucas? You can probably describe all the *gory* details better than I." The way he emphasized gory made Ava's stomach turn.

Lucas didn't say anything. When he met Ava's eyes, she saw endless regret in the deep blue of his irises.

"I didn't think so," Owen muttered. Lucas seemed to shrink into himself—his tall frame trying to disappear into the earth.

"Get to the point," Ava spat—nerves frayed.

"Patience, *sister.*" Owen said, raking her with his sarcasm. He continued, "Our Ares friend over here has told you about the Makhai—the 'elite' warriors hell-bent on killing off every last member of the Gaia, down to the babe in her mother's arms." Owen looked at Lucas with rage burning in his eyes, and Ava wondered once again what had befallen her Order. "Like all homicidal hate-groups worth their stripes, this one has an intense initiation process."

Owen pressed down on the same spot on Lucas's wrist, drawing another grimace. "Isn't that right, Lucas?"

Ava met Lucas's gaze, hoping to see denial there. Hoping that Owen's dramatic hints were just bluster, the last resort of an exhausted man. But all she saw was anguish. *Lucas was a Makhai.*

126

"The price of entry into this great brotherhood of hate is steep—the life of a Gaia." Owen's voice had dropped to a whisper. He was tracing his finger along the blade of his knife. "All you need to do is take a knife, just like this one and…"

Ava felt a pulse of grief from Owen. For the first time that night she felt sorry for him. The ground had shifted beneath his feet, just as it was now collapsing beneath hers.

There was silence for a few seconds. Long enough for Ava to come down from the drama of the moment. The scene almost made her laugh. Here they were, three teenagers drenched to the bone, sitting in a forest in Australia calmly discussing torture, murder, and ancient blood rituals. And yet, it was not even the slightest bit funny. An unexpected voice broke the stillness.

"Blood. I was raised to spill blood," Lucas said. He sounded like a child intoning the Pledge of Allegiance—these were words he had repeated many times before. "And when I did, I would become a member of the Makhai—a blood brother. If I completed the ultimate task, killing a Gaia, the knife that spilled the blood would be melted down. And then…it would be implanted into my body—into my heart, my neck, my wrists, and my ankles. The greatest honor a young Ares could ever dream of."

Lucas paused, closing his eyes. "These metal pieces, sangstones, complete the circle. They demonstrate eternal loyalty to the Makhai." He laughed bitterly. "And the Makhai demand nothing less than eternal loyalty. The punishment for betrayal is death at the hands of your brothers. They…we…are creatures of metal and fire. Of violence. Together, with powers combined, the brotherhood can manipulate the sangstones in the body of any traitor. Death can be swift." Lucas paused once more. "But not for people like me….traitors. Those that flee the brotherhood pay the price in pain. They are rewarded with a slow, agonizing death."

Ava tried to block out Lucas's words. She thought of something, anything else, to keep the truth away, a corrosive truth that would worm its way to the very center of her core and burn there for the rest of her life. She tried desperately not to make the connection between what Lucas was saying and what Owen had discovered when pressing on Lucas's wrist earlier in the night. But her mind refused to cooperate. *He killed somebody. A killer of Gaia.* And then another thought, *Owen was right.* Moments after this insight, the Lifetree's roots withdrew in a flurry of movement.

Owen noticed the motion and spun around to see what was going on. He looked at her, this time the ghost of a real smile playing on his lips.

She felt very old suddenly. She tried to keep her mind blank, but thoughts plucked at the periphery of her brain like seagulls after crumbs. How could the Order ever take her back after she had associated with a killer of Gaia? What would they do with Lucas? She and Owen couldn't just let him go?

Lucas interrupted her thoughts, "I didn't kill anyone."

Owen looked at him in disbelief—as if this cowardly denial were the worst of all of his crimes.

Lucas turned to Ava, repeating, "I didn't kill anyone." Ava's thoughts flashed back to that terrible night when Lucas had slain his father right before her eyes. Lucas's must have too, because he quickly corrected himself, "I haven't killed any Gaia. That was the first time…I swear."

He looked at her pleadingly. But she was so tired. And she had noticed something new. Now that she knew what to look for, she could feel the tiny pulses of evil coming from Lucas's body—barely perceptible waves of malevolence radiating from the sangstones.

Ava turned to Owen. "So that's why She's been so angry?" It was more statement than question. Of course Mother Earth would be devastated that the Alpha was cavorting with someone who had Gaia blood on his hands. Who wore that blood as a trophy implanted deep within his skin. The Makhai were monsters. *And Lucas was one of them.*

"Why save him at all? Why cut the sangstones out?" Ava asked.

"You," Owen said simply.

"Because I'm the Alpha?"

"We need you, Ava. If I couldn't bring you home…well then…I needed to give you a chance at surviving long enough to realize the truth on your own. Right now you two are leaving a trail the size of the Milky Way. Gaia is so angry at you." When Ava looked at him in disbelief he added, "Seriously, it's like fireworks are exploding above you wherever you travel. At least for those attuned to Gaia's emotions."

She and Owen had looked away from Lucas for a moment while they spoke. Only a moment. Ava got a flash of sadness and resolve from Lucas like a lightning migraine. Immediately she understood what Lucas was going to do and she shouted, "No!"

Owen echoed her cry and rushed back to Lucas's side. But they were too late. She knew what she would see before she turned around and it made her hesitate. Blood—Lucas had been so fixated on the word. How had she not heard the terrible foreboding in his words? It felt much longer than the split second it took to force herself to turn and look at the scene unfolding behind her. Owen was holding tight to Lucas's left wrist right above the tattoo—that damn tattoo. If she had never seen it, maybe they wouldn't be here. Maybe there wouldn't be so much red, shining sickeningly in the pearly moonlight.

She had forgotten. Lucas carried an extra knife hidden at his waist. He had cut through his bonds and stabbed deep into his own forearm to pull out the sangstone buried there.

"Ava," came the sharp prompt from Owen. "Help me."

Still Ava found she couldn't move. "I can't...I can't touch him," she whispered, tears in her eyes. Finally she jerked a foot free from the ground and hurried to crouch next to Lucas.

The Ares warrior wasn't moving. Owen worked to staunch the flow of blood from his artery. Suddenly Lucas's eyes shot open, bulging in his head, and he gestured frantically at a small object, no bigger than a penny, lying in the grass. He grabbed Ava with his good arm.

"I see it, I see it," she said soothingly, as she extricated her arm from his—terrified that her touch might injure him further. "Hold on, Lucas." *Hold on, I need you,* she added silently.

Lucas worked his lips desperately, still agitated, and managed to gurgle, "Sorry." For a moment, the most beatific smile crossed his face, and then awareness faded from his eyes.

Chapter 13

He's alive. He's alive. Ava whispered it to herself over and over again. She had become so accustomed to Lucas's heartbeat over the last several weeks of their isolation— thump, thump, thump, *you are not alone,* thump—that she knew its rhythm like that of her own. And although his pulse was weak, he had a pulse. For the last several hours Owen had fed him a little bit of energy—one hand dug into the ground holding a root of the Lifetree and the other resting gently on Lucas's heart. Ava, too afraid of what might happen if she touched Lucas, had tried to relieve Owen by connecting herself to the Lifetree's root and holding Owen's hand, while he held onto Lucas. As exhausted as she was from the events of the last day, Owen must have been even more so—he was forced to go for much longer stretches without her aid. Owen had urged her to sleep when she wasn't helping him. But she had spent much of the time huddled on the ground, knees drawn to her torso, eyes fixed on Lucas's chest—watching each labored breath anxiously.

She had another reason for refusing to sleep—the small voice in her head warning her not to leave Owen and Lucas alone together. After all, Lucas's death by his own hand would be the ideal outcome for the Gaia, and Owen had little incentive to keep him alive now that he had exposed Lucas's lies to Ava. But hour after hour, she had watched as Owen nursed Lucas, tender as a mother bear, blotting the sweat from Lucas's brow and checking his pulse as he used all of his own energy to help Lucas heal. At one point, watching Owen tip Lucas's head forward to feed him a drop of water at a time, it dawned on her that his threats to kill Lucas had been as empty as the desert at high noon. She tucked that knowledge away—she could learn something from Owen's poker face. As the faintest pink streaks appeared in the sky, signaling dawn, Ava could see that Owen was near collapse himself. But still Lucas had not awakened.

"We just need to give him enough energy for his body to start the healing process," Owen had whispered in the first minutes after Lucas had fallen into his coma—his voice a pillar of certainty. Certainty that Ava had clung to like a gymnast to the uneven bars, throwing herself into the task of getting Lucas as much energy as possible. He had added with a reassuring smile, "He's young and strong. I've seen warriors heal from much worse. And they didn't have the Alpha on their side."

His words had the effect of a stick poking a turtle—she pulled her limbs even tighter to her chest, tucking into herself. Owen didn't know it yet, but she knew—hers was a cursed touch. She had killed a man and brought a quaking city to its knees without even meaning to. The merest trace of her fingers would probably suffocate Lucas in his weakened state. Owen had looked at her like she was some kind of deity sent to save the Gaia, but she knew the truth—if she were any kind of immortal, she was a goddess of death and destruction. How had she become so poisoned—she who drew her power from the ultimate force of life?

But Ava saw no need to voice her anxieties—it was clear as the hours passed that Owen had plenty of his own.

Finally, unable to keep silent any longer, she asked, "Why isn't he waking up?"

"The sangstone was placed in such a way that it couldn't be removed without ripping through an artery. Lucas essentially severed that to cut it out, but…"

"But?"

"As I said before, I've seen Gaia warriors heal from much worse. So I think the sangstone must have triggered something. Look here—Lucas's wound hasn't closed at all." He pulled up the bit of Lucas's shirt being used as a tourniquet to show her. "The blood has barely clotted."

After another hour of using the Lifetree as an IV, Owen spoke, "Enough. He's stable for the moment and we're not doing him any favors if we both pass out here to let ourselves be ambushed by Makhai assassins."

He passed her a canteen, from which she drank thirstily. She forced herself to leave some water for her companions and looked up to find Owen giving her a questioning look. She shrugged, brushing off his concern. There was no need to throw yet another problem at him.

Lucas was still bare-chested. Owen hadn't had a spare moment to clean up the blood spilled over his torso. There were handprints of it all over his chest—war paint gone terribly wrong. Owen followed her gaze and put a hand on her shoulder. Without thinking, Ava leaned into the touch until her back was pressed into Owen's chest. The solidity of his form reassured her more than anything he could have said. After a few seconds, she shook her head, pushing herself away from Owen. She took the water bottle back from him and knelt next to Lucas.

Careful not to touch him, she gently poured water over his chest to wash off the bloody handprints.

Owen had started gathering up the camp. After a whisper from him, the soil rippled, drawing the bloodstained topsoil underground and replacing it with undisturbed dirt. "We've got to go."

"I know."

"We have to take it with us," he said, gesturing at the sangstone

"I know," Ava replied again. Instead of meeting Owen's eyes, she stared balefully at the hateful little hunk of metal, now glinting in the dawn light. Like a miniature disco ball smeared in blood. "Are you sure he can travel?"

"Yes," Owen replied although he didn't quite meet her eyes. She understood—Owen was no longer sure of anything. They were in uncharted territory. He had always been the older, wiser one—deeply trusted by the Order. But he was just as lost as she was. The thought made her shiver.

She had held off telling Owen about her strange affliction for as long as she could, but she had to tell him now before they broke camp and her weakness became all too obvious, a dangerous liability. She'd been loath to admit that she would be practically useless once she wasn't plugged into the energy of the Lifetree. But she'd run out of time. She opened her mouth to speak but Owen preempted her, asking, "How are you still standing?"

"What do you mean?" Ava asked.

Owen pointed at the newspaper—one of the things Lucas had stolen from the game warden's hut the day before—he was stuffing into his backpack. The front page featured a map of Australia filled in with a tie-dye pattern of reds, ochers, oranges, and a deep purple. Above the map a headline announced, "Australia Forced to Add New Color To Temperature Map as Heat Rises."

Ava blinked, unsure of what Owen was getting at. Quickly she scanned the first paragraph of the story. *To quote the immortal words of Nelly, "It's getting hot in herre." This summer's record-breaking temperatures have been attributed to global warming caused by carbon pollution. The most recent heat wave— unprecedented in both scale and scope—has broken every previous temperature record and required Australia's Bureau of Meteorology to add a never before seen colour to its scale—*

Owen interrupted her before she could finish reading the paragraph, "I mean I know I've been struggling in this ungodly heat. You don't even want to know how much I've been sweating. And the thirst—it never ends. If not for the thirst I would have tracked you guys down just outside of Melbourne...I've had to stop watching the news...all the stories of raging forest fires...droughts..." He smiled sadly, eyes twin pools of empathy. "Can you feel Her? How thirsty She is?"

"She—you mean Mother Earth, Gaia?"

Owen nodded. "I can only imagine that as the Alpha the heat would be nearly debilitating."

"You don't want to imagine," she said darkly. She didn't want to admit to Owen that she hadn't known that her connection to Gaia would make her feel like this, like her insides were slowly cooking. She turned away from him to hide her reaction and breathed a small sigh of relief. It wasn't a cure, but at least now she had an answer.

Pushing her spine straighter, she spoke with renewed confidence, "Ok, let's move south. Away from the equator. And we'll stick to the coast. We can move more quickly now that we're not being followed by some creeper."

Owen smiled at her. "You took the words right out of my mouth. Well not the creeper part. Obviously you were being followed by a stoic Gaia warrior."

She looked over at Lucas—saw the uneven rise of his breath, heard the ragged sound every time he breathed. "You understand why he has to come with us?"

He nodded, although Ava was sure that he didn't. In Owen's mind Lucas was still a Gaia-slayer. But she knew how much Owen wanted to return her to the Order. She was counting on that eagerness.

"Can you…" she trailed off, gesturing at the sangstone, hoping he would understand that she couldn't bear to touch it.

Owen obliged, reaching down to pick it up, then promptly dropped it with an anguished cry.

"You can feel it? Who he killed?" Ava whispered.

"Yes." Owen looked horrified.

Ava paled. She had felt a terrible foreboding about the sangstone. Remembering Lucas's urgent gesturing towards the strange object and his last whispered apology, she had been afraid of the secrets the metal might reveal. One secret in particular had plagued her thoughts throughout the night. *Please let it not be Isi. Please say Lucas didn't kill my best friend.*

Finally, Ava summoned the courage to ask, "Who?"

"I'm not sure how it's possible." Owen paused; Ava felt her heart fluttering in her throat as she waited for his words. "But there can be no doubt. That metal was used to kill the last Alpha, more than sixty-five years ago."

As Owen said the last part of the sentence, their eyes met—they had made a terrible mistake. Lucas was not a Gaia killer.

Chapter 14

Events transpired rapidly after Owen and Ava had realized their deadly error. Owen kicked the sangstone into his backpack, handed the bag to Ava, and scooped Lucas ever so gently up in his arms, making his six-foot frame seem weightless. Ava called for the Lifetree to lend her its roots one last time and they rose out of the ground like snakes coiling up towards a charmer's song. As the tree shuddered with a last gasp of life, Owen and Ava grabbed hold of its roots for a final jolt of energy for the long journey ahead of them.

With Lucas's wound barely closed, travelling by water was not an option. But they needed to get south quickly, where the heat would be less debilitating, and they would be better able to defend the unconscious Lucas. They both felt the terrible burden of his life and it forced them to act quickly.

As they ran, birds raced overhead, spreading the news throughout the forest, and a cacophony of life kicked up through the treetops as all manner of creatures hissed, howled, and clicked encouragement.

"I can feel the questions burning in your mind, Ava. Save your guilt until you know exactly how much of it you should feel. Trust me. Lucas can explain more when he wakes up and there's no point wasting your energy until then." After a pause, Owen added reassuringly, "He will wake up."

No words were spoken but Ava could feel the shifting alliance like she felt a sudden change in the wind, blowing her hair in the opposite direction. Owen was with them—there was a triangle where once there had been a pair. As long as Lucas could ever forgive her for doubting him.

Although they couldn't travel by water, they hugged the coast, where they found some relief from the brutal heat wave sweeping Australia. And then as dusk was falling on their second night on the run, Ava heard the best words of her life.

"Ah, the elusive Ares-Gaia bromance—what a beautiful thing," Lucas whispered, his voice hoarse, before nestling his head even deeper into Owen's chest from where he was being cradled in the Gaia warrior's arms. "I can see what you like about him, Ava," he said, poking a finger at one of Owen's biceps with an impish grin.

Owen stuttered to a halt, brows furrowed, before breaking into a wide grin. The Gaia warrior laughed, saying, "Cheeky little bugger, aren't you?" Although it was not clear exactly who he was calling little. Now that Lucas was no longer hanging limp in Owen's arms, the two were essentially the same height and girth.

"This is an image I will treasure for the rest of my life," Ava said, before gesturing Owen over to a tree. There he carefully set Lucas on the ground, propping him in a sitting position with his back against the trunk.

Owen and Ava hovered over Lucas, looking rather like a set of confused puppies.

Lucas studied the pair of them, rolled his eyes, and asked, "What does a guy have to do to get some water around here?"

Both Owen and Ava moved to grab the bottle from the backpack and bumped into each other. Blushing, Owen gestured at Ava that she should have the honor. She grabbed the bottle, unscrewed the cap and handed it to Lucas. Her outstretched hand stayed for a few seconds after Lucas had weakly grasped the canteen from her, as if she were proffering an invisible olive branch. The two Gaia warriors watched Lucas take slow sips, neither of them speaking. When the silence dragged on, Lucas spoke again, "I'm guessing from the tender moment Captain Planet and I shared earlier this evening," Lucas paused to wink at Owen, before continuing, "that you've decided I'm not the enemy."

"I'm so sorry—"

"Bad intel—" Ava and Owen blurted out, talking over one another.

Lucas looked surprised at their hurried apologies. "Why?"

"Erm. The whole scorpion, paralysis, knife-waving thing?" Owen murmured, blushing.

"Well I knew it wasn't personal," Lucas replied. He turned to Ava, saying, "I kind of deserved it. I lied to you. It just wasn't as big of a lie as you thought."

This seemed to invigorate Owen; she could see the cogs turning in his head—*yeah, that's right, you did lie.* Ava put up a hand to stop what she knew would be a full-fledged interrogation of Lucas. That would come soon enough. She rubbed her forehead, picking fretfully at the skin above her eyebrow.

Lucas looked at her. "I'm not mad. You *do believe* me don't you?" he asked with the ghost of a smile on his lips.

Lucas had set a neat trap. Ava smiled, conceding defeat. "You *are* a cheeky little bugger."

Lucas hooted weakly. "I'm going to get so much leverage out of this. You'll always have to believe me from here on out."

Ava rolled her eyes. "How does your arm feel?"

"My arm?" he asked, tugging at the make-shift tourniquet around his arm with the air of a magician moving the curtain to reveal that the woman he'd cut in half was whole again. "It's good as—" he stopped talking abruptly, the blood draining from his face. For what he had revealed was not a miraculously healed wrist but a nasty wound—inflamed and infected. Ugly red streaks were climbing up his arm from the site of the injury.

"Bloody hell," he exclaimed, adding a string of curse words under his breath. Recovering slightly, although he still looked stricken, he added, "That was not what I was expecting."

Owen had looked up from where he was cooking soup over a small fire. "You thought you'd heal normally?" he asked, clearly trying to sound as nonchalant as possible.

The forced indifference in Owen's tone was a terrible blow to Ava. She realized with a sinking heart that Owen had been waiting for Lucas to wake up—believing that the Ares warrior would be able to direct them on how to mend his injury.

"Well, yeah, I've never had any problem healing before and I've had much grislier injuries than this one." Ava wondered if the machismo in his voice was for her or Owen's benefit.

"But I can't even feel it," Lucas said, still staring at the ugly wound on his arm in disbelief.

"That could be the Lifetree. We were feeding you quite a bit of its energy—so if it couldn't heal you, maybe it took away the pain. Similar to morphine," Owen said, shaking his head in puzzlement.

Ava spoke, "Unfortunately, whatever relief the Lifetree provided you will only be temporary. So we need to figure out how to jumpstart your healing." Gesturing at Owen to bring some food over to Lucas she said, "You need to tell us everything you know about the sangstones."

Lucas looked at her, his face impassive. She hoped he wouldn't fight her on this. "I wouldn't ask now, when you've just regained consciousness, but if there's anything that might help you heal, we need to hear it." *Before you pass out again*, she added in her head.

Lucas's mouth tightened. Ava knew from long observation that the movement was a signal—he had come to a decision. He spoke, "Ok. Where do you want me to start?"

Ava plunged straight in, not wanting to waste Lucas's energy with frivolities, "Why do you have sangstones that were used to kill my great-aunt in your body?"

Before answering, Lucas gulped down a handful of trail mix to fortify himself for the story ahead. Ava settled in against the trunk of a tree—this could take a while.

Finally Lucas spoke, "I told you once that my father was obsessed with the Alpha. That the Makhai had been founded and baptized in the blood of the most recent Alpha—your great-aunt." Lucas paused for another bite. "Obsession may have been too gentle a word. After my mother left with my little sister, my dad turned to another, very demanding mistress—booze. Many nights I would find him, bottle of scotch close at hand, slowly tracing the lines of his tattoo and whispering to himself. I didn't yet know the full story then, so his confused mumblings about 'the Alpha,' 'Ella,' and 'destruction' didn't make much sense to me. I just thought he was a bad drunk. Besides," he said, putting out his hands, "even if I had wanted to work out the puzzle, I learned to avoid my father when he was in one of these moods." His eyes became more and more unfocused as he was swallowed by his memories.

"One time I found him passed out on our living room couch. He looked so forlorn and gentle in his sleep...I tried to cover him with a blanket. And then...I mean who knew blankets made such effective nooses?" he asked, trying to smile. "Anyway, his mumbling psychosis continued for months, years after my mother left. By that point I had learned the origin story of the Makhai, the threat of the Alpha, and I had heard of the sangstones. Only those who had bested a Gaia warrior in hand-to-hand combat got the honor of wearing the sangstones.

"Years later, I was braver—long recovered from the blanket-noose experience—bloated with confidence from the praise of my Ares teachers, and I grew curious about his mumblings." He put his hands up. "You see, I thought they might have something to do with why my mom had left—the mumbling had started right after she was torn away from me. I wanted to find out why. And I thought that if I could save her from the dreaded Alpha, maybe she could come back to live with me and my father.

"As you said, I'm a cheeky bugger. Being a cheeky bugger, I began to leave my father's favorite scotch in prominent positions around our kitchen—he never cleaned up after himself, so I had free reign with the place. I may have also made the scotch a little more potent..."

Ava shivered. Lucas's father would have surely killed him if he had ever found out about this little game of hide-and-seek.

"After laying my trap, I would sit at the bottom of the stairs and listen to his drunken whispers." Lucas shook his head. "So many hours wasted lying in wait for any tidbit about my mother. But alas, all he could think about was *you*," he said, turning to Ava. "Or at least the theoretical version of you—the next reincarnation of the Alpha." Seeing the disturbed looks on Owen and Ava's faces, he added, "Believe me, I would have been way more interested if I had known how hot the Alpha would turn out to be." He winked at Ava, adding, "You cast such a long shadow over my childhood.

"Anyway. One night while I was spying on him he sat up excitedly, his eyes bulging with sudden inspiration. At first I thought it was just another one of his many moments of drunken 'revelation.' He swept the bottle of scotch up with one hand, smashed it in half and threw it at the wall closest to me, shattering it into a thousand pieces." Ava could feel Lucas's pulse quicken and thrash as he recounted the memory. "I thought for sure he had discovered my plan and was on his way to kill me, for real this time. But then the most bizarre thing happened. He gestured at the fallen alcohol, calling flames up from where the liquid had spilled all over the living room. He began to hop and skip between the flames, laughing drunkenly. The fire responded to his manic energy, building and swaying—climbing almost to the ceiling.

"He was a master of fire, but I had added a particularly heavy dose of medication to his booze that night, and judging from the insanity unfolding before me, I was pretty confident the house would soon be burning down around him."

"Funny isn't it?" Lucas asked, laughing mirthlessly. "I saved him once from a burning house. Only to condemn him to die in another. Or I guess he was already dead by the time I lit that fire," Lucas murmured to himself, shaking his head. Ava felt his guilt, secreting from his pores like sweat. "Anyway, at twelve, I didn't yet want to see the only parent I had left die in a fire. I ran out of my hiding space and grabbed him by the forearms to steady him."

Ava was terrified for twelve-year-old Lucas, even though she knew how the story must end. Owen too seemed transfixed by the strange story.

"He just looked at me. Pure joy reflected in his unfocused eyes. 'Fire!' he yelled. And repeated it several more times." By now Lucas was acting the story out and he looked uncannily like his father as he gestured and pantomimed. Suddenly, Ava didn't know how much more she wanted to hear.

Lucas continued, "He looked at me then like a teacher trying to coax an answer out of a reluctant student. 'What do you get when you combine Gaia and Ares?' he asked and shoved me off of him, almost pushing me into the flames. Then he put his hands together in the form of a box—as if he were hiding the answer inside. And then, manic delight in his eyes, he opened his hands and sent a massive fireball towards the ceiling. 'Fire!' he shouted again before collapsing unconscious in my arms.

"It took me hours, but after I dragged my unconscious father outside so he wouldn't die of carbon monoxide poisoning, I finally managed to put the fire out and rescue most of our belongings." Ava caught a memory suddenly from Lucas—him carrying her limp form out of his house as a fire consumed the home—and his father's body with it. It was an eerie parallel.

"I almost ran away from home that night, I was so terrified of my father's reaction when he woke up to see the state of our house. But he was as happy as I'd ever seen him the next morning, and he didn't touch the bottle for the rest of his life. He didn't need to. From that moment on he had an otherworldly energy carrying him forwards, filling him with purpose."

Lucas looked mournful. "I was soon to find out why." He stopped to shovel more trail mix into his mouth. He took his time, getting a drink of water and washing off his hands before settling back against the tree comfortably, sure of his audience's rapt attention.

"What my father had realized, right before he tried to burn down our house, was that the ultimate undoing of Ella, the last Alpha, had been her attraction to a member of the Ares. Fire—the sparks of desire that burn almost unbearably hot between members of the orders."

Owen shifted uncomfortably. Ava blushed.

If Lucas noticed their reactions, he didn't let on. "And when does that fire burn out of control? *When the members of the orders are teenagers.* He had solved part of the puzzle— he knew how to attack the Gaia—go after the young, prevent an Alpha from ever developing, and strangle the newest generation of warriors before they even mastered their powers.

"It took him another couple of months to figure out the second piece of the puzzle: how to ensure the loyalty of young Ares warriors sent to seduce their prey? Warriors who would have to first plunge themselves into the flames of attraction and then kill the object of their infatuation.

"It was yours truly that finally provided him the answer. One day he caught me playing with the neighbor's dog, which of course I was doing just to make him angry." Lucas shrugged, sheepish. "What can I say? Rage is just another kind of fire. And I liked the way it burned—it made me feel alive when nothing else could." His eyes were far away, remembering. He shook his head, coming back to himself. "Anyway, just as I knew it would—the stunt with the dog provoked a vicious beating from my father. But no matter how hard he punched me in the gut, he couldn't wipe the grin off my face and it was infuriating to him. It was after he hit me with the handle of his knife, breaking my nose, and I just giggled, that it occurred to him—he would be better able to control me if he forced me to bear the sangstones.

"I was horrified. Both because, as a committed Ares warrior, I wanted to earn my own sangstones. And because my father was right—I would essentially be his puppet if he and his gang of Makhai could torture me into obedience. It was our little inside 'joke' for the next couple of months—any time we got into one of our wrestling matches he would make the threat. I didn't think he'd really go forward with it. Or rather, I did, but I felt secure in the knowledge that the Elders would never allow such a sacrilege."

Lucas took another sip of water. "How naïve of me, to think the Elders would protect me," he said, smiling sadly. "My father must have convinced them of the beautiful simplicity of his plan. I think the Elders liked to turn a blind eye to the Makhai. They knew the Makhai were winning the war and they didn't want to know exactly how—preferring to keep their hands clean and their consciences cleaner.

"They gathered us, the most promising of the young Ares—all in our teens. And my father did what he does best—put on a show. He spun the sangstone plan as if it were the most sublime offer. Most of the fools, already diehard ideologues, bought into my father's lies. They considered it the ultimate honor—we had proven ourselves worthy without even killing a Gaia member. And the perverse bonus of my father's plan? The young Ares were that much more eager to make the killing—to show that they deserved to be members of the Makhai. Not everyone was so easily convinced. Some of us screamed as the sangstones were implanted—for of course, as much as my father presented the sangstones as the greatest gift, none of us was actually free to turn this glorious gift down. But nobody screamed louder than I did. It took four Makhai to hold me down as I clawed and spat. Because I knew it was no honor.

"From that day on, I thought very hard before disobeying my father. But he grew complacent, thinking that the sangstones had given him total control over me. And…well, you know the rest of the story. Ultimately, he couldn't keep me away from you."

144

The magnetic look in his eyes drew Ava in. But she heard Owen shifting uncomfortably behind her and she changed the subject quickly, "And how does Ella fit into all of this?"

"Oh that? Another little stroke of genius from my father. He was very proud of that one. It was my father's idea of a joke. Since my mission was to kill the Alpha, he thought it perversely hysterical that I would seduce you with the blood of your great-aunt literally in my heart."

"And Isi?" Ava asked, glancing at Owen.

"Probably a casualty of the Makhai's newest strategy. They didn't share much information. I didn't know who anybody else's target was."

Ava shook her head, understanding the true beauty of the plan. "Every Gaia they seduced would give them more information, providing them with more targets. The Makhai must have already seduced somebody who knew Isi and me—they told you the details." Ava shuddered, wondering what childhood friend had fallen prey to the vicious plan of Lucas's father.

"Kind of. I got the sense there were two waves. The first wave was probably very subtle, with not that many Gaia targets. More for information gathering than bloodshed. But the second wave? We were all supposed to strike at the same time. To wipe out the newest generation of Gaia in one deadly sweep."

"So you're...they're going after the young now," Owen said, violence in his voice. Ava recognized Owen's flood of grief from the night with the Lifetree. This is what had been bubbling under the surface before. She couldn't wait any longer. She needed to know what had befallen her Order.

Ava turned to Owen and asked, trepidation in her voice, "How successful was the second wave? What happened? What happened before you came to find us? I know you were injured—my mother called me that night."

145

Owen took a moment before answering, "Mine is a story of fire and heat as well. But now is not the time for me to tell it. We need to keep moving. Eat up and we'll head out in fifteen," he said, moving away from them into the forest.

Ava listened to Owen's advice and shoved some trail mix into her mouth. But it was no use. There were other questions she had to ask, questions best answered while Owen was otherwise occupied. She turned to Lucas and asked, "Have you ever seen them be removed successfully?"

"Only when their hosts were, how do I say this delicately? In a better place."

"So why the hell did you do it—"

"Well I thought the Alpha would be able to save me. Think of it as a way to expand your powers," he answered. Ava glared at him—rising to his bait. He just grinned at her and continued, "Plus what would you two have done if I hadn't taken matters into my own hands? It would have been the end of us, of everything we've risked." He turned away, suddenly intensely interested in an ant marching across the ground below him. "Trust me, it was worth it."

That last phrase, whispered quickly and displaying a vulnerability Ava had rarely seen before, pierced her to the core. She had let him down. She wished the earth would swallow her up and then abruptly banished the thought from her mind. Because the earth would probably listen.

Struggling to understand the implications of everything Lucas had told her, of everything it would mean for them going forward, she had a flash of memory from the night Lucas's father had tried to kill them. "Why didn't your father use the sangstones against you that night? Do you think maybe that was his last small sign of love?"

"He was using my sangstones, just as I was using his. That's the genius of the sangstones—two hot heads who get into a fight can't do any harm to one another. It would even be difficult to kill somebody using the combined power of two or three Makhai. But if you are condemned to die by a group of the Makhai—well, nobody survives once the brotherhood decides."

More flashes of that terrible night came back to her— she saw the concentration in the eyes of Lucas and his father and it had new meaning for her. The perversity of the sangstones was chilling. And yet it was such a brilliant way of controlling the strongest, most uncontrollable warriors of the Order. *Except it didn't always work.*

She had worked up the courage to ask her final question. "Why? Why didn't you tell me?"

"You know why."

Her face was unmoved—she was not going to let him get away so easily, even if he was injured.

He sighed in surrender. "Because. You kind of got me to believe in this crazy mission of yours. And I didn't want you to give up just because I was a dead-man walking." He smiled at her. "Or, more accurately, a dead-man carried."

Chapter 15

Lucas insisted on walking on his own after they broke camp. When Owen looked relieved, Lucas laughed. "You can't tell me you're not secretly disappointed, Captain Planet."

"You're heavier than you look," Owen retorted easily, and Lucas huffed. Neither Owen nor Ava complained about the slow pace being set by the injured Lucas. From their flushed cheeks and brows drenched in sweat, it was clear to see that they too were suffering. But as Lucas's shade of green went from pale olive to something bordering on lime as the miles wore away beneath them, Ava insisted that they break for camp somewhere along the coast.

While they paused, Owen quickly consulted a map. Lucas peered over his shoulder, brows furrowed in suspicion, and asked, "Why are we going back to Melbourne?" When nobody answered, he continued, "You can't take me to a hospital—the Ares will be all over us in a second."

"We're running out of options, Lucas, and I have a friend who's an excellent surgeon," Owen replied, his tone neutral.

A look of comprehension dawned on Lucas's face. "You want to leave Australia. I won't go, not without seeing my mother."

Owen and Ava looked at each other—this is what they had feared. Owen replied, "We're sitting ducks here. We're sitting ducks who have shot a giant duck flare over our heads to advertise our sitting duckness."

"Well this duck is staying put," Lucas said, folding his arms across his chest. "Although I prefer to think of myself as a platypus."

"You can't joke your way out of this one, Lucas," Ava said, gently.

Owen nodded. "We need to regroup, get stronger, and then…we can talk about returning and trying to find your mom. You're not even sure that she's here."

"Nobody's following us now. Right?" Lucas asked.

Ava thought about it for a moment, replying, "I haven't felt anything."

"Well, no," Owen said. But he couldn't quite meet their eyes.

Lucas had picked up on Owen's discomfort. "What is it?"

"A lot happened that night you ran away," Owen answered hesitantly. He paused—from his look Ava could tell he was on the brink of telling them something important.

Ava sighed, equal parts terrified and excited to finally get an update on her Order and her family. But what Owen said next, she was not expecting.

"You two weren't the only ones to disappear."

When Owen didn't elaborate, Lucas sighed heavily, turning to Ava. "That night with my father was supposed to be the start of the second wave. We were all going to strike together…take out our targets while the Gaia forces were otherwise occupied…"

"You mean they killed them, the other Gaia teens?" Ava asked, unable to hide the horror in her voice.

"We're not exactly sure," Owen said. He turned to Lucas. "Haven't you thought it was a little strange how few Ares have come after you?"

Lucas nodded. "Yes. It's been…disconcerting to say the least. I've been worried about it."

Ava looked surprised—Lucas hadn't mentioned anything about this fear. Apparently she wasn't the only one trying not to burden her travelling companions with secrets.

Lucas sighed. "Of course," he mumbled. He traded a meaningful look with Owen. "They're distracted."

Ava put the pieces together. "You mean the other Ares teens might not have been able to go through with it either—killing their targets? They might also have gone AWOL?"

"We're hopeful. It's not like the Makhai to be modest about their victories—usually we find the bodies of their victims pretty quickly. But no bodies have turned up yet…" Owen trailed off.

Ava shook her head. "The Order must be in total disarray. All those young Gaia warriors disappearing—"

"You can't imagine," Owen said darkly.

Lucas let a bark of laughter escape, and then he was howling with mirth—tears streaming from his eyes as he rolled on the ground. Owen looked at Ava but she just shrugged—she had no idea what this latest outburst was about.

Finally Lucas managed to speak through his tears, "His plan. It failed so miserably. He always warned me—fire was the most potent of weapons but also the most dangerous with its quicksilver changes in direction and intensity. He set this fire—unleashing the young Makhai to seduce the Gaia—and it consumed him."

His eyes were bright, unnaturally so. Sweat was pouring off of his brow. "We have to find them...the others."

Ava grabbed a water bottle and moved over to him. "Lucas, have some water. Calm down for a moment."

He was frantic with excitement—with the manic light burning in his eyes and the agitated hand gestures, he looked uncannily like his father. At the thought Ava faltered.

Owen looked unruffled. "So you'll leave with us? If we work to find the others?"

"No," Lucas said—his tone decisive. Owen's face darkened at the brusque response.

Lucas realized his mistake; he put his arms up, trying to placate Owen. "I'm not just being stubborn, Captain Planet, I promise. I think my mother would know how to get the sangstones out. And we'll need that knowledge to have any chance of successfully recruiting the other AWOL Makhai."

The two stared at each other mutinously, one steely calm and steadfast, the other stubborn and smoldering with passion.

Mindful of Lucas's precarious health and trying to keep the peace, Ava broke in, "We don't have to decide tonight." She turned to Owen, saying, "In the meantime, let's rest and maybe you can tell us about the rest of that night, the night where the Makhai were supposed to attack. It might help us fill in some of the pieces. Which could help us decide what our next move should be."

Owen said wearily, "I'm tired of talking." Ava looked hurt. Owen's face immediately softened. "But that doesn't mean I won't show you."

Ava's eyes widened. "No...you know how to create a linea?"

"Yes," Owen replied, unable to keep a small smile of pride from his face.

Lucas was looking between them clearly confused.

Ava noticed his confusion. "It takes a lot of skill, but some Gaia can…I'm not sure how to say it without showing you. I guess the best way of describing it is to say they can invite others into their memories. I'm talking about a full-on reliving experience."

She shivered, reliving the memory of free-falling her grandmother had invited her to see when she was little. She had been staying with her grandmother while her mother was on a particularly long mission, and she'd thrown a terrible tantrum one night—she'd wanted her mom to read her a bedtime story. Her grandmother had instructed Ava to lock forearms with her and then—she was falling, the wind in her hair and her stomach in her mouth until the whooshing parachute had jerked her up and she had floated gently down, staring at the ocean below with wide eyes. It had only been a couple of seconds, and her grandmother had never explained where the memory had come from. In fact, she'd been so tired after performing the linea that she'd fallen asleep in bed with Ava. Ava cherished that memory—the two of them curled up facing one another. Ava hadn't dared to fall asleep. She'd been so lonely without her mother, she'd just wanted to soak up every moment of nearness—watching the gentle breathing of her grandmother, still wearing all of her jewelry—

"So can he show us both at once?" Lucas's question jerked her out of her sweet reminiscing and she let out a small gasp at the visceral loss of being wrenched away from the memory. The smell of peppermint tea—her grandmother's favorite—seemed to fill the air around her and she smiled sadly at the sensory mirage.

Owen and Ava traded looks. "I think it's best if Owen just shows me for now," she said.

Lucas looked hurt. "Why?"

After a moment, Ava replied, "It's not...it's not like watching a movie. This won't be a relaxing display of his memories. We'll feel like we're there with him. We'll feel the same sensations that Owen feels—fear, heat, exhaustion, pain..."

Lucas looked like he was going to say something in protest. But then he just put his hands up, surrendering. "Fine. I'll just stay here. Count the number of mosquito bites I get. You'll be sorry you missed out on all of the fun."

Before Ava could respond, Owen whispered a few words in the ancient tongue. At the sound of his voice, rough and guttural, spiders climbed down out of the trees in droves. Lucas's eyes widened. But the spiders just scurried and spun—until a giant egg-shaped web enveloped Lucas. Ava sighed—the thousands of tiny crisscrossing lines of web sparkled with iridescent beauty in the sunlight.

Owen smiled shyly at Lucas. "This should help with the mosquitoes." Then the Gaia warrior turned to Ava and asked, "Ready?"

Ava nodded, trying to quiet her nerves. The linea was a thrilling experience. But she knew what she was about to see would bring her terrible sorrow.

Just as her grandmother had so many years before, Owen locked forearms with her. He closed his eyes in concentration. Ava's heart sped up in her chest.

Owen murmured, "Just follow me. I'll guide you." His voice was full of gentle reassurance. Just as Ava closed her eyes, Owen added a whispered warning, "And don't forget to breathe."

Chapter 16

Ava forgot to breathe. For a terrifying moment she felt like she'd been jerked underwater—liquid flooding every surface of her body and blocking out all of her senses. And then, just as quickly as it had begun, it finished.

"Open your eyes…and *breathe*," a faraway voice whispered. Ava gasped for air and obeyed the command of the disembodied voice. She found herself standing next to Owen—an Owen who looked noticeably less haggard and more clean-shaven. He was scanning his surroundings intently, a worried look on his face. Behind him a lyrical voice was speaking, "…and then Pele chased Kamapua'a into the sea. Isn't that a beautiful legend? I do feel a special kinship with Pele—the Hawaiian Goddess of Fire."

Ava's heart skipped a beat. She recognized that voice. She turned and there was her grandmother, Lena, standing in front of a small group of children—they were sitting at her feet and staring up at her with adoration. Little kids had always loved Lena. Her grandmother spoke again, "This is a sacred place for our Order. Can you feel her here—Gaia? This is a place we bring our children to catalyze a true connection with the Earth Mother. If you open your mind—remember how we practiced?—she'll come to you. She'll speak to you, each one of you, helping you discover where your true powers lie—revealing whether you are a creature of water, of air, of earth, of bears and birds and bees or even, *of fire*." As she said the last part, she placed a weathered hand to the ground and drew it upwards with a flourish. A miniature geyser of lava followed the motion of her hand and the children giggled in appreciation.

"Can I be a creature of the elephants?" asked a little girl—freckles covering her entire body.

"Can I be a creature of butts?" chimed in one of the little boys, a hint of glee in his eyes. He beamed, dimples rippling, clearly exceedingly self-satisfied with his question.

Lena whispered something in his ear, and the self-satisfied smile slid off his face. Then she turned gracefully to address the children once more, "I know this might seem strange, but I want you to try something. Place your

153

hands on the ground—do you feel that heat? Visitors come here, to Kīlauea Iki, from all over the world to feel the crater still warm to the touch sixty years after it last erupted. They marvel at its mystery and snap many pictures, trying and failing to capture their moment of awe for eternity. It moves many of them to tears." She had the rapt attention of her crowd, even the little joker, at this point. "But what they feel, as beautiful as it is, is nothing compared to what you will experience when you connect with Gaia, when you immerse yourself in a great chain of life stretching back billions of years. Calm your minds and open your hearts."

Owen caught Lena's eye and she excused herself from the group of children to stand next to him. He whispered to her discreetly, "Are you sure they're ready?" Owen ran a hand through his hair. "I didn't go through the Ritual of Fire until I was fourteen."

Lena looked at him, sighing. "The world is changing. Even the very young must be able to protect themselves in this savage war."

"Can we wait for the other Elders to arrive?"

Lena looked uncharacteristically nervous. "I'm not sure that we can count on them getting here. Gaia has been skittish all day, and it's only getting worse. Something is happening…" Lena trailed off, her blue eyes unfocused.

"What is it?" Owen asked apprehensively. "What do you feel?"

"I fear for Ava."

"Ava?" Owen said, sounding truly surprised.

Lena looked suddenly haggard. When she spoke, her voice was low, somber. "I've felt this fretful energy from Gaia only once before. Nobody was more successful at provoking Gaia than my sister Ella, the last Alpha. Joy, rage, affection—she could make Gaia feel it all." Lena shook her head, smiling in remembrance. "But the last time Gaia reacted like this was the night Ella was killed." At the murmured phrase, Lena's eyes hardened in steely resolve—lethal resolve. "Whatever is coming we need to be ready. The young ones must prepare for the Ritual of Fire—immediately."

Putting a hand on Owen's shoulder, Lena said, "You must lead them in the ritual."

Owen pulled away from her and opened his mouth as if he were going to object but Lena spoke again, "No. You will take them. As for me, I am old—"

"Lena, please, you take the children."

Lena smiled at him, clearly still half-consumed by memories of her sister. "I am old, but I'm not dead yet. There's a reason I'm so drawn to the story of Pele. She's not the only goddess of fire here today." Her words crackled with power as she spoke the last part. "Now, go. Take the children."

This time Owen just nodded solemnly.

"I'll follow soon behind, I promise," Lena added.

With a quick whistle and a few whispered words, Owen herded the children towards a path—it led up to the dense rainforest surrounding the crater. Although they were very young, they had obviously been on many other training excursions because the children hiked with military precision—their eyes scanning their surroundings warily. Ava followed Owen and the Gaia youngsters for miles as they wended their way through the rainforest. With every passing mile, the children grew more hushed—the occasional murmurs and burst of giggles fading to utter silence. The children had noticed Owen's anxiety—so palpable that the earth shuddered at his every step.

Suddenly Ava heard it, a faint whirring. She moved to Owen to warn him, but as she whispered to him she remembered with a sickening jolt that he could not hear her. There was nothing she could do to change the situation. Owen and the children were on their own.

A helicopter buzzed overhead. Owen put his head back and released a primal roar into the forest, "Lena!" And then, hands gesturing wildly at the sky, he yelled at the children to take cover. The children were all well prepared for the situation, and Ava watched as they found clever hiding spaces—some disappearing under the ground with a quiet whoosh as the earth parted to accommodate small bodies and quickly reformed, some shimmying up trees and disappearing into the canopy. She knew that at least some of them, the older children, would be sprinting back through the treetops to warn Lena and summon backup from the Elders.

Meanwhile, responding to Owen's frantic gestures, the wind had begun to pick up, whistling through the treetops, and lightning forked across the sky. A bolt struck near the helicopter above, and it jerked backwards, flying rapidly away from the danger. Ava smiled at the triumph, but the smile disappeared with a gasp. Two camo-clad dots had leapt out of the retreating helicopter and were falling quickly towards them. They were wearing some kind of winged suit that allowed them to aim precisely as they fell. They landed not twenty feet from Owen—who realized, eyes widening in dismay, that one child, the littlest of the bunch, had gotten stuck mid-waist in the mud. The little boy turned to look at Owen in terror and Ava recognized him—it was the joker.

The earth bucked beneath Owen as he pushed a wave of dirt at the camo-clad figures, but one of the Ares managed to snatch the child and start running.

There was a split second when Owen looked at the little boy hanging in the arms of one of the Ares, and then looked back to where the rest of the children were hiding. With a grunt, he did the one thing every moment of training had forbidden—he left the group and chased after the Ares warriors.

With a shake of her head, Ava ran after Owen. Owen screamed ahead—once again releasing a primal howl that shook the trees around them and must have been audible for miles. Ava took a few more running steps and saw what had caused the outburst—a tiny shoe lodged in the dirt. Next to the shoe was a splatter of blood. Owen moved faster, calling the earth to propel him forward; the earth obliged, shooting him ahead through the forest like a slingshot. The trees bent backwards with a wooden creak to facilitate Owen's furious pursuit. Laughter rang out through the canopy—it was terribly cruel, the kind that spewed from sadistic teens torturing a captured animal. "Catch," somebody yelled, the cruelty threading through the words as it had the laughter. Owen looked around wildly, drawing the earth up into a miniature shield. And then the air filled with dense smoke.

Ava's vision went black for a moment. The memory shifted, like a movie skipping scenes. It was nighttime in this new patch of memory. Owen was lying on some kind of metal sheet. His hair was sticky and matted with blood. Her heart jumped into her throat—he looked dead. She reminded herself that if she was seeing the memory, he must be not only alive but conscious. He must have passed out back there in the forest—that's why the memory skipped.

Ava could just make out two shapes in the darkness—the two men who had jumped out of the helicopter. One, a sandy-haired blond, was on the phone. He hung up and turned to the other, a hulking brunette. "Word is they're holed up somewhere. Some kind of fortress. Apparently a bunch of reinforcements showed up."

"So it's working," the brunette replied, his voice gleeful.

"Except our forces aren't in position."

"What d'you mean? Why were they delayed? This is our chance—fools all came to gather in one place."

"Dense fog, apparently," the blond muttered. "One of the Gaia witches no doubt."

The beefy brunette cursed under his breath. "Still, they're all here and—let's just burn 'em to the ground. The General called it perfectly—they wouldn't leave their precious children to die."

"Don't be stupid. That many Gaia warriors gathered in one place—they'll be...formidable. Could risk a lot of casualties to attack 'em now. Especially with the bloody fog."

"Whatever. We don't even have to engage. Let's just use the copter to douse the whole rainforest in lighter fluid and then..." He snapped his fingers and a flame ignited in his palm.

"As if the copter could fly—they'll raise hurricane-force winds before we get within ten miles. Plus, we have people in the forest. That was the whole point of the operation—to surprise the Gaia on their own turf."

The brunette one looked annoyed; clearly he didn't like being corrected. "What about these two? Should we take them inside?"

"General warned me not to get any blood on the carpets."

"I don't think these two have much more blood in 'em."

After a few minutes of silence, the blond nudged the brunette—clearly trying to placate him. "Guess what else I heard—the Alpha witch's family is all here."

"Nah..." the other one said smirking. "Seriously? How fitting that the Alpha and her family would all die on the same night."

Ava shivered, terrified of what dark secrets Owen's memory might reveal. Had all of her family escaped? Or had Lucas been wrong.

She was distracted from her fears when the blond one continued reverently, "Another glorious movement in the General's master symphony. Word is he's on his way now to watch the Alpha witch die at the hands of his own son—wanted a front row seat."

Too busy laughing, the two men hadn't noticed the goose bumps that had spread over Owen's body at the latest turn in conversation. Ava had, and she had noticed something else. The metal handcuffs Owen was wearing had begun to corrode at supernatural speed—they wouldn't bind the warrior's hands for much longer.

A dense cloud of fog moved towards the little group, turning everything in Ava's line of vision a dark gray. Visibility was nonexistent.

From the direction of the two men there was muttered cursing. "Not again."

One of them, it sounded like the blond, although Ava couldn't see for sure, spoke, "I'm going to check in with command. This is no natural fog. Maybe something's happening." He sounded tense.

There was muffled noise as the blond, who was apparently in charge, consulted with central command. After a moment, the blond spoke again, "Something's up. They want us to do one more round with these two. Remind the Gaia that we have two of their own…at our mercy."

"Should I heat it up again?" This was the brunette's voice. There was violence in his tone. Ava couldn't see what the hefty brunette was gesturing at, but she guessed he was referring to the slab of metal Owen and the little boy were lying on.

"Yeah. Word came straight from the General himself. He wants us to really make 'em scream this time. It seems like the Gaia witches may not be picking up on the emotional distress radiating from our hostages. But we can fix that…"

Ava heard a series of guttural whispers. Whatever the brunette did, the metal must have begun to heat up because the little boy let out a whimper of pain.

She could just make out Owen's body lying next to her and she crouched down—desperate to protect him from whatever torture the Ares were preparing, but she knew her efforts would be useless. Tears welled in her eyes, rolling down her face and onto her arms. She almost missed the drop of rain that splashed on her forearm, at first mistaking it for another tear. Almost. Quickly, she turned to the motionless form on the ground. Owen's eyes burst open and the sky split like a speared piñata—spilling drops of water bigger than Ava had ever seen before. The fog had cleared slightly, and Ava could just make out the scene unfolding before her through the rain. The Ares warriors had a moment to share a look of surprise before the water hit the metal sheet and erupted into great billowing curtains of steam. Owen directed these pillars of boiling vapor at the Ares warriors—lashing the curtains of steam like a whip. Then the Gaia warrior was springing up, scooping the little boy into his arms, and hobbling into the forest—the shrieks of the Ares warriors at his back.

His breathing labored, Owen moved at an ungainly pace through the trees. One leg was scaly and blistered over in burns and he was dragging it behind him. He was whispering frantically; in response to his words the raindrops merged and wrapped themselves around the little boy's exposed skin like liquid cellophane. Ava hoped that it would be enough to leech the poisonous heat from the boy's skin—he wasn't yet old or powerful enough for the skin to heal completely on its own.

Owen looked wildly around in the rain. At first, Ava thought he was looking for the Ares warriors camped throughout the rainforest. But as his searching became ever more frantic, she realized he was looking for some bird or small mammal with which to warn the others of the Ares' plot. But no animal appeared—evidently they had been scared away by the combined threat of torrential rain and the Ares' invasion of their territory.

Owen slowed as the miles fell away—the slower he went, the more the rain let up, until it was nothing but a fine mist. Finally he broke through the thicket of trees to see the edge of the crater below him.

Ava gasped. She had scanned the crater earlier that day, while her grandmother was telling the children the legend of Pele. It had been shaped like a giant footprint—dark, hardened lava in an oblong shape encased by nearly sheer cliff walls that led up to a verdant rainforest. It had not looked like it did now. Now, on the opposite side of the crater roared a four-hundred-foot waterfall. Icy blue water pounded down from the rainforest into the crater floor where it erupted into great clouds of mist. Ava had to shake her head as she looked—there was something wonky about the spectacle. It reminded her of a surrealist landscape. A second later she realized why—there was not one waterfall, but two. Or rather, there was a massive curtain of water flowing over the cliff edge, hitting the crater floor, and then shooting upwards and back to the cliff top—creating an endless waterfall loop. The gathered Gaia must have been sheltered behind the sphere of running water.

It would take an unbelievable amount of power to create this symmetrical waterfall—Ava hadn't even see a river near the crater as they'd crashed through the forest earlier that day. The kind of power that only a group of practiced Gaia working together could generate—her family. Her family was behind that waterfall. The Ares thugs had said as much. Driven by that knowledge, she stared fixedly at the panorama in front of her. She was staring at it so intently that when the water began to part she had a long moment to scan the scene unfolding behind the protective sweep of the water. She caught a glimpse of a dense forest, thick trunks and roots twisting and vaulting into a miniature fortress. After the waterfall had fully parted with a graceful ripple, a small figure moved through it. The mist rising off of the watery curtain lent the figure, a woman, the air of a high priestess emerging through the mists of Avalon from another world. A bridge formed before her, leading her down to the center of the crater. The woman strode across the bridge of water confidently until she reached the flat of the crater. Stepping down from the bridge, the woman made a deft chopping motion. Instantly the bridge withdrew, arcing back into the waterfall, and the curtain of water rippled closed behind her. She was alone.

Ava choked on her breath—the woman was her grandmother. But she looked nothing like the Lena of Ava's childhood memories—an old, world-weary woman, still mourning the separation of her family and the death of her beloved sister. This woman, mist churning around her in ethereal splendor, stood with clear, unafraid eyes and head held high. She was regal in that moment—queen of the water. *But she had said she was the goddess of fire.*

Lena opened her mouth to speak and when her voice came out it had the power of Stentor, ringing through the entire rainforest, "You have ten minutes to return the child and the warrior."

A lone snicker rose up from the forest in response to her words. Moments after the laughter, something whistled through the air towards her grandmother's chest. Ava inhaled sharply. Lena made a gentle motion with her hand, the half wave of a monarch in a long public procession, and a tendril of water shot out of the waterfall to knock the spinning knife away easily.

"I would prefer not to spill blood in this sacred place. But I have before and I will again if the two are not returned."

Ava was watching Lena so carefully she had forgotten to keep track of Owen's movements next to her. Out of the corner of her eye, she caught a ruffle of feathers and had a moment to observe Owen whispering to a sleek white and black bird perched on his shoulder before it leapt into flight. Gaining height, the bird flew towards Lena near the center of the canyon and let out a piercing cry.

Lena's cobalt eyes darted upwards and she locked eyes with the bird for a moment; her whole body tensed as she received whatever message Owen had sent. Ava could guess the gist of it—a report on the terrible injuries endured by Owen and his ward, and a warning about the

Ares hidden in the trees. She had an agonizing moment of fear that Lena would sacrifice herself to protect them. Lena concentrated for a moment, clearly communicating with the creature. It cried again, this time turning its head to direct its message towards Owen. The bird gave another piercing shriek and this time Ava heard the message ringing through every corner of her brain. *Water.*

Owen gestured feebly at the sky—calling the last of the mist to condense in a globe of ice around himself and the little boy. Nothing happened for a moment and Ava crept closer to observe her grandmother in the crater below.

Lena knelt to the ground, her head bowed as if in prayer. And then the earth erupted—fire spewing everywhere. Long sheets of lava streamed out of vents in the crater—their vertical precision making them look like pyrotechnics at a concert. The lava shot into the air, fifty, then one hundred, then two hundred feet. Lena looked up from her kneeling position, a gleam in her eye, and with a trembling of earth, a vent opened directly beneath her. A column of lava rocketed her up into the sky.

Ava cried out in dismay. Was she about to witness her grandmother's death? Is this why Owen had been hesitant to show her the memory?

There were now four different curtains of lava, including the column lifting Lena—pillars of fire reaching into the sky. The earth let out a strange keening sound and the columns of lava began to coalesce. Ava squinted, unable to believe what she was seeing. The lava was forming into a solid, towering mass—a woman. There was the curly hair, the eyes, the lips. And Lena was standing on top of the woman—a tiny dot on this giant fiery Amazon. The figure reached a molten hand towards the forest next to where Ava was standing, slowly extending an accusatory finger at unseen enemies.

There came a strangled cry from the forest—of surrender? Defiance? Terror? Ava wasn't sure. But the fiery figure was unmoved. With the same eerily human sound, lava erupted out of the Amazon's pointed finger. The molten creature swept around in a circle, fiery trigger finger extended, covering the rainforest around the crater in lava. Ava heard screams echoing up through the forest and turned to see how Owen would protect himself. But their little corner of forest had been spared. Although heat was pouring off the lava surrounding them, and Owen's ice globe was melting quickly, it was holding for the moment.

Ava craned her neck to watch her grandmother direct this fire creature and for one long moment it seemed like her grandmother looked down and met her gaze. And then everything went black.

Chapter 17

"What?" Ava exclaimed, coming to in the sweltering Australian night. Adrenaline still humming through her veins, she spoke rapidly, "What was that? How did my grandmother do that? Could she see me? Was that Gaia, in the lava?" The questions tumbled out faster and faster. Ava looked at her own hands in wonder—*could I do that?*

And then she caught sight of Lucas, crouched on the ground looking pale and anxious. Owen was already standing over him, his hand resting lightly on Lucas's shoulder.

Ava felt hot shame snaking up her chest, around her neck, and into her cheeks, leaving its trail of crimson across her skin. As much as she had just seen her Order triumph in an unbelievable show of power, she had also just witnessed Lucas's friends and fellow members mowed down by a monster wrought of fire.

Lucas turned to her. "What is it? What did you see?" he asked.

As anxious as she'd been to speak before, words now deserted her. After a pregnant pause, Owen leaned over and began whispering in Lucas's ear. Red climbed higher up Ava's face, burning all the way to her earlobes. She had let Owen be the one to share the news. This seemed always to be his task, the stoic messenger, his broad shoulders strong enough to carry the heaviest burdens of grief.

After a long whispered conversation, in which Lucas slumped further and further down against the tree trunk, Owen straightened. "I'm sorry," he murmured.

Lucas acknowledged Owen's words with a quick nod of his head. After a few moments he looked up at the Gaia warrior. "The little boy? The one captured with you?"

Owen shook his head, and Ava felt the familiar pulse of rage coming from her old friend. "He made it. But…he'll carry those burns for the rest of his life. They were too severe for even our most adept healers." His voice strangled with emotion, Owen added, "And we lost another…a little girl…to the Ares laying in wait in the forest." Ava looked away, heartsick. Now she understood the source of Owen's rage.

After a few moments of silent mourning, Ava thought of Lucas's question. It reminded her of something—she turned to see how Owen's burns had healed. Scanning up Owen's body, she realized she hadn't once truly looked at him since he had joined them in Australia. Maybe she was afraid of what she would find. Or more likely, how it would make her feel. She stared at the angry red scabs on his legs and understood that Owen too would carry the scars from the torture for the rest of his life. Unable to resist, her gaze moved up his legs to his torso, taking in the ripped t-shirt and broad shoulders. His face was dirt-smeared and covered in a week's worth of blond scruff, but the mischievous green eyes and slicing cheekbones were unchanged.

Under other circumstances this would be the setting of one of her daydreams—stuck in a remote Australian coastal setting with two men who looked like they had stepped right out of an *L.L. Bean* catalogue. As it was, the strange energy pulsing between the three of them was unsettling. She could feel the emotions swirling around her, tugging at her clothes like a riptide, currents of attraction colliding with guilt, jealousy, distrust, affection, hope, and a little tug of despair. Perhaps, most unsettling, she felt less the center of the triangle than the odd woman out. Her relationship with both Owen and Lucas was stalled—plagued by betrayals on her part and on theirs. But the two men had clearly begun to find common cause. Why did the small moments of affection between them, while sweet, make her so uncomfortable? These moments could exist, here in the wilderness, but she could scarcely imagine a future where Owen and Lucas could be real friends. Things were going better than she ever could have imagined, besides that whole kidnap and torture thing earlier in the week. Lucas and Owen were palling around like old friends. And yet…

She was interrupted from this train of thought by the faintest trace of laughter. She turned to find both the guys staring at her, eyes crinkled in mirth.

"Wh—" the question died in her mouth. In front of her, ants were marching in a perfect miniature triangle— the points of the shape roughly correlated to where she, Lucas, and Owen were arrayed around camp. Another group of ants had shaped into a larger triangle. And another, and another—the perverse incarnation of nested Russian dolls. After a second, the ants began to move, rotating the triangles in perfect precision. The ant version of spin the bottle. Where would they land? Who would she choose?

Ava blushed deep purple, asking, "How long have they been doing that?"

Owen replied, "The last three minutes at least. Every thirty seconds or so they pause and start rotating in the opposite direction. What's the fixation on triangles?"

Lucas chimed in, "Is this your subtle way of telling us you want to see the pyramids, Earth Mother?"

Earth Mother. He hadn't called her that in so long. She couldn't tell if he was harkening back to the past as a gesture of endearment or distancing himself from her like he did from Owen by calling him Captain Planet.

"Who says I'm the one the ants are responding to? You guys are both Gaia," Ava murmured in response.

"I think you just did. With that little nose crinkle," Lucas said, turning to Owen. "Why didn't you guys train her to be a better liar?"

Owen shrugged his shoulders, grinning at Lucas. "We tried. But some things just can't be taught. Have you ever heard this girl sing?"

Ava looked haughtily between the two self-satisfied smiles and retorted, "What, like you two deserve a parade for being such good liars?" The moment the words were out of her mouth she regretted them.

There was an uncomfortable silence for a few moments as each teen pretended to be deeply engrossed in preparing camp for the coming nightfall. Ava was secretly seething that her private thoughts had been transmitted into the insect equivalent of Shakespearian theater, and she kicked resentfully at the ground. What would be next? A cache of butterflies descending upon the next person she dared to have a crush on, fluttering in lurid imitation of a heart?

Finally Owen broke the standoff. He moved over to Lucas and gestured for him to stick his injured arm out. Pulling off the bandages, he examined the wound—which still looked red and raw.

"How does it feel?" Owen asked.

"Ok."

"Better or worse than before?"

"Um…"

"No need for stoicism," Ava interjected.

"Worse. Definitely worse. But that could just be my pride speaking. I've never not been able to self-heal an injury before," Lucas muttered.

Ava remembered that the Ares had a different healing mechanism than the Gaia, one that involved manipulating cells to heal faster. "Do you have any better idea of what it is?" she asked hopefully.

Lucas examined the angry red streaks climbing his arm from his injury. "Hmm. Yes. It's a most rare affliction. Pajamitis. Makes the afflicted look like he's perpetually wearing striped pajamas."

"Weak. Could have gone with candycanitis. Or conjunctive zebratitis," Owen said, with the slightest hint of a smile.

Ava rolled her eyes. "My God. Lucas, you've done the impossible. You've found someone who's even worse at telling jokes than you are. Like two peas in a terrible pun pod."

Owen shook his head, gesturing at Ava. "Sorry about this one. No appreciation for good humor."

Lucas replied, his face deadpan, "No, she's right. Best not to get our roles confused. You're the strong, silent one. And I tell the jokes."

They all had a good smile at that one, although Ava was sure she was not the only one left thinking about what role she actually played in their strange little threesome.

Turning more serious, Owen put his hand on Lucas's shoulder. "This stoic mute doesn't like the look of those red lines. Let me try giving you some of my energy again."

"No—"

Owen interrupted him, "It's better for all of us if you can keep up. And whatever those streaks are, I don't want them moving any further up your arm."

Lucas nodded wordlessly. As Owen held onto Lucas's shoulder, his face lined in concentration, Ava felt the faintest pulse of energy being transmitted.

Lucas grimaced as the energy flooded into his body. "Those guys who…hurt you and the little boy. They're not really Ares," Lucas mumbled.

Owen and Ava waited for him to continue. "They're bottom feeders, thugs. The Makhai turn away a lot of Ares interested in joining—my dad wanted to keep the ranks small. You know the old trick—turn enough people away and you can trick them into thinking anything is elite and prestigious. All the more unsavory types wanted to join, and when they were turned down, they latched on that much harder—eager to be lackeys of the Makhai." Lucas sighed. "We don't all take such pleasure in violence."

Ava was trying to think of what to say to soothe Lucas when Owen spoke, "I know."

"Really?" Lucas asked.

"Of course. I'd be a terribly ineffective soldier if I thought all Ares were robotic killers. A good ideologue but an awful soldier."

Lucas replied, "I always thought the Makhai were good ideologues and good soldiers. Better than good. But now…if there are others who disappeared the same night as Ava and I…"

Owen nodded thoughtfully at Lucas's words, looking suddenly decisive. "I think you were right before, Lucas."

Lucas tried to cover the surprise on his face.

Owen said, "This is our opening, the last one we may ever get given the discipline of the Makhai. We have to find the others…the ones who disappeared the same night as you two." Turning to meet Lucas's eyes, he continued, "And you were right—it'll take more than just finding them. We'll have to figure out how to neutralize the power of the sangstones. I guess it's time to find your mother."

"How do we do that though? If she hasn't found us yet…" Ava trailed off, looking at the sorry state of their huddled group. They wouldn't be able to muster much energy to pursue somebody, let alone a powerful member of the Ares like Lucas's mom. She added, "I'm not taking

169

any more chances. I want to be able to control my power before the next time we're ambushed." She gave Owen a pointed look as she said, "After all, even our oldest and dearest friends can surprise us."

Owen put his hands up in a gesture of surrender, saying, "The lady doth make a good point."

"That she doth, that she doth," Lucas replied, grinning and doing his own best impression of old English. "Alas the lady doth frown at our unparalleled wit. And now she doth pulleth her golden ringlets in dismay."

Ava pretended to kick Lucas in the shins. To her dismay, he grimaced in pain—she must have inadvertently nicked him. "I'm so sorry," Ava said in a rush.

But Lucas was already beaming at Owen, who reached out to high five him.

"Ah, the old soccer flop," Ava said with a wry smile.

Owen draped his arm over Ava's shoulders and Lucas's grin dampened a few watts. "I have a terrible plan," the Gaia warrior said.

Ava turned her neck to smile at him. "Perfect. It'll fit right in."

Owen fished a coin out of his pocket and held it up to Ava. Before he could begin Ava let out an "ohhh." Pointing at Lucas, she said, "Take notes, Lucas. This one brings props for his inspirational strategy speeches."

Owen cleared his throat, trying to regain the attention of the peanut gallery. "As a Gaia—the Alpha Gaia—you have your animal side and you have your human side." As he spoke, he flipped the coin. "It is essential to build control over both sides."

Ava put her hand up, gesturing for Owen to halt his explanation. "Wait, I'm sorry. How many sides are there again?"

When Owen didn't so much as crack a smile, Ava realized that he was nervous. Very nervous. What was he about to tell her?

"Right, forget the coin." He chucked the money into the backpack. "I should warn you that what I'm about to tell you is largely conjecture—pieced together from conversations with the Elders and my own, sometimes illicit, research."

Ava nodded. "Warned. Now get on with it...you're freaking me out."

"You remember that time you called the thunderstorm when we were little? We were learning hand-to-hand combat and you refused to go inside with the others? That was the first inkling I had that you were different, you were special."

"You've known for that long? The Elders, my family—they've all known?" she said, the accusation clear in her voice.

Owen held up his hands in a calming gesture. "Don't judge them too harshly, Ava. At first they only suspected. And then...I think they kept it from you because being the Alpha is dangerous."

"Yeah, but I was always the Alpha, I just didn't know it."

"There is power in identity, in knowledge. You've felt more powerful since finding out, right? And in turn you've opened your mind to the possibility of harnessing more power."

Ava nodded despite herself. There was truth in Owen's words.

"But that's not the only reason they kept it from you. I think it's also dangerous to take on the mantle of the Alpha. A baptism of fire as it were."

Ava's eyes lit up at the word fire, recalling the giant Amazonian creature wrought of lava that her grandmother had summoned.

Owen pursed his lips. "Ok, that was not the reaction I was expecting. And it doesn't involve actual fire. Just the opposite actually."

Ava's curiosity was piqued. *Water?*

"Your grandmother…Lena…once told me a story about her sister Ella…" He paused to tug his hands through the scruff of his new beard. He was deep in concentration, recalling the details of the story. "Back before the start of World War Two, Ella had suggested that she and Lena go swimming off the coast of California. She was sixteen or seventeen and apparently she'd been acting erratically for months. Lena was young then and still frightened by the open ocean, but she could never say no to her older sister. At some point during the swim, Ella disappeared. The Elders called a massive search party, terrified that she might hurt herself or others."

Ava thought of the earthquake she had initiated in San Francisco. She could empathize with her great-aunt.

"Anyway, Ella showed up hours later, eyes wide. 'Manic,' that's how Lena described her. She kept mumbling about sharks—the beauty, the connection of the sharks. And her power had expanded exponentially. For days she wandered dazedly, the prodigal princess— wherever she walked flowers burst into bloom, even in winter, roots poked out of the ground just to be near her. She soaked it in, sucking up the energy around her. But Lena could never quite get the full story out of her. Apparently, Ella had decided to push herself to the very limit, maybe to escape what was happening to her— swimming far out into the Pacific. She had some kind of epic encounter with great whites."

Ava murmured. The Gaia had immense respect for the great whites, so much so that even they kept their distance from the creatures. Great whites were apex predators— alphas of the sea. And the Gaia didn't have the same facile connection or understanding with these predators as they did with other creatures.

"As I said, the details are foggy. But something about that swim, about learning to communicate with the great whites, pushed Ella to her limits. Not only was she more powerful, she was more adept at using her power. The difference was immediate—she had much more control over the way she reacted to the natural world and, in turn, how the natural world reacted to her."

Ava's jaw tightened in anticipation. "Well, luckily, we're in Australia. Shouldn't be too hard to find something that wants to kill us." Her voice dropped. "And you think if I can control it more, I should be able to…Lucas and I…I could touch whoever I wanted?"

Owen's face tightened. "Yes. Although as I said I can't make any guarantees."

"So I could heal him?" Ava asked hopefully.

Owen nodded. After a moment of hesitation, he added, "That's not all." He shook his head. "The Elders are going to kill me for telling you all of this. But apparently Ella wanted even more control over her power. She hypothesized that if freeing her primal side might expand her power, then freeing her human side might as well. Against everyone's better judgment, she shucked her powers and did…a little exploring of human nature."

"What are we talking? The usual temptations? Boys, booze, and…" she trailed off, her face lit with curiosity.

"Absolutely not. I put my foot down at that," Lucas broke in, his eyes fluttering open.

"*Excuse me?*" Ava asked. When Lucas looked sufficiently chastened, she continued, "So you're saying you'd rather I swim with great white sharks that hang out with humans without my powers?"

"Er…yes," Lucas murmured.

"A true brother of the Gaia now," Ava said with a wicked grin. "I like it."

"What do you think, Ava?" Owen asked.

"I'm with Lucas. I'll start with the sharks…And then we can tackle the real danger—humans."

Owen rested his hands lightly on her shoulders, giving her an earnest look. "You won't be alone in any of this."

"I know."

Lucas chimed in once more, "As long as we're suggesting terrible plans. I have one of my own."

Owen and Ava looked at him expectantly.

"I know how to get my mom to come to us."

Ava saw the look in Lucas's eyes—she knew exactly what he was about to say. Forestalling his proposal, she said, "Nope. We're not using the necklace." She folded her arms tightly across her chest.

Owen's eyebrows raised in surprise at the mention of the necklace. Quickly recovering his composure, he said, "Good, you have the alliance stone with you. Lena wasn't sure…"

Lucas's brow furrowed. "You know I'm right. She'll come. She won't be able to ignore it." His voice dropped and he added, "Nobody will."

"The Makhai will come," Ava said sharply. *And they'll kill you—as easily as swatting a fly as long as those cursed stones are in your body.*

"Let them come," Lucas replied stubbornly. "Look, if you get to do something stupid and reckless, then I get to do something stupid and reckless."

"Words of a champion. I finally understand why they never let Gaia teens take on real missions—at last the Elders and I agree on something," Ava said, anxiety over Lucas's safety making her voice sound more sarcastic than she had meant it to. And then she understood. "You want to draw them out like we did in San Francisco. Get them to attack prematurely, when they have less of a tactical advantage."

Lucas nodded. "They're going to come for us no matter what we do. At least this way we could pick the time and place. Where you two would be at your strongest. It's the best way of finding my mom and making it out of Australia alive."

Owen looked from one to the other of them. "How are you two still alive again?"

174

Ava shook her head. For tonight she was tired of arguing. "No necklace until after I've mastered my powers," she said decisively. *And maybe not even then.*

Lucas too looked like he was tired. "Fine. Just as long as you promise not to gobble any millennials while you swim with the sharks."

That drew a giggle from Ava, and then she threw her head back to laugh in earnest—happy and terrified to be making her own plans again, even if they were terrible.

***

When Ava woke up the next morning, she saw Owen already packing up camp. While he was off filling their canteens at a nearby spring, she took advantage of the moment of respite to study Lucas's sleeping visage, his long lashes fluttering gently as his breath rose and fell. She counted the trail of freckles across his nose and cheekbones. Leaning over him, she savored the rare closeness, and whispered, "Rise and shine, sleepy head."

He didn't move. She stayed where she was, wanting to be close to him as he rose out of his gentle sleep. But even after a few seconds of her whispered name-calling, he remained motionless. "Wake up, Lucas," she said, louder this time.

"Owen, he's not waking up," Ava called to the Gaia warrior, trying to keep the panic from rising in her chest. She listened for the familiar beat of his heart. It was there—but weaker than usual.

Owen emerged from the brush and leaned over to shake Lucas gently. When still Lucas didn't respond, Owen grabbed his shoulder and murmured. It was clear the Gaia warrior was feeding him a burst of energy.

Lucas's eyes popped opened as if he'd been shocked. He let out a garbled string of curses ending with "Captain Planet!"

"You wouldn't wake up, you lazy bum," Owen said with a smile.

"Hm. Things do seem to be deteriorating over at Casa de Lucas," the Ares warrior said as he looked down at his arm, which was now covered in angry red marks. "Mistake. That was a mistake. Shouldn't have looked at that."

"Luckily, we can make it to Melbourne tonight. From there we'll have easy access to the airport if any emergency arises," Owen said reassuringly.

"But we're going to try and find my mother first, right?" Lucas asked.

"Yes. Although it seems like we may have to accelerate our plans slightly." Owen's calm tone belied the anxiety in his eyes. Turning to Ava, he asked, "How do you feel about going for a little swim?"

Ava paled, and then, looking at the crimson streaks climbing Lucas's arm, her face hardened. "I'm good to go."

"Slow down there, lady. Even a terrible plan needs some kind of vague stirring of strategy before it qualifies as an actual plan. We'll take today to scout the best location—one where Lucas and I can keep a close eye on you. And how's your shark knowledge these days?"

"Excellent. Right up there with my mastery of giant sloths," Ava quipped in response.

"So you need to bone up on it?"

"Just a tad. Nothing a few episodes from *Shark Week* can't fix."

Lucas raised his hand like a schoolboy trying to get the attention of a preoccupied teacher.

Ava and Owen broke off from their intensive strategizing to stare at him expectantly.

"I'm guessing you won't have much use for me today," Lucas said, his face unreadable.

"Well, to be honest, no," Owen answered.

"Well then…I have a request," Lucas said, exaggerating a grimace of pain and wiping elaborately at the sweat on his brow. He coughed, much more loudly than usual. Ava was not fooled—she and Owen were not going to like whatever it was Lucas was about to say.

"I'd like a last night out with my buddy Greg while you two reenact *Jaws*."

"No way—"

"Absolutely not—" Owen and Ava said at the same time.

"Well at least you two can agree on something. But you do have one little problem," Lucas said with a grin. "You won't be able to recreate *Jaws* and babysit me at the same time."

Owen groaned. "Cheeky bugger. Don't make me regret saving your life."

"Question. Does it still count as saving someone's life when you're the one who put them in danger in the first place? Possibly by injecting them with scorpion venom and waving a sharp knife in their face? Just hypothetically," Lucas asked, pulling the corners of his mouth down and shrugging in an exaggerated motion.

"Fine," Ava said, and both men looked at her in surprise. Owen's eyebrows lifted towards the sky and Lucas grinned triumphantly. "But we're coming with you," Ava added firmly. Lucas's grin faded slightly and then slipped off of his face while Owen's eyebrows only rose higher.

Ignoring both reactions, she tossed a water canteen at Lucas and one at Owen. "Let's go. Wouldn't want to keep them waiting."

"Who?" Lucas queried.

"Any of the multitude of creatures wanting to kill us."

"Right," Lucas said with a dry smile. And with that, they set off into the forest once more, Owen moving wordlessly to put an arm around Lucas to support him as they walked.

177

Chapter 18

"This is so stupid," Owen murmured. They were standing outside of an Irish pub off of Lygon Street—Jules had informed them earlier that evening that it was a favorite of college students. Lucas was already inside with Greg.

"Life is short. Shorter for us," Ava said with a shrug. She winked at Owen and added, "Plus while you were scoping out the perfect shark adventure spot, we did a little something that might keep the Ares distracted. At least for a day or two."

Owen put a hand to his forehead in despair. "What did you do?" His tone made it abundantly clear that he did not really want to know.

Ava pulled out her phone and queued up a video. Two people in Ninja Turtles masks and matching pajamas—which, judging by the vast amount of calves and forearms left exposed by the material, were made for children—were dancing goofily to a techno song. After a few seconds, Owen shook his head. "I can't watch this. Just give me the quick and dirty."

"Well, they keep dancing like that for a while—I think Greg starts doing the Running Man, which is really quite impressive. Then they show off their abs. And eventually Lucas shows the camera a close-up of his tattoo. He describes how he was abducted by a cult—naming some important Ares headquarters as the secret hideout of the cult—and forced to get the tattoo on his arm. Then he mentions that he only feels safe while in costume and warns everyone to beware of the tattoo."

"Oh my God. It's like I've teamed up with Andy Samberg to save the world." Owen tried to look serious, but Ava caught the smile hiding on his lips.

"Let's do this," Ava said, grabbing Owen's hand, getting a jolt of energy as she did so, and leading him into the pub.

They found Lucas and Greg ensconced in a corner table, deep in conversation while clutching their pints. Owen sat down next to Lucas, forcing Ava to sit between him and Greg. Lucas was wearing a long sleeve shirt to cover his injury and looked to be in good spirits. But his eyes were just a little too bright and his knuckles just a little too white as they clutched his stool.

Lucas had already ordered beers for them and gestured that they should drink up.

"Join us, join us," he said cheerfully. "We're right in the middle of a D and M."

"D and M?" Owen queried.

"Deep and Meaningful," Greg explained.

"Ruth Bader Ginsburg," Ava blurted out.

All eyes turned to her questioningly. She shrugged, explaining, "Well if you're discussing the meaning of life in your D and M, the answer is clearly Ruth Bader Ginsburg. The notorious R.B.G.—baddest supreme court justice around."

Greg beamed appreciatively at her. "Do you always talk like this? Does she always talk like this?" he repeated the question to the two men on either side of him, evidently a little tipsy.

"Like a manic tour guide?" Lucas responded.

"Like a drunk librarian?" Owen offered.

"A stuttering suffragette?" Lucas tried again. "That's a tongue twister."

Lucas and Owen looked at each other. "Yes," came the simultaneous and resounding answer.

Lucas took a long swig of his drink. Ava sighed inwardly—alcohol was uniquely potent for members of both orders, and the last thing they needed was for Lucas to do something to mess up their plan before it had even begun.

After he put his glass down, he addressed the table, "Sorry to disappoint you but we weren't talking about the meaning of life. Or only obliquely. We were talking about transience."

Greg nodded solemnly, putting a massive hand on Lucas's shoulder.

"Transience sucks," Lucas sputtered through a mouthful of beer.

"Well, that is both very deep and very meaningful," Ava said dryly.

Lucas pouted at her over his glass.

She shot him an apologetic look. "Fill me in."

"I haven't seen Greg here in two years," Lucas explained, gripping Greg's shoulder. "Two whole years. And it hurts me," he said, grabbing his heart dramatically, "that life can pass so quickly without the people we love in it. I want those days with him back. Think of all the things we could have done together in those two years." He smiled impishly at Greg.

"So what?" Ava asked. "Is it better not to connect? To create those impossible lines of affection spanning oceans and time zones?" An image flashed in her mind—the curmudgeonly crab trying to snap those human connections, so fragile and so fleeting. Especially when stretched so far across the globe.

"Of course not," Owen said, shooting her a meaningful look. Good old Owen, so full of confidence, so assured of the black and white nature of the world. She felt a hand on her quad, resting there—gentle yet possessive. *Or maybe not so good.*

Flustered but not displeased by Owen's move, Ava rushed to hide her surprise by speaking, "It hurts me too. Knowing that I will only see my father…my brother…my grandmother in periodic blips. That they will lead full lives without me…lifetimes I will see only as icebergs—catching the faintest glimpse of those lives, the icy tips, but missing the rich depths, the meaty substance beneath the water."

Greg jumped in, "That's why we choose one. One person we don't have to share, one person we can mark our days with. Not an iceberg but a shadow—laughing, dancing, crying, celebrating…and drinking with us." He raised his pint glass to the group in a silent cheers, and everyone raised their glass to clink with his.

Greg continued, "In that way, we conquer transience. Transience is nothing when you face it with somebody else—they are your past, present, and future."

They had fallen under the spell of the big, eloquent redhead—who spoke with such prescience. The grip on Ava's thigh grew firmer while Lucas caught her eye, giving her a smoldering look. *That's why we choose one.* Ava suddenly felt very warm.

She stood up abruptly, knocking the chair over behind her. "Anyone up for a dance?" She did her best to ignore the two pairs of eyes trained on her, questions swirling in their dark depths.

"I thought you'd never ask," Greg replied, bounding out of his own chair with the frenetic excitement of a puppy.

Ava clapped delightedly. "Yes! Why don't you rally the troops?" she said, gesturing at the college students dotting the pub, "and I'll see what I can do about some music."

Shaking her head, Ava moved away from the corner table, flustered fingers tapping lightly over the wood of the nearest table as she walked. The expanse of oak shuddered at her touch—she was losing control—and she snatched her hand away quickly. In the front of the bar a group of tables was arrayed around a small stage. College students gathered in circles, forming wagon wheels of friendship with gesticulating hands extending from the circle's center like spokes. Ava smiled as she caught snatches of elaborately embellished stories—*and then, I swear, all of a sudden we were flying for real*—as she wended her way through the crowded bar. Laughter washed over her like water—merriment was all around her and yet she had no part in it.

She saw Greg already bending over a cluster of students, chatting with them excitedly, and she blinked—what was she pretending at? This was not her life. But it could be, just for this night.

She finally made it over to the counter and she forced herself to smile at the waiting bartender. After a whispered conversation with the mustached man she moved away from the bar, smiling widely at Lucas and Owen with a raised eyebrow.

The song Ava had requested blasted through the speakers of the pub. It was the kind of music that made teachers sweat as they scurried around the high school dance floor in a losing effort to keep students from dancing too closely together. But there were no teachers here tonight.

Greg met up with Ava in the middle of the bar. As they walked towards the stage, Ava let off a little of her energy into the room—a potent combination of recklessness, excitement, and defiance.

The college students didn't need any more encouragement—droves of them moved to the little stage and an impromptu dance party was born. Ava wasn't quite prepared for the ecstatic movement of the dancers around her but she followed suit, spinning and whirling like a top.

About twenty minutes into the frenzied dance party, Ava opened her eyes. She noticed that the movement around her was much more languorous—the language of dancing had moved from arm waving and head swinging to slow hip movements and subtle stomach rolls. There looked to be fewer people on the dance floor until Ava realized there were just way more couples—students pressed so closely together that they appeared to merge into one being. Greg had disappeared somewhere and she felt the air go out of her, the frantic energy that had propelled her all night dissipating instantly. She looked at the couples longingly—she wanted to feel that close to somebody.

She shivered—a hand brushed the small of her back. "May I?" came a whisper in her ear. The heat rushed to her stomach as her heartbeat quickened. The gravelly voice belonged to Owen. *What should she do? Was it unfair to Lucas?* But his touch was magnetic—she turned slowly to face him, her lower body pressed against his. His hands were now on her waist, she was acutely aware of them, of the heat of his touch. She looked into his eyes, saw the same uncertainty that she felt mirrored in their green depths, almost as if he didn't quite know how he had gotten out on the dance floor. He blinked once as if waking up from a dream, but then a languid look slid over his eyes. There was an inexorable quality to their movement—her body wouldn't move from his if she tried to pry her legs away. But the uncertainty from the moment before had stung—there were questions in those eyes that she didn't want to think about, not now. Instead, she turned her back to his chest until she was nestled into his body, their bodies fitting together like Legos. Pressed against him like this she had a moment to remember his muscular height, the sturdy breadth of his shoulders. And then the bass started and Ava's world narrowed. The music wrapped around her, pulling her body—a demanding mistress. All that she knew was the heat of Owen's body, the pulsing sound of the bass, and the power of her movement. She felt a tickling sensation on her shoulder—Owen's stubble brushing against soft skin. Again she shivered, this time out of pleasure. And then came the heat of his breath on her neck. He trailed his fingers across her thighs, hooking them into the cuff of her shorts as they danced. Ava kept moving, slow, sinuous movements, pleasure overwhelming her senses. When she opened her eyes she found that Lucas was only a couple of feet away on the dance floor, staring at her with feverish fascination.

Having forgotten everything but sensation and sound, she reached for Lucas. Without thinking, she grabbed the collar of his shirt and pulled him in towards herself and Owen. She had a moment to see the horror rising in his eyes before fire exploded upwards from where her hand was touching the skin of his chest peeking out from his shirt. The flames seemed to erupt out of his heart before racing towards the ceiling. Ava and Owen stood watching the fiery destruction, seemingly paralyzed by the pleasure of the evening. Lucas heaved his chest, inhaling deeply. With the movement, he sucked the fire back from the ceiling and into himself before collapsing onto the dance floor, his head hitting the wood with a sharp crack.

Ava reached out a hand towards Lucas's fallen form before Owen grabbed her and shook her angrily.

"What are you doing?" Owen barked as he threw himself over Lucas.

Screaming college students began to stampede towards the exit. As they pushed past Ava, jamming her with a stray elbow or shoulder, Ava felt little fizzes and pops of their emotion. The emotion of the crowd was strangely homogenous—disturbingly so. Usually standing in a throng of people, like she was now, she would feel hundreds of separate strands of emotion. Granted this crowd had a singular focus—getting out of the burning building—but still, Ava sensed something was off. In the aftertaste of emotion hanging on everyone's skin, she could sense only one feeling—desire. Someone had been manipulating the emotion of the crowd—it was the only plausible explanation. Even she and Owen had fallen prey to it. Although he was clearly no longer feeling that way as he stared daggers at her. Lucas. It had to have been Lucas. But why?

"He's mumbling something," Owen said urgently. "Can you hear him?"

Ava leaned over Lucas, careful not to get anywhere near his exposed skin, and asked the air to refract the cacophony of the chaos in the pub away from the cone of space surrounding the three of them.

"Dance...dance. Enjoy your night, my young friends. Live." Lucas's eyes were gleaming but unfocused as he murmured to imaginary dancers. Why would he do this? Why would he deliberately bring Owen and her together? The answer hit her like a punch to the gut.

Ava turned to Owen, whispering, "He thinks he's dying."

"He is dying," Owen replied softly.

"Stop." Ava's throat constricted and she pushed back the swell of tears from her eyes with determination. The last thing she needed was the earth to swallow up the pub in an earthquake—a possibility only too real after the last couple of weeks. She wanted to dismiss Owen's words. But they would explain so much—Lucas's insane antics tonight. And his request for a last night with Greg. And his insistence on seeing his mother. Each thought brought a new wave of tears that Ava struggled against. *Why hadn't he said anything?*

Greg appeared behind them. "Is he ok? I wasn't sure...whether to call an ambulance." The way he said it brought another shocking realization for Ava that night— Greg knew what Lucas was and obviously didn't care one bit. She was overwhelmed with affection for the gentle giant.

Greg leaned over the fallen teen, mumbling, "Lucas, you're ok buddy," over and over again until Ava thought her heart might burst like an overfull water balloon.

She put a hand on Greg's shoulder. "Shh...we're going to take care of him. Can we use your dorm room tonight?"

Greg nodded silently without turning away from his fallen friend.

Owen once again hoisted Lucas into his arms and followed Greg back to his dorm room. Ava trailed behind the group, immersed in guilt.

She stopped by her old friend, the oak, before following the boys into the dorm. Bowing her head, she watched her tears fall into the dirt below. A gnarled root snaked out of the earth and wrapped around her waist. She sagged against the support, too tired and grief-stricken to stay on her feet. Another root poked out to pat her gently on the head and the leaves trembled slightly, sounding like a mother comforting a distraught child. "Shh…shh," came the sound from the rustling branches, over and over again for the next half hour as Ava sobbed quietly. Finally she straightened up, whispered a thank you to the oak, and headed towards Greg's dorm room.

This time as she made her way up the grand staircase at the heart of the dorm the graying photos on the wall seemed to taunt her, boys in pinstripes and bow ties laughing at her for her blindness. Turning down the corridor she saw Owen and Greg engrossed in conversation—Greg was gesticulating anxiously while Owen seemed to be trying to calm him.

Just before the men noticed her presence, she caught the tail end of their exchange, "Are you sure I shouldn't call an ambulance?" Then Greg caught her eye and fell silent.

Without waiting for either man's approval, Ava strode toward Greg's room, pushed past the two sentinels, and opened the door. The lights were off. Lucas was lying on his side in the fetal position. Looking closer, she realized he was cradling his bandaged wrist near his heart. She walked over to the bed, grabbing a pillow and placing it behind Lucas's back. She took another one, positioning it behind his knees. Then she draped herself behind him, assuming big spoon position. The pillows provided the necessary buffer to prevent another fireball fiasco. But even still it was the closest they'd been to cuddling in months, and Ava snuggled into the pillow.

They lay like that for a long time—their heartbeats gradually slowing and syncing until they beat as one. Finally Ava broke the silence, "You're an ass."

"I know."

"You tricked us. We let down our guards to celebrate with you and you manipulated us."

She couldn't see Lucas's face, but she could feel his smile.

"It was a pretty good trick. I wasn't sure if I'd be able to pull it off. As weak as I was. But my father taught me well. I can master fires of all kind. Even the fire most fickle—human desire." He was pausing for breath between every sentence.

Ava didn't like the ragged sound of his breathing. "Should I let you sleep?"

"No," came the adamant reply.

"Ok. But let's not talk for a while," she murmured. "For tonight at least, it's much easier for me to like you if you're not talking."

Lucas snorted. But they didn't speak for a while. The silence stretched so long that Ava felt herself drifting off, heavy lids straining to close.

Finally, Lucas shifted in front of her, jolting her out of her half-sleep. He was shaking his head, holding his injured arm up to his face for inspection. "I should have known. The Makhai would never make it that easy." His tone was rueful.

Ava swallowed her words. Now was not the time to debate whether or not cutting something out of your own wrist was easy. "Why'd you do it? Why'd you cut out the sangstone?" The question was mostly rhetorical, she had asked it before and he had tried to explain, but the freshness of her grief drove her to ask again.

"Ava. I was a ticking time bomb as soon as I raised a hand against my father. As soon as enough Makhai tracked me down…" He shrugged. "I wanted to go out with my head held high and the only person I cared about not hating me. And I even made a new friend. Captain Planet and I have developed a pretty beautiful bromance."

This time Ava snorted. Her heart hurt.

"Will you get Captain Planet for me?" Lucas whispered.

Ava didn't respond, reluctant to leave this moment of peace with Lucas.

"I need to talk to him. Explain…what I did…that you weren't yourself tonight. I don't want you to have to carry the burden of my mistakes."

"Oh, buddy, don't you worry. I won't be. I'm not letting you get off that easily. You're going to live." It came out more fiercely than Ava had intended.

"For what?" There was no fight in his words. He sounded like he was floating out to sea on a raft, hands behind his head, eyes focused contentedly on the cloud configurations in the sky.

"For me, *babe*. I'm going to save your life for the second time. Not that anyone's counting."

"Haha, ok." He paused for a breath, and Ava could tell that he was very tired. As she was moving to leave, Lucas whispered at her back, "I just wish I'd seen my mom."

***

While Lucas and Owen conversed, Ava kept vigil outside of Greg's room. Sitting with her knees drawn up to her chest, she listened for Lucas's heartbeat.

When Owen returned, looking somber, he and Ava held a whispered conversation in the corridor outside of Greg's dorm room.

"Should we risk using the necklace tonight?" Owen asked.

"I'm not even sure how to use the necklace," Ava admitted sheepishly. "I've only ever activated it accidentally. And only when I was touching Lucas. Actually I've been thinking it might only work when I'm touching him. It's the only thing that makes sense especially because my grandma never took it off—she couldn't have been activating it all the time." She shook her head. "But, now that he's so frail, I'm afraid I'd kill him just trying to activate it."

188

Owen looked at her, eyebrows raised questioningly.

Ava blushed and continued, "The last time we triggered the necklace…it went…*less than smoothly.*"

When Owen's eyebrows did not descend, Ava realized she was going to have to explain more fully. "We bumped into each other accidentally while I was teaching Lucas how to harness the power of water. And then we almost died…twice. Once when boiling water expelled us hundreds of feet in the air. And then when said water withdrew unexpectedly and left us to free fall to our deaths."

"Jesus, Ava. I didn't realize how terrible a plan this 'terrible plan' really was."

"Well that's why I wanted to learn how to control my power before we used the necklace," Ava said defensively.

"Ok." Owen stroked the scruff on his cheeks as he analyzed their predicament. "We may not need the necklace. If you can pass Gaia's test and reach your full potential while learning to control that power, you may be able to heal Lucas all on your own. And then we can figure out some other way to track down Lucas's mom."

"So no pressure or anything," Ava replied.

Owen changed the topic abruptly, "About tonight. I'm sorry. Lucas told me what he did."

Ava shook her head, not wanting the apology. In her mind, she wasn't entirely certain that Lucas's mischief was a sufficient excuse for their actions. At Owen's words a rush of sensations from earlier in the night came back to her. The heat of his breath on her neck, the feeling of his hands on her thighs. Her face flushed and she turned away from him for a moment, borrowing coolness from the air.

Owen must have sensed her discomfort because he saved her from her memories by turning quickly back to the strategy at hand. If he was flustered there was no trace of it in his voice. "Lucas can't travel like this. It would be suicide. Especially if we got ambushed at the airport."

189

"I say we accelerate the plan. I'll go swim with the sharks tonight," Ava said, stifling a yawn as she finished the last sentence.

Owen caught the movement betraying Ava's exhaustion. Wordlessly he moved behind her and placed his hands gently on her shoulders. After a few moments of massage, Ava was lolling against his touch, yawning freely.

"Get some sleep, Ava. The sharks can wait." Owen noticed her hesitation and added pointedly, "I'll keep watch out here."

She nodded at him, and reached for the handle of Greg's door. "I'm sleeping here tonight."

Owen nodded, his face impassive—she hoped he understood. Once inside, she arranged herself once more around Lucas's sleeping form, a big spoon several inches shorter than the little spoon she embraced. She drifted off listening to the sound of his heartbeat.

Chapter 19

The next morning Greg volunteered to drive the three of them to the beach Owen had scouted out the day before. They had several hours of road trip ahead of them before they made it to the Great Ocean Road. After mumbling feverishly about how red Greg's hair was—"like rubies"—Lucas had promptly fallen asleep in the front seat. Owen and Ava were in the back—the middle seat a safe buffer from the forced proximity of the car. But still, Ava felt acutely the closeness of Owen and Lucas as they drove.

After reviewing shark information for several minutes, Owen said, "I have something I need to show you." He fished a small notebook out of his backpack.

Ava recognized it. "My grandmother's journal—did she give it to you?" There was more than a hint of envy in her tone.

"Yes," he said simply. She could always count on Owen not to sugarcoat the truth.

"She never let me read it," Ava said wistfully. "But as she flipped its pages I would sometimes sneak a glimpse of the illustrations—at once beautiful and terrifying. She was such an amazing artist. It was only in those drawings that I caught a hint of my grandmother's true self—the woman she transformed into when summoning the lava creature out of that crater."

"That wasn't her true self. Or, that wasn't any truer than the version of herself she shared with you, Ava. We all have our secrets." Ava thought she caught a hint of double meaning in Owen's words. *What are your secrets, old friend?*

"Anyway. She gave me the journal. But only so that I would be better prepared to help you." He shook his head, grinning. "All roads lead to Ava."

Ava shrugged off his explanation, still saddened that her grandmother had entrusted the journal to Owen but not to her.

"Lena is a woman unto herself. Just like you. And if Lena couldn't stop you from your rogue mission, she wanted you to have every possible advantage."

At Owen's words the smell of peppermint tea once again seemed to linger in the air. Ava remembered that afternoon in her grandmother's kitchen, warm sunlight dancing across the patterns of the room, as Lena had explained the true history of the Gaia and Ares— disobeying a direct order of the Elders. As if her grandmother had known Ava might end up here, in this car, far from her Order and her home, and in grave danger. She smiled. "Show me."

Owen opened the book carefully. Ava watched intently, trying to make out the pictures as he flipped through the pages quickly. She shivered, catching a glimpse of a picture of someone who looked like herself, eyes closed in eternal repose. Ella. Would she meet the same fate?

Owen stopped on a page with an image of the same woman, her great-aunt Ella. This time her great-aunt was clearly alive, but she looked...unwell. In the drawing, her hair was tousled and there were deep circles under her eyes—although the eyes themselves were lit with a manic glow.

November 11, 1942

Ella is still not herself. It's been five days now since she returned from whatever happened to her in the Pacific. I've been tasked with keeping an eye on her but nobody will tell me why or what I should be looking for. It's very frustrating—the Elders haven't treated me this way since I was very young. It's clear that Ella is more powerful than ever physically. But mentally—she seems slightly unwell? Nothing too obvious—you know Ella, she hates to seem anything but perfect. But sometimes I catch her when she thinks she's alone. Whispering to herself, she's always whispering to herself. And giggling.

I couldn't make out what she was saying until last night. I made dinner for the two of us. I even agreed to sneak some of mother and father's wine with her, hoping it might loosen her inhibitions and get her talking about her time in the ocean. Then I begged off with a headache and sat in wait upstairs, listening for the familiar jabbering. This time I caught snatches of her words. "I passed...I passed the test. Her test," Ella would repeat over and over, giggling to herself.

I am beginning to understand what has happened, why the Elders have been tiptoeing around her. I hope I'm wrong but I can't think who Ella would be referring to but Gaia herself. Which would mean it's true—Ella is the Alpha. Gaia has chosen her. Through some kind of test apparently. I might not even believe it—chalking it up to the hysteria of those hours lost in the Pacific, swimming with the sharks—if it weren't for all the other things. The way flowers bloom in her wake, swelling to crimson splendor, straining against their stalks just to be near her. In the middle of November. The way the earth rumbles when I chide her for being careless in her training—as if warning me not to trifle with my big sister. The way she trails her fingers through the air, smiling dazedly at me, as clouds form at her barest stirring. And then…of course…there's the way we found her. Leaping out of the ocean and stretching towards the sky, as if she could fly—I've never seen any Gaia do that before. I tried it myself two days ago, just to see. But the air would not, could not lift me…

I write here, being a terrible sister on paper so that I can be a good one in real life. Wringing my jealousy out as if from a sponge to be soaked up by these pages and banished from my thoughts. That is the hope, anyway. I had heard the rumors, of course, but I had tossed my head, pretending not to care. "The mighty Fae sisters—two potential Alphas in one family." I hadn't dared to believe it—the Elders had said it wasn't time for another Alpha, that not enough generations had passed since the last one. But the rumors drove me, made me train harder, swimming and digging and climbing while Ella and the others socialized in their free time. Apparently the Elders were wrong—Gaia was ready to choose another Alpha. It just wasn't me.

I'm happy for Ella. Worried, but happy for her. For all of us, really. The Alpha could change everything. She could shift the balance back in favor of the Gaia.

But here, late at night, tucked into my bed, I can ask: why didn't She choose us both? But the real question, the one making me burn with guilt: why didn't She choose me? I was stronger and faster than Ella—I trained harder.

Ava looked up at Owen, her eyes wide. "This is not quite the version of the story my grandmother told me. I had no idea she wanted…" She shook her head, *it didn't matter now.* This emotion, although fresh and raw to Ava, was long spent. She had to focus on the present. But pulling herself away from the swirl of her grandmother's emotions was like trying to extricate her foot from knee-deep mud. It sucked her in greedily, leaving her at once desperate to know more and wary of reading even one more sentence. It seemed unfair to violate her grandmother's privacy in this way—a journal was a terribly vulnerable thing.

"Does she mention anything more about the test? About how Ella passed it?" Ava asked.

"Unfortunately not."

"Did she tell you anything else when she gave it to you?"

"No. And honestly, I don't think she knew any more."

"Why not?"

"Ella lived another several years after this entry. Lena chronicled as much as she could of the unrest between the orders during World War Two in this journal, any trace of Gaia knowledge or Ares scheming..." Owen ran a hand through his hair. "She did mention in an entry dated about a month after this one that Ella was back to her normal self. Although she was more powerful than Lena ever could have imagined."

"Ok. Good. So any psychotic break brought about by this mysterious test will only be temporary."

Owen put up his hands against the sarcasm in Ava's tone. "Hey. I don't make the rules."

"You just follow them," Ava retorted.

"Still a little mad about the Lifetree incident, I see?"

Ava held up her two fingers pinched together. "Just a smidge. You're lucky you're so useful. Run me through some more Gaia lore, please."

"The Elders carefully collect and store knowledge over centuries, risking pain and even death. And you want the Cliffs Notes version?"

"Yup."

"Sure, I'll distill seven centuries of knowledge in ten minutes."

Greg's ears perked up at this line of conversation. He met their eyes in the rear-view mirror. She saw Owen shift uncomfortably and Greg must have noticed as well.

"Don't worry. I kept Lucas's secret for years," the redhead said.

Ava couldn't stop herself from asking, "Why?"

"Because he asked me to," Greg said simply. "And 'cause he promised to make me the happiest man in the world on my eighteenth birthday."

"And did he deliver?"

Greg just smiled—the smile of a very happy man indeed.

"Well. We've got your twenty-first birthday covered," Ava offered.

Greg laughed. "You don't need to." His eyes were far away, clearly remembering the aforementioned birthday bash. "But I confess, I won't turn you down….an offer that good, I can't turn you down."

Owen and Ava caught each other's eyes and laughed—at the ridiculousness of the promise, at the ease of Greg's compliance. She had never once told anyone outside the Order her secret. She could bet that Owen hadn't either. And now they were trading the knowledge of their deepest secrets in return for an epic twenty-first birthday party. *And I don't regret it for a second. I just hope I'm still around to attend.*

The smile slid off of Greg's face. He cleared his throat. "Actually. I don't care about the party. Just promise me that Lucas will be around for it. My twenty-first."

That sobered everyone. After a strained silence, Ava, whispered, "I'll do everything I possibly can." Forcing an upbeat note into her voice, she said, "On that note, Owen, hit me."

Owen rubbed a hand through the scruff on his chin, and then pulled at the corners of his mouth, evidently deciding where to start. He cleared his throat and asked, his tone hesitant, "I'm guessing you and Lucas haven't always created a fire hazard when you two touched?"

"No," Ava said quickly, the heat rising in her cheeks at the onslaught of memories.

Again Owen ran a hand through his blond beard, tugging at the wiry bristles. And then he dove right in, "Gaia is…diffuse. She pulses through every organism on the planet—from the mighty elephants to the humble plankton. But She is also part of the atmosphere and the physical mass of the planet itself. She is omnipresent, but not omnipotent. Don't get me wrong. With the entire planet at Her disposal, She is immensely powerful, but that power is dispersed." Seeing the puzzlement in Ava's eyes, Owen paused, and then tried again, "Have you ever seen someone use a magnifying glass to start a fire?"

Ava nodded.

"Well…we…members of our Order act like those magnifying glasses, concentrating Gaia's power in one place. The most powerful of our Order can channel so much of the Earth's energy that they can impel Gaia to take physical form. Remember that goddess of lava summoned by your grandmother?"

Ava nodded, her pulse quickening in excitement.

"The Alpha," Owen stopped, correcting himself. "*You* are the ultimate lens channeling Earth's energy. The connection between you and Gaia is all-consuming."

This time Ava shivered. *Consuming.* Owen didn't realize how close he'd come to the truth with his word choice. She had felt like she was being consumed by an outside power these past couple of weeks. If she didn't learn to control it, it would surely destroy her.

"Unfortunately, at this pivotal moment in our planet's history, your connection to Gaia is both the ultimate blessing and the ultimate curse. Through thousands and millions and billions of chemical processes and minute environmental changes, Gaia has worked to create the optimal conditions for life on our planet. The warming climate is changing those conditions, shifting them much faster than Gaia can adapt. All manner of creatures, even members of our Order, are suffering as those conditions accelerate," Owen said, his voice sad.

Seeming to shift gears, he asked, "You know She tried to do something on Her own? To slow the warming?"

Ava shook her head no. Why had they kept everything from her?

"It was before we were born. 1991. Mount Pinatubo, in the Philippines. All the news coverage I've read described the eruption as cataclysmic. It injected millions of tons of sulfur dioxide into the atmosphere."

Ava's eyes widened. "Sulfur dioxide. That much released into the atmosphere would combine with other particles to act as a shield, reflecting the sun's rays. Which, in turn, would lower global temperatures."

"Exactly. It did. But not for long."

"Will She try it again?" Ava asked, her throat suddenly dry.

"Maybe. It must have taken an immense effort. But I'm beginning to understand that there's no telling what Gaia will do if sufficiently provoked." His eyes were far away as he spoke, and Ava thought again of the lava woman— shooting fire into the surrounding forest like a terrifying, avenging angel. She shivered—now indelibly connected to such a force.

"She's thirsty, I'm thirsty. She's angry, I will be a puppet of her anger," Ava mumbled.

"Unless you can control your power," Owen said, his tone steadfast. She clung to that solidity, that confidence exuded by Owen.

"She hates Lucas…I hurt Lucas," Ava added in a whisper.

Owen shook his head. "No. I don't think so. You and Lucas were able to touch before. And then you must have woken Her somehow, gotten Her attention in a big way?"

"The night with Lucas's father?"

"That could do it. Remember, Gaia is omnipresent but dispersed. She's awake to things happening all over the planet. Think of the ancient empires—they expanded across the globe, building their power. But as their empires

197

grew, leaders couldn't react quickly enough to events unfolding all over the world."

"Really pulling out all the metaphors tonight, Coach," Ava said with a smile.

Owen just grinned at her and continued, "It would take a serious disturbance to grab Gaia's attention. And there was a lot happening that night, a lot that might draw Gaia's focus. Her ire. Lucas tricked you into shucking your powers. The leader of the Makhai almost killed you—"

Ava cut in, "Lucas used his Gaia and Ares powers simultaneously. The Gaia were being attacked while the Alpha ventured out on her own with a member of the Ares. Yeah. I can see how that might draw attention."

"I'm not totally sure. But I think that once Gaia was focused on you and Lucas, on your interaction, She became aware of the sangstones. They could have triggered a primal rage. An instinctive reaction. To Gaia, Lucas's sangstones probably felt like caustic sores, and once made aware of their agonizing burn, She could no longer ignore them."

Ava felt momentarily hopeless—what could she possibly do to overcome Gaia's rage?

As always, Owen was quick to pick up on her distress. His tone reassuring, he continued, "I can empathize with Gaia—I had the same instinctive reaction to Lucas. I could feel those angry little pieces of metal, feel the sacrilege and the pain that they embodied. But then I began to understand what you saw in him—you won me over despite myself. Now it's up to you to convince Gaia, however you can, that Lucas is not that enemy. I'm living proof that it's possible to override the instinctive animosity. And if you can, then I believe you will be able to help Lucas heal. I've been reading your grandmother's journal—and trust me, if you can learn to control your power…"

Ava felt a wave of hope from Owen, but his words troubled her. "Convince Gaia? The lava Amazon? How could I even begin to do that?"

Owen nodded. "Think of the Earth as a human body. It's a unitary form—generally working in concert. But there are millions of parts that have to function independently for the body to function. Like the billions and billions of organic life forms great and small that churn and grow to keep ecosystems working."

Ava put up a hand. "I took AP Bio." She twirled her finger in a circle, signaling that Owen should get to the point.

Owen's face became unreadable—the green eyes inscrutable. She wondered if she had offended him. When he spoke his voice was husky. He leaned towards her, moving into her space. Looking in her eyes for permission, he trailed his fingers along the inside of her arm. "Look." Ava followed his gaze, suddenly very warm. "The hair on your arms is standing on end. Responding to a stimulus. Your body responds independently to my touch even though your brain might be telling it not to."

Ava blushed. The very tips of his fingers were still touching her skin. She felt frozen, paralyzed by his knowing gaze—how much could he see? How far did that gaze reach?

"Gaia is much the same. The natural world reacts independently to outside stimuli. That's why, even if Gaia might be angry with you, individual trees and rivers and animals will still respond to your energy. When Gaia takes tangible form she is essentially acting as the brain, the command center of the planet—and she has billions of years of memories, emotions, wisdom, and experience at her disposal. It is from this form that she can rally action, like the eruption of Mount Pinatubo."

"You," he said, tracing his finger down until he reached the palm of her hand, where he laced his fingers into hers—wordlessly communicating his belief in her, "have to convince Gaia, in her tangible form, that you are a true Alpha. And that Lucas is not the enemy."

Greg cleared his throat, obviously trying to get their attention. "We're here." Catching their eyes in the mirror, he asked, "Should I park it here and wait for you guys?"

"No. This could take a while," Ava answered, her tone holding a note of foreboding.

Chapter 20

Lucas rubbed at his eyes sleepily in the front seat of the parked car, like a little boy waking from a deep slumber. Ava marveled that even Lucas, warrior that he was, reverted back to childlike form when unwell. Pain was the great equalizer, bringing even the Gaia and Ares to their knees. Taking in the dark curls dampened by sweat falling across his forehead and the pink flush in his cheeks, Ava half expected him to start sucking his thumb.

"Are we here?" he asked groggily.

When Ava nodded, he asked, "Did you enjoy the Great Ocean Road?"

In truth she and Owen had barely looked up as they spoke but she remembered her promise to Lucas to enjoy the fabled beauty of the drive. She nodded again, smiling soothingly.

If Lucas knew she was lying, he didn't let on. He looked around and his eyes lit up in pleasure. "Lorne. I didn't know that's where Captain Planet had decided on for this great 'test.'"

Ava looked around, taking in her surroundings with wide eyes. The view was breathtaking. White sandy beach stretched out invitingly in front of her before fading into water, shimmering blue-green in the sun. Green cliffs framed the shoreline panorama and the scent of pine wafted through the air. As if that were not enough sensory stimulation, children scurried and darted everywhere, taking advantage of the elaborate playground and trampoline park wedged between the beach and the downtown. One feature of the landscape though gave her pause.

"Apparently these other five hundred sun-kissed citizens and I are all going to undertake the test together." She gave Owen a look, narrowing her eyes. "I thought you were going to find somewhere secluded. *Somewhere without any bystanders.*"

"It's the summer. We're in Australia. Of course there'll be 'bystanders' on the beaches. But that's why I came prepared." He rubbed his hands together with a grin and dark clouds began to roll in overhead. "Nothing a little rain can't fix."

"Australians don't strike me as the kind of people frightened by a little rain," Ava replied.

Owen nodded. "You're right. Of course." He waved his arms as if conducting an orchestra and lightning began striking in time with his gesturing. He started humming a tune and watched with satisfaction as the lightning and thunder kept in synch with his song. "Can't beat classical music and a thunderstorm," he murmured.

Punctuating the music of the storm were the cries of frustration from the people scattering towards cars for shelter.

"Do you want me to keep this up the whole time you're out there?" Owen asked.

"Yeah. It's the only way to keep everyone away. Keep them safe," Ava replied.

"It'll sap my strength." He looked at her through the rain, his green eyes filled with concern.

She turned away from his gaze before she could change her mind and started striding towards the ocean. Owen followed her.

They were already drenched. Ava turned, her hair whipping around her face. "Get back to Lucas—get him into that building," she said, gesturing at a simple metal structure that housed public restrooms and concessions. "He'll be safe and dry there. And make sure Greg doesn't stick around. No telling what's about to happen."

Owen grabbed her wrist. "One more thing, Ava. You know how Gaia is more powerful in certain places around the Earth? How it's easier for Her to impose Her will? One of those places is the crater where your grandmother summoned her lava friend. The open sea may be another one of those places. Just be careful. You could be venturing into Her territory."

"Well we are the Order of *Gaia*—shouldn't it be thrilling to venture into Gaia's sacred territory?" Ava quipped, trying to laugh through her unease.

"You know better than I, that you can respect and revere that which you also fear."

"Eloquent. Even on a beach. In the middle of a raging storm. Don't worry. I'll be back for more of your wisdom-infused poetry, *Captain Planet*."

She threw him a salute before turning back to the stormy sea, her face steeled in concentration. She scanned the scene in front of her—momentarily transfixed by the lightning forking along the horizon in rhythmic intervals. Then she unlaced her shoes, tossed them on the beach, and charged into the rough waves without a backwards glance. The dark blue surf swallowed her up greedily.

Initially she followed the game plan Owen and she had devised in the car, saving her energy by tugging at currents of water that shot her out to sea. But there was a wild energy to the storm-riled waves, and she couldn't help but plunge herself into their frenetic movement. She rode up twenty-foot tall waves, somersaulting out of their peaks to fall into the writhing sea below. The sea was her own personal waterpark, and she let the water toss her high in the air—up, up towards the electricity humming through the clouds. Gliding effortlessly up another swell, she threw her hands out to her sides as if she were a winged butterfly. Quickly obliging, the ocean fashioned her a

202

magnificent pair of wings—jeweled in dark, swirling blue and frothy white. As she was flying, a bird of the sea, a whoop of joy tore out of her. She was free.

She glimpsed another wave, towering darkly on the horizon, at least forty feet tall. She let the water pull her up, like a roller coaster cranking slowly up the hill before a drop, anticipation thudding through her veins. Right as she was cresting the wave, hands out to her sides in the classic *Titanic* pose, she caught a glimpse of something. There was a shape in the wave in front of her, sporting vaguely human features, with the spray coming together to form a long tumbling mane of hair.

Ava faltered, losing concentration for a split second, and the wave slammed into her body, crashing over her and plunging her deep into the depths of the ocean. For a moment she was utterly disoriented—it was so dark. But she steadied herself and pulled on a current of water, shooting to the surface. As she broke the surface she gulped for air and searched desperately for the figure. The rain had only increased its force and she motioned to clear the airspace ahead of her. A feeling snaked up her leg and into her chest. Primal predatory competence. Single-minded purpose. *Yes, they had come for her.* Was she ready to face the great whites?

And then, the feeling was gone. Replaced by a raucous cacophony of affection. Ava sighed, kicking with powerful strokes to maintain her position in the rough seas. Her dolphin friends were back. Astrid, the matriarch, and her pod were heading towards her quickly. She couldn't see them, but she could feel them—the rich, many-layered ties of their social bonds, the fretting anxiety over their young human friend. She thought about asking them to stay away, to keep from disrupting her mission. But she was now miles away from the shore and all she could see stretching out in any direction was dark sea—massive waves sloping like sombreros on the horizon. She was just about to signal that she would appreciate their company when she sensed confusion. A spike in the pod's anxiety. And then resignation. The dolphins were moving away from her.

Sharks wouldn't trigger that kind of reaction from her dolphin friends. It was Her, Gaia. She must have instructed them to leave. Suddenly not wanting to be static in the ocean, she started swimming. She reached out for a current to shoot her even further out to sea but as her hand passed through the water, there was nothing to grab. The invisible channels of water, threads of power the Gaia learned to find and utilize, had disappeared. Ava was left to her own power in the ever-roughening seas. Ignoring the little bead of anxiety in her head, she kept swimming, senses probing to find where the dolphins had been last, and headed in that direction. She hoped they would return to her. But deep down she knew they wouldn't.

She was moving towards a rapidly approaching monster of a wave. Steeling herself, she pushed to swim up the face of it—at times feeling like her body was almost vertical as she moved. And then as she reached the peak, invigorated with a flash of triumph, she pirouetted on the wave. It was a wasted show of bravado—the figure in the waves had disappeared. But She was somewhere close by, and Ava wanted Her to know that she was not afraid. Balancing in those few milliseconds, face upturned to the pounding rain, Ava felt viciously alive. And then her heart clamored into her mouth. She had a moment to gasp for air before she was dragged underneath the water—as if a hand had stretched up from the bowels of the Earth and snatched her, pulling her down into the deepest depths of the ocean.

The grip on her ankle was rigid, unforgiving. Ava struggled frantically, clouds of air bubbles swirling around her, first to slow her rapid descent and then to catch a glimpse of whatever had clamped onto her ankle with that iron grip. But to no avail. She was dragged deeper and deeper. After thirty seconds, she stopped struggling and hung limp like a rag doll. If escape was futile then she needed to conserve energy and oxygen for whatever awaited her deep at the bottom of the ocean. As she relaxed, a small pale figure in a dark, stormy world, she caught glimpses of gray and white—massive bodies lurking at the edge of her peripheral vision.

Of course, Ava sighed, appreciating the irony despite the anxiety that had begun squeezing her chest. *Of course this is when the great whites would choose to show up.*

Finally, hundreds of feet below the surface, the force below her slackened, and Ava slowed her descent. Seeing an opening, Ava kicked her foot frantically to shake off its captor. The pressure ceased almost as soon as she began moving. Shivering with relief, Ava began kicking upwards. She jolted to a halt and opened her mouth to scream in frustration before remembering that she was underwater. She flipped her body, swimming towards the ocean's hidden depths to see what her foot was caught on now. She discovered a tether, made of some kind of incredibly strong and dense plant material, looped around her ankle and stretching into the darkness below. Panic would only waste the precious supplies of oxygen she had left in her lungs. Although panic seemed exceedingly appropriate right about now. Especially because an entire gang of great whites was now circling her position, spiraling closer with every passing second. These were the biggest great whites Ava had ever seen—dwarfing her nearly six-foot frame many times over.

From what she had learned in the preceding moments, she doubted she'd be able to summon an air bubble—Gaia was apparently cutting her off from her powers—and she didn't want to waste energy and hope on a futile effort. Instead she took a few seconds to study the apex predators swimming around her—the vicious teeth, the sleek heft of their body. They were truly a beautiful sight.

The water began to churn; sediment clouded Ava's vision. In the ensuing darkness—with nearly every sense deprived of function—she focused on her breathing, clinging to her composure like a rock climber to a crumbling ledge. As the sediment began to settle, Ava beheld a tangled mass of seaweed writhing and swirling like ribbons in a tornado. Although at first it seemed to be without pattern, without logic, she saw the seaweed whipping and twisting into the shape of a woman. The figure turned a featureless face to Ava and made a sweeping gesture. From Her hand emerged a glowing orb, the globe gathering speed and size as it raced towards Ava until, with a gentle pop, it enveloped her. Ava gasped in relief as oxygen flooded into her lungs. But after a few seconds of breathing, the bubble quickly dissolved. It was clear that Gaia was trying only to keep Ava alive not comfortable. Now the face looked more and more like a woman, features emerging as if molded out of clay by an invisible hand. She thrashed Her arms as if cracking twin whips and seaweed spiraled out from Her hands, covering Ava in a sinuous pattern.

She panicked as the strands of plants slid and slithered all over her body. *Not this again.* But then she forced her limbs to still, floating motionless in an attempt to placate the creature in front of her. She looked down and gasped. She recognized the pattern that had been fashioned all over her body by the long strands of seaweed. It was Lucas's tattoo. Gaia was asking about Lucas.

That thought was followed immediately by another, more troubling. *How do I explain? How do I explain to a woman—a force—alternately dancing in seaweed, bubbling in lava, and sprinting through the wild waves of an ocean storm?* Options ran through her mind. Or rather images seemed to amble before her, synapses processing information slowly as oxygen was scarce. For some reason her mind kept drifting to the moment on the bridge in San Francisco. She swatted the memory away like a nagging fly—Lucas hadn't even been there with her. When it would not leave her alone she struggled to find the connection—why was this memory so important? There, back on the bridge, she had opened her mind to the earth around her—making herself a permeable membrane. And the earth had certainly felt and then reacted to her emotion. But that wouldn't be enough, here, now. Ava recalled Lucas's admonition on the plane ride to Australia—the Gaia too often saw the world in shades of black and white, eschewing nuance for moral clarity. And Owen had said the Gaia had a primal hatred for Lucas and the pulsing sacrilege of his sangstones. She desperately needed Gaia to see the nuance of her relationship with Lucas. She needed to do something more direct.

Staring at the body of a great white—now circling so close that she could reach out and touch it if she wanted—an idea lit up her brain. *Oh man, another terrible plan.* Taking a moment to calm her nerves and warm muscles tightening in the cold, she had a moment to think, *well, She probably won't kill me.* And then Ava elbowed the great white passing next to her before rocketing downwards, causing the tether to slacken. She could feel the predator chasing her, gliding effortlessly through the water, and she smiled. She knew from bingeing on *Shark Week* that great whites could go as fast as thirty-five miles per hour. She would have to go faster. She sliced through the water, looping and cutting. But the great white was locked onto her like a heat-seeking missile. Again, she felt its deadly competence as a hunter, and the smile slid off her face as she forced oxygen-starved muscles to move faster. Finally, just as it seemed the great white would catch a bite of her ankle if it were so inclined, she threw herself to the side as hard as she could—causing the tether around her ankle to catch in the shark's mouth. With a toss of the great white's head the tether snapped and Ava was free.

She shot straight towards Gaia, muscles burning as she pushed to go ever faster. She saw Gaia lunging back from her. But the Earth Mother was too late—Ava had caught Her by surprise. Ava grabbed the creature's wrist and held on for dear life. Gaia's face darkened in rage and She started thrashing violently to shake Ava off. Tendrils of seaweed unraveled from Gaia and wrapped around Ava's trunk, prying forcefully. The water directly between Ava and Gaia began to boil and churn and Ava felt her skin blistering. But still she held on. All the while she opened her mind to Gaia—the memories of her time with Lucas flashing through her brain.

"*Enough, sister,*" boomed a voice unlike anything Ava had ever heard. Gaia had spoken in the ancient tongue and it took Ava a long moment to translate the primordial language. But she needed no such translation for the emotion of the tone. It was infinitely rich—encompassing layers of sound from the scratch of the cricket's legs, to the howl of the wolf, the skitter of sand blown through harsh desert, the ice cracking as it melted under the beating sun, the insistent thrum of raindrops against hard earth, and many more.

As a last image of Lucas—shirtless and commanding the river back in the canyon lingered between the two of them, Gaia spoke again, "I understand."

Ava had a wild desire to retort, *I'll bet you understand,* with a wink and a nudge. But she bit down hard on her tongue and chalked the idea up to lack of oxygen. Owen would be proud of her restraint. Lucas, on the other hand, would be terribly disappointed at the wasted opportunity. Besides, unlike the sea nymph in front of her, Ava had not yet mastered the whole underwater speech thing. As this wild chain of thought spiraled through her head, Gaia scrutinized her, tilting Her head. As if She could hear every word, every last inane word.

"*I am sorry, sister.*" Gaia's words were threaded through with a sigh. And this time Ava heard not the whisper of wind through long grass, or the flutter of a robin's wings, but the splintering of wood in a raging forest fire, the rattle of cage bars by a forlorn baby chimpanzee, and the thrashing of a dolphin trapped in a discarded fisherman's net. The effect was the total inverse of Gaia's initial words—evoking in Ava's mind a thousand anguished images. With every grating syllable, she saw the natural world ravaged and plundered. More subtle was the ancient sadness layered over Gaia's words like a fine coat of dust.

Ava understood. Gaia was sorry for the violence of their underwater struggle, for the burden Ava would be forced to carry as the Alpha. But Ava also understood something else—maybe there was no grand quest, maybe this was the real reason for the underwater journey. Her burden was an easy one to bear when compared to the suffering shouldered by Gaia. She floated, red hair drifting behind her, Gaia's wrist still clutched in her hand, waiting to see what would happen next.

Gaia spoke again, *"Do you still wish to proceed with the test?"*

Ava swallowed hard, accidentally inhaling a mouthful of seawater. *That wasn't the test?* But she nodded, the image of Lucas still fresh in her mind.

"Are you sure, sister?" The way Gaia spoke, Ava had the distinct impression that She wanted Ava to decline.

Gaia's hesitance—whether stemming from concern or doubt—smothered the last of Ava's flickering resolve. Déjà vu enveloped her. She felt like she was once more sinking through the dark water—the hope, energy, and ingenuity that had buoyed her spirits escaping, leaving her weighted body to descend to the ocean floor. Lucas was dying. The world was burning. Her Order was doomed.

She was distracted from her thoughts by a light shining in Gaia's palm—no bigger than a quarter. The globe of light expanded rapidly, reaching the size of a beach ball in a few seconds. She offered the globe solemnly to Ava, who took it with an equally solemn face and brought it towards her mouth. As soon as her nose and mouth passed through its barrier she inhaled deeply—oxygen flooded through her cells. With the oxygen came hope—tingling along her synapses. Watching the ancient guardian before her, Ava felt her spine straighten. *She has not stopped fighting. Nor will I.*

Gaia nodded. *"Let it begin. Good luck, sister."* And with that She stuck up Her right hand—out of the seaweed emerged wickedly sharp talons made of shark teeth. Quick as a flash, She brought the talons down across Ava's chest, right above her heart. The resulting gashes were shallow, but they produced a cloud of blood that swirled around the two of them for a moment. Then Gaia began to spin rapidly, strands of seaweed unraveling in all directions. In a moment She was gone. Ava was alone.

Or not quite alone. The great whites had dispersed, dismissed by Gaia earlier in the afternoon. But apparently they had not gone far. Ava felt fifteen alien intelligences hone in on the cloud of blood before her. She didn't wait to find out more; she shot towards the surface as fast as she could. For the second time that afternoon she was engaged in a lethal game of tag. With her senses on full alert—probing for movement within a twenty-foot radius of her careening body—she discovered two sharks locked onto her position and closing on her fast. What did Gaia want her to do? She couldn't want her to kill the sharks? Maybe it was a ritual to see where Ava fit in the hierarchy of dominance upheld by great whites? What better way to determine if she was the true Alpha?

She needed to buy herself enough time to discover the goal of this mysterious test. Frantically she tried to recall what she had learned about the species. Although great whites did not purposefully hunt humans, the cloud of blood had focused their attention on her. Looking down at her chest, she cursed. A steady flow of red was streaming from her wound. She swung a hard right, hands clasped into a fist in front of her—a poor imitation of the sleekly aerodynamic form of her pursuers. She had given up on swimming and was instead calling the water to thrust her forward as if she had a propeller attached to her feet. Her feint had done nothing to shake her pursuers. The sharks had cut their teeth hunting seals, who were fast swimmers themselves, and Ava would not present much of a challenge, especially as tired as she already was. She felt experimentally for the seaweed and, much to her relief, great strands of it unfurled like banners in front of her.

She had no advantage underwater. All of her training insisted that she needed to create one. Maybe the seaweed would allow her to move in unpredictable ways, arming her with the element of surprise. She grabbed ahold of a long strand, keeping the force of water at her feet steady, and hoped the combination would swing her in a giant arc. The plan almost worked. Ava did indeed swing around in a giant loop. But just as she reached the end of her huge arc, grinning to herself as she left her pursuers behind, she saw a third shark directly in her path. She let go of the seaweed with a gasp but it was too late. She slammed bodily into the twenty-foot creature.

Time slowed as the contact gave Ava a split-second window into the world of the great white. She knew from her research that they were an ancient species—many times older than humanity. But now she *felt* that primeval power, that ancient presence. She could see why Gaia used them as her honor guard—apex predators who had maintained their position at the top of the food chain for millions of years. In that instant of contact, she experienced the ocean depths as the great whites did, tapping into a sixth sense inaccessible to humans. For an instant she could sense the electromagnetic fields pulsing in alien patterns around her. As Alpha, could she too tap into such a sense?

The shark thrashed, tossing Ava off easily and breaking the connection. It turned in the water to face her. They locked eyes and Ava felt paralyzed by its deadly grandeur. From her brief moment of connection, she knew the shark was a male, about fifty years old. "Ok, Grandpa. What are we doing here? Should we duel?"

A whisper sounded slowly, gently from the sea, "*Ava.*" She ignored it, desperately trying to focus on the great white in front of her. She could feel the other sharks closing in around her and she needed to make this count. The water grew more insistent, "*Ava...Ava.*" And then a wall of water slammed into her from below—bringing with it a scream, "*Ava—they're here!*" The voice was Owen's, transmitted by the water across miles of ocean.

No need for her to ask who *they* were. The sharks had already taken off, racing towards the shore—the whole ocean alive to Owen's panic. Ava darted up, pushing herself as fast as possible, and managed to hook a hand onto the dorsal fin of one of the great whites, whispering apologies under her breath. But the shark made no move to shake her off.

The miles raced by. Ava desperately asked to borrow strength from the water as they came within sight of the shore.

She slid off the shark with a miniature salute and ploughed towards the shoreline. As she launched herself out of the waves, something grabbed her midflight and pulled her backwards into the water as if a hook had lodged under her collar. *Gaia.* Shaking her head at her own impetuousness, she crouched in the surf to assess the situation. Trembling with adrenaline she thought for sure that whatever was out there would be able to hear her heart thudding in her chest along the eerily quiet beach.

She blinked, doing a quick double take. Where before there had been a sturdy metal building housing public restrooms and concession stalls, there was now a horribly misshapen hunk of metal. The roof had collapsed in on itself, as had the walls. Bending as if...as if to crush whoever had been inside. Her heart moved up from her chest into her throat. Something beyond the building, closer to the parking lot where Greg had dropped them off, was catching rain in a strange pattern, drawing her gaze. Her eyes flashed the iridescent yellow of an eagle as she focused on the shapes in the distance—two people frozen mid-action in blocks of ice. *Owen's work.*

It was still raining, although much less intensely than before, which meant Owen's energy was waning. Unable to wait any longer, she slithered out of the surf and onto the wet sand. A shout rang out across the beach. Ava jumped, rolling away from the noise. But she realized that it had come from a distance and turned to find its source. About a mile up she saw Owen surrounded by a group of people. Body completely flat, she began to shimmy her way up the beach—calling the sand to camouflage her movement. She could feel the thousands of tiny grains skittering across her back—keeping a constant layer of sand over her body so she would blend in with the beach. Where was Lucas? In minutes she had covered more than three quarters of a mile. She now had an excellent view of Owen and his opponents and she cursed under her breath. *Makhai.*

Three Makhai assassins had formed a loose circle around the Gaia warrior. With the two imprisoned in ice, that made at least five attackers. Just as Ava was wondering why the Makhai were standing down, one of them—a dark-haired woman with sharp metal teeth—tore off a chain from the swing set on the beach. She snaked it around her wrist and began swinging it overhead like a lasso. The metal on her arm burned red with heat—the color spreading to the section of the chain being whipped in the air. As the woman spun her weapon, the other two Ares warriors circled behind Owen, trying to divide his attention.

The sound of ice cracking came from somewhere behind them on the beach. All four of the warriors heard it—Ava was sure. They were all too disciplined to show it, but Ava caught the telltale signs—the slight perking up of ears, the hair on the back of necks standing on end. Which meant they all knew that the tides were about to turn. Ava thought again, *where's Lucas?* A vision of the crushed restroom flashed in her mind, but she pushed it away. She had to help Owen—if the other two freed themselves from their prisons of ice he would be far outnumbered.

Obviously encouraged by the sound of ice splintering, the woman lashed out at Owen with her makeshift weapon. Ava bit down hard on her tongue to keep from yelling out; her mouth filled with blood. But Owen needed no shouted warning. He spun gracefully—evoking an Olympic skater—and with a spray of sand he disappeared into the earth. The woman cursed loudly as her chain fell harmlessly on empty ground. The Makhai darted forward to inspect the spot of Owen's disappearance.

Ava heard a final splinter—the other two Makhai warriors must have escaped from their frozen bonds. Their main target would be Lucas. She had to find him. She trusted that the earth had informed Owen of her return. He had sent no further message since the command in the water. Trusting her own instincts, she headed back to the metal structure to keep an eye on the Makhai now sprinting down the beach.

And then the earth moaned—a mournful cry—that caused Ava to freeze in her tracks. The sound came again, from somewhere far beneath the beach. No not the earth. That was a human voice—Lucas. Owen must have hidden Lucas somewhere underground to protect him from the Makhai. It was an old trick—one that all Gaia children were taught. But the Elders had always warned them that the maneuver must only be used when they were truly defenseless, because it would leave them blind to their attacker's whereabouts. Lucas must be in terrible shape.

The wail had caused a burst of activity from the Makhai, who convened quickly to strategize and then spread out in careful precision across the beach. The five Makhai warriors were now grouped in a loose semicircle near the misshapen concession stand. Ava grunted in frustration—in the hands of the Ares, the metal structure was as good as an ammunition silo. Two of the Makhai

214

dropped into the earth near where the sound had seemed to originate from as the other three kept wary eyes on their surroundings. Their lips began to move in concert and Ava strained to hear—they were chanting something. The only word she caught was "sangstones," but that was enough. They must be concentrating on the tiny pieces of metal lodged in Lucas's body, willing them to vibrate and burn—wreaking havoc on his blood vessels and arteries, and causing an incredibly painful death. A shriek of agony came, but not from where the Makhai were digging. It seemed to originate further up the beach, closer to Ava. The Makhai began sprinting straight at her.

Ava tensed her muscles, preparing to leap up and attack. But she was too late. The earth trembled and with another wave of sand, Owen thrust out of the beach twenty feet in front of her. He emerged from the sand mere inches from the Makhai leading the charge down the beach. With a snarl, he head-butted the figure—drawing a vicious crack of the skull—and dropped back into the earth. The whole attack had taken only a second. A few moments later came another tremble from the earth. Owen erupted next to another one of the Makhai. This one—an incredibly tall warrior with a shaved head and a neck tattoo—was ready for Owen's attack. He elbowed Owen in the face. There was a crunch—as if Owen's nose had broken—and the Gaia warrior stumbled backwards. As he was falling, the tall Makhai drove a foot into his right knee. The accompanying crack of bone and cartilage made Ava wince. Owen fell backwards onto the beach, scrambling on his elbows to get out of the way of the advancing Makhai. And then the Gaia warrior sprang up and, with a grunt of concentration, threw sand in the Makhai's face. When the resulting cry of pain came much louder than Ava expected, she looked more closely at the tattooed warrior—there were shards of glass embedded in his skin. She murmured, half in appreciation, half in disgust—Owen had changed the sand into glass. She watched in awe as her old friend took a running leap and dove head first into the earth, which swallowed him eagerly. No wonder he had advanced through the Gaia ranks so quickly—he was a natural fighter.

The sounds of agony coming from beneath the sand had subsided—Owen had temporarily succeeded in distracting the Makhai from Lucas. But she noticed with a sinking feeling that the rain was much lighter, coming in spurts. Owen must be near exhaustion. She needed to give him time to rest; it was her turn to harass the Makhai and keep them from focusing on Lucas's sangstones. She took stock of her options. Already exhausted from her time in the ocean, her only advantage right now was that the Makhai didn't know she was there. Ava would have one chance at a surprise attack—she would have to use it well. The Makhai warriors were re-grouping and tending to each other's injuries—a well-oiled, cold-blooded machine.

She felt a hand clamp down on her ankle and then she was being dragged underneath the beach, grains of sand flooding her mouth as she opened it to scream.

"It's me."

Owen.

"Cover your eyes for a moment," the Gaia warrior said, his voice commanding.

She felt earth shift around her and then settle. Owen's warning about her eyes had come a moment too late and she shook her head frantically to dislodge the grit caked to her lashes. But it wasn't just the sand—beneath the ground all was black—and Ava's stomach filled with dread at once again being in the dark, far outside of her element. Something poked her gently in the back and she whirled around, muscles tensed to attack. But, eyes straining, she realized it was just a root, sticking through the sand. She had a moment to wonder how the root had traveled so far afield before a bright light flashed in her eyes. Blinking against the glare, her eyes readjusted to find Owen standing in front of her, holding a flashlight. But he wasn't

216

looking at her. Ava followed his gaze and inhaled sharply. Hundreds of roots were now pushing through the sand walls of the underground chamber, like worms rising through mud. With a whisper of rippling sand and grating wood, the plants twisted and knitted together to reinforce the structure of the chamber. They also must have threaded through to the surface because the air suddenly felt less stale and tiny circles of sunlight filtered into the compartment. Ava inhaled deeply, grateful for the small respite from the darkness.

"Don't waste your energy," Owen said brusquely, gesturing at the cathedral of roots. There was a hint of emotion in his eyes—fear? dismay? hope?—Ava couldn't tell. *I didn't do that*, she thought.

But she didn't waste her breath repeating it aloud. Instead she studied Owen. He was standing about a foot away from her and he did not look good. She could see bloodied tatters of his shirt—those must have been from earlier in the day. She thought of the warriors encased in ice. He had clearly paid a steep physical price to hold off so many Makhai; he was terribly injured. She reached out to touch his nose, which looked swollen and broken. But he brushed her off.

It was a small space, but he moved around it with single-minded focus. He tore off parts of his clothing to staunch his various injuries and put a hand to the sand in concentration as if checking on a pulse. This was soldier Owen—competent to the brink of collapse.

"Thank God you're back. Lucas…" His eyes betrayed a deep exhaustion—this one of the spirit. "I tried to move him but I couldn't." As he spoke she noticed for the first time the wonky angle of his shoulder; it looked dislocated.

Ava did not want to interrupt Owen—this militaristic ritual of task and speech must be keeping him functioning under unbelievable pressure. She waited for him to slow and look at her.

"Where is he?" she asked finally

Owen pointed to his left. "About four hundred feet to the north and thirty feet down."

Ava nodded.

"You've got to concentrate. The sand is tricky—it can shift under you, Ava."

She smiled reassuringly at him and stuck an arm into the earth in the direction Owen had pointed. With quick circular movements she coaxed the earth into a tunnel formation. "Should I move him deeper?"

"No. Bring him here. You're going to have to distract the Makhai for a while. I'll try to heal as quickly as possible to relieve you."

Ava sprinted through the tunnel she had created, back hunched over and eyes screwed up in concentration. She strained her ears to hear that familiar heartbeat; near the far end of the tunnel she began to catch the faintest traces. The heartbeat reverberated from so far beneath the ground it seemed as if the earth itself were pumping away. She stopped at the end of her horizontal rabbit hole and plunged a fist into the earth below her, carving out a steep drop. She leapt into the darkness below. Landing catlike in another little warren she scanned the inky depths for Lucas. He was slumped against one wall surrounded by canteens and granola bars. Owen had prepared him to be underground for a long time.

He was unconscious. Ava examined him quickly—his veins stood out horribly all along his body. The angry red streaks that had so worried Owen before were now climbing up the skin of all four of Lucas's limbs and spreading out from his heart as if his whole body had been dunked in crimson tie-dye. Although she was desperate to talk to him, Ava was glad to find him passed out—his screams of agony still burned in her ears. She slung him over her shoulder, her thoughts flashing back to the first time she had carried him like this, after his bar fight last year. She found herself wishing perversely that his biggest injury was a glass bottle to the skull—he was going to need a lot more than her simple ministrations this time.

Grabbing the granola bars and canteens with one hand, she asked the earth to rise under her feet, creating an elevator effect that raised them both back to the horizontal tunnel. Not wanting to drag Lucas's head through the sand, she took a few moments to widen the tunnel and then quickly sprinted down it to return to Owen with her precious cargo.

Owen had been busy during her brief foray to retrieve Lucas. There was already another tunnel sloping off from the underground chamber. And a bed-shaped form crafted out of sand—Lucas could rest there.

"What's the other tunnel for?" Ava asked, fearing the answer.

"I'm going to do a little moaning of my own today," Owen replied softly. He looked at her, his green eyes full of regret.

She understood—Owen was going to pretend to be Lucas, drawing the Makhai away from their grievously injured friend. It was a terrible risk—it would be just as big a coup for the Makhai to kill one of the Gaia's leading warriors as it would be to kill the betrayer, Lucas.

She refused to part on a sorrowful note. Just in case. Grabbing Owen up into a tight hug, she whispered, "Moan away, good friend. Moan away." When she moved to withdraw, his arms tightened around her.

Sounding vulnerable for the first time that Ava could remember, Owen whispered back, "Not the most fabled way to go down."

"Pshh…You're not going anywhere my friend." She was not as confident as her words suggested, but she would never let Owen see that. "We have unfinished business."

"How ambiguous of you."

"Just more incentive for you to stay alive."

"Be careful," he whispered. The affection, the love, in his tone momentarily stunned Ava. Then she pulled away, smiling a hard smile and rubbing her hands together in anticipation. "Let's show 'em what the dirty hippies can do, shall we?"

They heard shouts above them. Owen looked at her and cried, "Go, go!" They both knew Lucas would not survive another bout with the sangstones.

Ava was still smiling fiercely as she sprinted down Owen's newest tunnel, took a running jump, and erupted out of the sand. In her rush to draw the Makhai away from Lucas, she hadn't timed her jump well and she had the bad luck to emerge right next to one of the Makhai—the deadly competent woman with the chain. The assassin still had the weapon in her grip and she swung it instinctively at Ava's crashing form. Ava spun backwards and away but the chain had become a metallic snake in the woman's hands, anticipating the move and darting forward to entangle her waist. In a split second the rest of the chain had wrapped itself around her, coils of hot metal pressed into her flesh. The other four Makhai circled her with cold eyes, muscles tensed in preparation for any foolhardy escape attempt.

Ava threw her head back and screamed—weeks of pent up frustration and pain bursting forth from her lungs. With her head to the sky she eyed the dark clouds overhead. She screamed again, flexing her muscles—shoulders, forearms, quads—straining against burning metal to break the bonds of her imprisonment. But the metal seemed to respond to her movement by coiling ever more tightly around her. The water began to pound against the beach, waves stretching greedily towards the band of Makhai. The waves crashed and snapped like the jaws of a beast, but fell short, tethered by the ocean. The earth thrummed and rumbled, sand shifting underneath the feet of the assassins. But still, the woman held. Another Makhai lashed out with his own makeshift chain, further ensnaring Ava until none of her flesh was free from the metal bonds.

The Makhai began to circle like sharks smelling blood. They could see the end was near as Ava struggled and gasped. A few began to taunt her like a caged bear, cajoling and baiting her. "You're the mighty Alpha?" they whispered and laughed.

Heat. It was an inescapable foe. It had taunted her these past few weeks—syphoning the moisture from her mouth, suffocating her body in its inescapable embrace, and sparking into flame at even the most innocent touch between Lucas and her. The chains were the prison of heat made tangible. Her flesh was burning—she drew in upon herself, desperate to break the contact, the chains like knives slicing at her nerve endings. But the heat would not be stopped. Not content to ravage her skin, it crept into her organs, gnawing away at her muscles and tendons. She wanted to cry out at the agony, needing a relief from the prison of her pain. Instead, as it all became unbearable, she began to laugh, a wild reckless laugh of despair. The other Makhai smirked—at the crazy Gaia laughing to her death. But the woman in front of her showed a hint of fear in her eyes; she alone had remained silent as the others taunted.

Without a trace of warning, a bolt of lightning split the sky in half, stabbing to the ground like a neon pitchfork and striking Ava as she laughed. The energy pulsed through her body and into the chains around her—slamming into the two Makhai holding the weapons. With a spasm the two dropped to the ground, the smell of singed hair wafting off of them. Realizing their mistake, the other three Makhai scattered to make themselves more difficult targets. But it was too late. Ava spun wildly, shedding the metal chains like a snake shedding its skin. Her flesh raw and smarting, she welcomed the curtain of rain that followed seconds after the lightning. The water smothered the heat burning up her skin but not the fire in her soul.

The Makhai had retreated away from her, forced back towards the ocean. Ava jumped into the air, and driving the weight of her body into her hand, she slammed a fist into the ground. A crack spread out from where Ava's fist had made contact with the beach—the gap widening with every passing moment. She scrambled onto the side of the chasm closest to the parking lot and furthest from the ocean. She had a moment to stand on high ground, staring down at her attackers with burning eyes. And then, with a whoosh, an avalanche of sand tumbled down the newly created cliffside and slammed into the Makhai warriors below. Their forms disappeared for a moment under the weight of the sand. She saw a foot sticking out of the beach near the ocean surf. The water lapped frantically at the limb, almost close enough to devour the assassin. The frantic motion energized her—she needed to get her attackers into the ocean. But how?

Doing a quick three-sixty to scan her surroundings for inspiration, she caught sight of a black car in the parking lot. Some terrified beach-goer would be getting the shock of a lifetime. Shaking away the wet hair clinging to her face, she turned back to the ocean; there was nothing she could do for the unlucky civilian. She had more serious problems to attend to.

Putting a hand up to block the rain streaming into her eyes, she studied the rough waves of the ocean—the height and ferocity of the walls of water crashing reminded her of a stallion rearing up on its hind legs in a show of power. Behind the waves she found what she was looking for. Fins. Lots of them. Gaia must be here, watching with her honor guard of great whites.

"Gahh," Ava snarled in pain and surprise as something metal tore through her shoulder. Below her the avalanche of sand had shaped the beach closest to the water into a steep hill. Another chunk of metal tore into her shin. She realized that the Makhai were trying to distract her with an onslaught of shrapnel as one of them clawed his way up the cliff of sand. The Makhai were resourceful—they had repurposed metal from the concession stand into shrapnel and climbing stakes—and they were still working as a military unit. As one neared the top of the beach, Ava reacted instinctively. She reached down to the sand below and lifted it up as if she were peeling the sheet off of a bed. She was amazed at how the earth jumped to do her bidding—allowing her to pick up hundreds of tons of sand as easily as a sheet of paper. Thinking quickly, she flapped the layer of beach, shaking the wrinkles out of the blanket of sand. The oscillation created undulating waves of earth that made it impossible for the Makhai to maintain their footing. Dislodged by the ever-shifting sand, the Makhai tumbled to the ground. Ava flapped the layer of beach again, more powerfully this time. The Makhai tumbled and rolled all the way into the ocean. Waves grabbed at them, tearing at their clothing. And then they disappeared under the surface, snatched by the undertow.

Ava threw herself off the cliff, landing in a front flip and using the forward momentum to leap into the tossing water, as if jumping into a mob of concertgoers to crowd surf. The water felt like a thousand friends buoying her, keeping her head and shoulders above the surface easily. She scanned the water for traces of the Makhai assassins.

A cry came from behind her on the beach. Ava had a moment to see one of the Makhai standing over a stretch of beach deep in concentration—cold spreading through her veins as she realized her terrible mistake—before Owen hurled himself at the assassin.

A scream, this one sounding like the dying gasp of an injured creature, reverberated up from deep below the beach—Lucas. The scream echoed over and over in Ava's head. She closed her eyes, hoping the action might drive out the sound. It was not logical, but there was no logic in a moment like this. She was helpless to protect Lucas. Helpless. Her heart was beating so hard she thought it might bruise the inside of her chest. It was not fear driving the rush of blood through her body but rage. *Was the rage hers or Gaia's? It didn't matter.* She tore at the wound in her shoulder, watching the blood-colored water churn around her. The sharks came then, as she knew they would, encircling her. A quick exchange with the apex predators confirmed that they were on the same page—nobody would be leaving the ocean today. But she got first dibs. And then the great whites dispersed to swim in a great wheeling circle. She watched the fins for a moment—poor warning of the hundreds of tons of killing power lurking beneath the surface.

She yanked viciously on the cords of power in the ocean, searching for the location of the Makhai. When she held them in her hands like this, taut like the strings on a guitar, they would vibrate if they came into contact with any object. Another scream shuddered through her—the incessant replay of Lucas's agony driving away thought and caution. After a moment, she realized this scream was no trick of her imagination. It had come from nearby; the Makhai must have discovered they were not alone in the water.

And then the water was spinning out of her control. *Gaia.* The ocean was an inexorable force in the world—tide in and tide out. But in this little corner of the planet, that energy had been badly thrown off. The water began to swirl counterclockwise. Ava let it carry her body, content in her all-consuming rage to allow Gaia to take over. The current picked up, dragging Ava in its insistent circle. *Could it be?* There it was, a disturbance in the ocean several hundred feet from her. *A whirlpool.* Like the vortex of water created when the plug is removed from a bathtub, but infinitely more forceful. The center of the whirlpool widened—a great dark maw opening wide to devour the three Makhai being swept around in its grasp. It was an inescapable force, tugging everything unmoored towards impending doom. Ava's hair fanned red around her, tugged towards the power. She smiled as the water spun her ever faster—embracing destruction in her fury.

The water was matching her mood, yanking at the exhausted Makhai, who were struggling—muscles bulging—to pull themselves from the current. Their morale could not have been bolstered by the gray fins circling just outside of the maelstrom's pull. Gaia had created a modern day Scylla and Charybdis. If the Makhai escaped the danger of the vortex they would have to confront the peril of a band of great white sharks. The moment had a terrible beauty to it—the symmetry of the water and the raging sky, the swirling grays and greens and blues, and the fins spaced perfectly like some kind of giant studded bangle. It was a masterpiece of utter despair. Not even the old masters could have dreamed up this much chaos. Ava kicked herself into a spin, putting her hands up as if she were on a carnival ride, her mind still besieged by the echo of Lucas's scream. She was whirling within the great looping pull of the vortex, spinning and spinning until she couldn't hear the scream anymore. She was lost to the movement and the rage and the energy of the water. Salt crystals clung to her eyelashes, salt burned in her wounds, and she welcomed the pain.

She lost all track of time. The next thing she knew, strong arms were looped around her in the water. "Enough," Owen whispered in her ear.

He shook her gently, repeating, "Enough, Ava."

"It's not me. It's Gaia," Ava murmured. *It's out of my control. Always out of my control.* But Owen's presence forced Ava to come back to herself. She saw the three Makhai warriors, exhausted, arms looped around each other's waists to meet their fate together as they were tugged dangerously close to the center of the whirlpool. Ava reached out to Gaia to plead for mercy. But there was no response. In fact, she didn't feel Gaia's presence at all. *Oh my God. It's me.* At the thought, she collapsed into Owen's embrace; the water stopped churning immediately and the vortex disappeared.

Without the rage and adrenaline propping her up, she could barely stay upright and she leaned heavily on Owen as he helped her out of the waves. She looked over her shoulder to check. The sharks had not abandoned their posts—the Makhai would not be going anywhere for the moment.

As they emerged from the water they were confronted by the cliff wall Ava had created earlier. She couldn't face scaling the nearly vertical wall of sand and she didn't have the energy to summon a helping hand from the earth.

"I was admiring this on my way into the ocean. You don't do anything by halves, do you?" Owen asked. His tone was light, but it was a forced lightness, and Ava's heart felt even heavier at what she was about to face on the beach. She would have known if Lucas were dead— that much she was sure of. But Owen's tone told her all she needed to know about Lucas's current condition.

Ava nodded weakly, too tired even to smile. Owen put a palm to the sloping wall. It shuddered and a staircase of sand began to emerge, starting from the top and working its way down to their feet. The effort seemed to sap the last of Owen's energy—he slumped under Ava's weight. They dragged themselves up, each leaning on the other. Ava wanted to rush, to dig through the sand and see Lucas. But for what? They hadn't known how to save Lucas before this disaster of a day. And now he was that much worse…and Ava hadn't even finished the test.

They were dragging their feet along the sand when Ava heard the skidding of tires and looked towards the parking lot. The car she had seen before was now racing down the beach towards them. They broke away from each other, weakly assuming fighting stances, totally unprepared for this next threat.

A woman leapt out of the car. She had dark hair, dark skin, and bright eyes. Ava gasped; she recognized her. It was the woman from the memory Ava had accidentally stolen from Lucas's. She whispered to Owen, "It's Lucas's mom." She sensed the same mixture of hope and anxiety that she was feeling pulse off of Owen at her words.

Without preamble, the woman asked, "Where is he?"

Neither of them replied right away. Ava was sure Owen was thinking the same thing as she—could this woman be trusted? But Lucas didn't have the time for them to figure it out. Ava strode up to the woman and grabbed her wrist. Owen moved to intercept her when he realized what she was doing but he was too late. The woman didn't move, just stared at Ava unflinchingly. And Ava felt the emotions coursing through the woman—fear, worry, love.

Ava broke away. "I trust her." Owen nodded.

The Gaia warrior tried to describe Lucas's condition, but he was tired and his words came out in a confused tangle.

The woman brushed his explanations aside with a wave of her hand. "I know. I've been following them. The Makhai. I wasn't sure why they were here, why they were in such a rush. But after watching you today…" Abruptly, she switched gears, saying, "Bring me to him."

It could be a trick. But Lucas was dying and Ava and Owen didn't know how to help him. So what did they have to lose really? And the emotions seeping off of the woman seemed genuine. Ava nodded at Owen and he disappeared under the sand.

She stared at the woman, delirious after the physical and emotional exertion of the last twenty-four hours. She couldn't imagine worse circumstances to meet the mother of her boyfriend. Especially since her maybe-past, maybe-current other boyfriend was here. And could Lucas even be called her boyfriend when they kept setting each other on fire with the merest touch? And to top it all off, Lucas had killed this woman's husband.

The woman's eyes widened. Ava realized in horror that she had been speaking her thoughts out loud.

The woman gave her a little shake. "Tell me about his injuries. What have you already tried to help him?"

And Ava told her, even down to the fact that she had attempted to take on the mantle of the true Alpha to save him.

The woman nodded her appreciation. Putting a tender hand to Ava's forehead, she whispered, "Thank you."

At the woman's touch, Ava's eyelids fluttered, suddenly impossibly heavy. "You tricked me," she mumbled before collapsing into the older woman's arms.

Chapter 21

The sun's rays woke Ava out of a deep slumber. Blinking, she put up a hand to shade her eyes.

"Sorry," came a melodious female voice. She recognized it immediately—Lucas's mother. "I thought it was time you two got some sunlight."

You two? Ava pushed herself onto her elbows, a surprisingly difficult task, and examined the room around her, hope making her pulse flutter in her neck. She silently cursed how slowly her eyes were adjusting to the light. When was the last time she'd seen the sun? She was in a twin bed and she could make out another twin bed squeezed in among piles of books and potted plants in what looked to be a cluttered professor's office. There was a form looming in the half dark. Lucas. It was Lucas. She scanned his face greedily, looking for the telltale signs of illness. But she saw only rosy cheeks, bright eyes, and veins that had faded—no longer standing out like vines wrapped around his body. Her eyes trailed to his left arm. The red streaks were gone, as was the gaping wound, replaced with a small scar. It was almost an affront for the scar to be so delicate—compared to the unending agony to which it had subjected its owner. She was sure Lucas would feel as much. And then her eyes met his. She felt that jolt of opening a favorite childhood book for the first time in a long time—the flood of old memories, emotions, and stories pulling her completely into its clutches, as if no other world had ever existed.

He broke eye contact, grinning cheekily. "About time, lazy bones. You've got to stop falling asleep right in the middle of the action."

"That's rich coming from you. Who would you prefer to carry you today? Me or Owen?" At the thought of Owen, Ava scanned the room. *Where was he?*

"Don't remind me," Lucas snorted ruefully. "Hopefully my swaddling days are well and truly over."

He looked up at her with that big goofy grin—like a puppy waiting for praise—the one that always appeared after he thought he'd said something funny. But he must have read the question hovering in Ava's eyes because his tone turned more serious and he said, "Don't worry. Owen's fine. He visited but you were busy...drooling up a storm. Drooler," he added in a whisper, so his mom couldn't hear.

"That's not a word," Ava mouthed back.

"He had some kind of mysterious errand to run. That kid—always with his secrecy...and do-goodiness...and silent hero thing. Do you think his whole life is some kind of secret body spray commercial?"

"Like this whole inter-order war thing was invented just to get a few candid shots of Owen's forearms looking amazing in combat?"

"Exactly."

"It would make a lot of sense. Now that I think about it, my life is probably a shampoo commercial—specially curated by the gods of consumerism to showcase this curly mane in action."

Lucas snorted. "I think you'd have to wash your hair more if you wanted your life to pass as a secret shampoo commercial. Or else they'd be sorely disappointed. What's the damage these days? Once a week?"

Lucas's mother bustled over from the tiny kitchen tucked away at one end of the room, a steaming cup of tea in hand. She ruffled Lucas's hair as she handed the mug to him. "Watch it, bud. He who lives with eternal bedhead should not cast the first comb."

Lucas shrugged good-naturedly. "At least now you know I come by my terrible sense of humor naturally."

Ava cracked a smile—she liked this woman more and more with every passing moment. She reached a hand out to Lucas's mother. "I'm Ava. Shampoo model, and occasional Gaia warrior."

The woman shook her hand warmly. "Taylah. Stand-up comedian, and occasional resistance leader. Delighted to meet you properly, when I'm not casting a sleeping spell on you."

Lucas shot a look at his mother, embarrassed. "Mo-om."

At the teasing "mom," Taylah's face crinkled in pleasure. Ava could have studied the lines of that face for ages—there were so many stories tucked away there. At present, Taylah's joy was palpable, which could only mean that she had felt terrible sorrow about leaving Lucas behind when she'd left his father—why had she done it? How? And Ava was burning with curiosity at that casual tidbit Taylah had tossed out in her introduction. *Resistance leader?*

"Tea?" the woman asked, turning back to Ava. "And I am sorry about before…on the beach. I thought it might be kinder for you to be asleep when I removed the sangstones. After all you'd been through." Her voice sounded so knowing—had she heard about the great whites? How much had Lucas and Owen told her?

"Are they…" Ava trailed off.

"Yes," Lucas said gently. "Well, all but one." He tried to smile. His hand moved to his heart.

His heart. She felt tears well in her eyes and she turned away—she would not let Lucas see her anguish. He'd been through too much already.

Lucas reached a hand out to close the gap between his bed and hers. At the last moment he changed course from reaching for her arm and tugged at the bed sheet wrapped around her legs. "It's not as bad as it sounds. Really. Now that there's only one sangstone it would take a whole army of Makhai to take me down."

"It's true," Taylah added, although Ava recognized a brave front when she saw one. It was, after all, the same facade Ava had been projecting for the last several weeks. The way Taylah was standing, back straight and arms crossed across her chest, made it clear that whatever army of Makhai came for Lucas would have to get through her first. Ava immediately felt another burst of affection for the woman—they had this fierce protectiveness in common.

Ava just smiled, not trusting herself to speak yet—the sorrow still causing a lump in her throat. After a few moments she regained her composure. "How did…" Ava stopped her question mid-sentence. She had noticed faint white scars on Taylah's wrists, at the same points where Lucas had said his sangstones were located.

Taylah caught her staring. "Perceptive. Lucas was right about you." She sighed. "The trick with sangstones is to coax them out."

"You mean—" Ava started to say before Taylah cut her off.

"Yes. I took Lucas's sangstones. *Invited them,*" she added sarcastically, "as the Makhai would say. It was one of the many Makhai secrets I picked up from Lucas's father over the years. Secrets I have put to good use." She smiled—the smile of the cat happily digesting the canary.

Lucas looked between Ava and his mother, his fingers fidgeting with the tasseled ends of the blanket in his hands.

He said, clearly trying to change the subject, "Owen told us that the test was interrupted."

"Yeah," Ava replied, shaking her head. "You know the Ares, always trying to crash the party."

"My mom described what you did on the beach," he said, excitedly. "I can't even imagine what it'll be like when you have full control of your power."

Lucas's mom shot Ava a look, saying, "Whatever happened down there—I've never seen anything like what you did on the beach.

"What was it like? Did you meet Her?" Lucas asked eagerly.

Ava thought of what Gaia had shown her and felt suddenly exhausted. She leaned back against her pillows again for a moment, glad for their decadent softness after the last several weeks. Taylah put a hand on Lucas's shoulder, holding him back from further questions, and Ava was once again grateful for this woman, who seemed to see so much. Just like her grandmother. The thought of her grandmother made her even more tired. She soaked in the simple pleasure of a pillow and soft bed and felt her eyelids fluttering.

"My mom's been filling me in on a lot of stuff. There's a lot you need to know."

Ava's eyelids opened. She remembered the tidbit from before—*resistance leader.*

"Not now, Lucas. All in good time. She just woke up," Taylah said and there was hesitance in her voice. *Fear.* Ava looked away, embarrassed that Taylah would fear her.

But Taylah came closer, laying soft fingers on her arm. "You mistake me, my dear. I'm not afraid of you. I'm afraid for you." Ava blushed more deeply—Taylah was even more adept at reading emotion than her own grandmother.

"What you saw on that beach was the first wave," Taylah explained, her tone wry. "The Makhai version of killing two birds with one stone—sacrificing a few warriors to test the power of the Alpha while simultaneously killing a reviled betrayer." Lucas fidgeted. "They did not succeed in killing Lucas—thank God." She turned towards her son. "But they did provoke you into showing your powers. And whatever you may think—your powers are immense. You are the proverbial phoenix rising out of the ashes of your people's desperation. The Makhai will do anything to kill you before you can fully spread your wings."

Unnerved by the intensity of Taylah's gaze, Ava asked, "But nobody escaped, right? What happened to the Makhai we captured?" The elephant in the room loomed beneath her questions—*where was Owen? What was his secret errand?*

But nobody took the bait and she didn't want to preempt whatever information Taylah was about to share. She bit down on her question. Lucas's mother reached for a cup of tea and Ava was reminded again of her grandmother.

"The Makhai never attack alone," Taylah said.

"Of course they don't," Ava replied, thinking of the military precision with which the Makhai had executed every action while fighting her on the beach.

"There were people, most likely Ares spies, watching that day on the beach. I could feel them," Taylah murmured. There was a deep sadness in her voice.

Lucas jumped in, "Unfortunately, the Ares now know that my mom is still alive…and that she's resurfaced."

"*Resurfaced?* So, Lucas's theory was right?"

Taylah reached to grip her son's shoulder affectionately. "Yes. He told me what he did. And I told him that I had tried and failed to kill his father long before he tried and succeeded."

Ava couldn't hold back the surprise in her eyes.

Taylah met Ava's gaze, and when she continued her voice was frank, unapologetic, "Yes, I wish I had killed that sadistic ass years ago." She didn't elaborate, and Ava guessed she was lost in her memories.

Lucas nudged his mom. "You can tell Ava…"

"Lucas's father, Max, recruited me to join the Ares." *Recruited?* Again it was as if Taylah read her mind, answering Ava's unvoiced question without skipping a beat. "It's rare. But the Ares do recruit members. And I was causing quite the stir. It was the late eighties. Here I was, an Indigenous athlete burning up the track, not only qualifying for the Olympics, but flat out destroying my competition—embarrassing male and female athletes alike.

"Everybody was trying to get me disqualified one way or another. They made me take this test and that test—was it steroids? A chromosomal abnormality? Of course, as you know, the Ares monitor international news very carefully. And they realized exactly what was behind my extraordinary athletic success. Max took it upon himself to come to Darwin. He pretended to be recruiting me for college in America." Taylah sighed deeply. "He was so handsome, so charming."

Ava realized with a jolt how young Lucas's mother must have been when she met Lucas's father.

"When he finally told me why he was really there, I was excited. He made it all seem so noble—joining this ancient order of protectors of the human race. Advancing peace and prosperity. And all the training and secrecy? I felt like I was preparing to become a spy."

When she saw the look on Ava's face—some combination of disbelief and pity—Taylah paused.

"Oh I was naïve, no doubt. But they don't treat the recruits like the others, the ones born into the Order. They ease us in—brainwash us over years and years. It's not as easy to swallow the reality of the Ares' mission if you're not steeped in it from birth."

She shook her head. "By the time I realized the full truth I was in too deep—two small children deep. Of course Max had planned it that way. He wasn't going to let me leave. Not me, or any of the other recruits."

"That's why the Ares ranks have been growing so large," Ava said.

"Partly," Taylah replied.

There was something terrible Lucas's mother wasn't saying. Ava remembered all the times she'd found bruises scattered across Lucas's body and guessed that he was not the only one to suffer abuse at Max's hands.

"Anyway you don't need to hear all the details. Not today. But—"

Lucas interrupted his mother with an excited smile, "My mom's been building a loose network of resistance. Starting with the other recruits—those less embedded in the ideology."

Ava returned Lucas's smile. But she was distracted by her previous exchange with Taylah. It was clear enough that the woman had tried to escape the sadist while protecting both her children, and having failed at that attempt, she had devoted her life to rectifying her mistake. But there was something else, something more—a current of emotion humming beneath her words. Was it deadly conviction? Desperation? Ava couldn't quite put her finger on it, but she knew it was important. Taylah's cause was noble. But what gave her such unyielding commitment?

Something slithered around her wrist. She shivered— memories of past bonds still fresh in her mind. But she looked down to realize it was just a vine, stretching from one of the string of potted plants ringing the little room. The plant had fashioned itself into a delicate bracelet, set off by tiny blooms burning red like garnets. Something clicked in her brain—*this must be the source of Taylah's conviction.*

When she looked up she found a young girl smiling sweetly at her. She was about twelve or thirteen and her mischievous eyes marked her unmistakably as another one of Lucas's relatives. Of course, this was the sister—it was clear from the delight on Lucas's face at her appearance. So Lucas wasn't a fluke; his sister, too, had Gaia powers.

When Ava didn't speak, Taylah covered the awkward silence, "Ah, Kira, that was very sweet. But you may not want to surprise poor Ava for the moment. She's had more than her fair share of excitement recently."

The little girl look chagrined, and the vine bracelet withdrew quickly.

"No, no. It's ok." Ava nodded at the plant closest to Kira, calling on the vine to shape into a delicate flower crown, threading through Kira's mass of dark hair. She had a moment to smile inwardly—Kira suffered from the same bedhead as her brother. And then she watched as the plant she had summoned kept moving, unbidden, growing and blooming before her eyes. It expanded into a miniature arch over Kira, vibrant blooms tumbling as they expanded and filled the room with a heady scent. The other plants in the room began to reach and thread and braid together, forming a miniature throne.

Enough, Ava thought, alarmed. "Enough," she repeated, this time out loud, to the greenery crowding the room. Everyone turned to her. Each wore a different emotion— Kira genuine delight, Taylah concern, and Lucas sympathy.

It was Lucas who broke the silence this time, "It's ok, it's ok, Ava. We'll get this under control." Lucas's face was full of worry, responding to Ava's panic, but he couldn't hide the excitement in his voice. "You'll pass the test soon. And my mom thinks that we might be right about the other Makhai and their Gaia targets disappearing...the same night we did. That they could still be alive and in hiding."

His words sounded far away. The overreaction of the greenery had shaken her. She remembered Taylah's comment—about the phoenix rising out of the ashes. For some reason the only image she could summon was Plumpy, her favorite stuffed animal—an ungainly goose. Imagining Plumpy's clumsy body trying to push out of a cloud of ashes, she stifled a giggle. Lucas was still talking, babbling with excitement over strategies and plans, people she had to meet. Lucas was happy, loved, anchored again in the world. She felt a slight loss—he didn't need her. It was she who was so very far from her family. A family she had continued to disappoint. Her grandmother's journal entry flashed in her mind. The inky scrawl seemed to mock her—her grandmother had been so desperate to be the Alpha, to lead her people. And Ava would gladly trade. All she wanted to do was curl up with her pups and a bucket of ice cream. That pitiful truth hit her like a truck. She had felt so strong, so brave back in Brookvale—saving worms and stopping bullies. But it was so much easier to be brave in the suburbs. *Maybe this is why they didn't tell me— they knew I was weak and soft.*

Ava had pulled herself into a sitting position, and was swinging out of bed, much to the dismay of the room's occupants. But she needed to get out, outside, out of the bed, out of her head.

"I just…I thought Gaia and I had connected. I thought I might have more control…" *God, that had been presumptuous of her.*

"You did," Taylah murmured, reassuringly. "You just need to practice. Think of it as being like a tennis player. You just got a much stronger racket—you have to learn to hit more gently. Nature will be incredibly responsive to you."

Ava shook her head. She felt the tears coming and she was horrified to look so weak in front of Lucas and his family.

Taylah moved towards her. "I found something when I was dressing your wounds." She hesitated. "You have a scar…"

"I have many," Ava said, torn between pride and sorrow.

"This one is very new. And quite…unique," Taylah replied, her tone mysterious.

Ava looked at her questioningly, wondering what she was getting at.

"It's over your heart," Taylah added.

Ava felt three sets of eyes on her as she pulled down the collar of her shirt to examine the skin over her heart. She inhaled sharply, tracing a finger over the slightly raised scar. "My God."

She met Lucas's eyes. "How?" he whispered.

"It's from Her. She must have given it to me when She scratched me during the test," Ava replied.

"What is it?" Kira asked, clearly bursting with curiosity.

The shape was rough, but its outline was clear. "An alliance stone," Ava said, her voice full of wonder. "She wants us to make peace."

Taylah spoke, "Or at least to try." Her voice held a note of warning. "It won't be easy, but I'll help in whatever way I can. I'm going to start gathering my people. Can you be patient?" Ava heard the veiled question within the question: *can She be patient?*

Ava reached deep down, stretching her senses into the bowels of the earth—searching, probing for the presence that she now knew to be Gaia Herself.

"She can wait." *But not for long.* Again she had the sense that Taylah could hear the unvoiced commentary—her dark eyes locked onto Ava's. No wonder Max had recruited her.

But whatever Taylah heard or didn't, she put a smile on her face, matching the excitement in Lucas's expression. "Then there is no time to waste. Let's begin."

"Owen's back!" came a shout from Kira, who was peeking out the sole window in the room. "And he brought a friend," she added, breathless with excitement.

Ava and Lucas exchanged a glance. She looked away quickly, not wanting him to read the excitement in her face. She had just thought of something—a possibility—and she couldn't wait a moment more to test her hypothesis. She had to act. Before calm, wise Owen

238

stopped her. Before things got messy and complicated—
with the three of them. With the orders. With the world.
She reached a determined hand out and placed a finger on
Lucas's wrist—on top of his tattoo. She felt Lucas freeze
at her touch, saw his look of uncertainty. But she just
smiled at him. Moments passed and her smile widened—
the telltale heat had not crept up her arm. There was no
smoke curling off their skin. She slid her hand down his
wrist, reveling in the small touch, and laced her fingers in
between his. She held on tight. Tight as she'd ever held
onto anything in her life.

About the Author

G.E. Nosek was born and raised in New Jersey. She graduated from Rice University and Harvard Law School and works in public interest environmental law. She's never met a dance party she didn't want to join.

Connect with G.E. Nosek

http://genosek.com

https://twitter.com/GENosek

http://avaofthegaia.tumblr.com

https://www.facebook.com/pages/Ava-of-the-Gaia/216944938353122

.